Nina and the Orange Dog

Nina and the
Orange Dog

Jane Clarkson

The manufacturer's authorised representative in the EU for product safety is Authorised Rep
Compliance Ltd, 71 Lower Baggot Street, Dublin D02 P593 Ireland
(www.arccompliance.com)

Troubador Publishing Ltd
Unit E2 Airfield Business Park,
Harrison Road, Market Harborough,
Leicestershire. LE16 7UL
Tel: 0116 2792299
Email: books@troubador.co.uk
Web: www.troubador.co.uk

ISBN 978 1836282 044

British Library Cataloguing in Publication Data.
A catalogue record for this book is available from the British Library.

Printed and bound in Great Britain by 4edge Limited
Typeset in 11pt Minion Pro by Troubador Publishing Ltd, Leicester, UK

To my family

Part One

Chapter one

'It's trivial stuff,' said Nina, handing over the list. His hands were calloused. She'd expected someone indoorsy and effete, maybe wearing cords, or with a studious goatee and round wire glasses. Not this hearty weather-beaten man.

'Nothing that is important to you can be dismissed as purely trivial,' Niall said. 'It matters to you, so it matters.'

'Psychobabble.'

'So you keep saying. Now, as you've taken the trouble to write some things down, let's at least have a look.' He started reading:

Things that make me angry:
People with paper tickets at the barriers.
Children on scooters on the pavement.
Fat people.'

'I know, it's a bit judgy. Especially when you say it out loud.'

'Your list, Nina. Things that matter to you. What's important is that it's authentic. Why do you say it's trivial?'

'It's completely trivial. Petty. It's not exactly manning-the-barricades stuff,' she said. 'It's just how annoying people are, all the time, every day. It shouldn't make me furious, but it does.'

'You find people annoying?'

'Not just people. Bank machines that thank you for using them. Ripen-at-home fruit that doesn't ripen. That yellow you've painted this room.'

Nina stopped herself. The room was awful. Primrose walls. Deep green rugs, that bit too small to cover the scuffed wooden boards. Shelves of books with polysyllabic titles. A shiny peace lily in a wicker pot.

'I didn't used to be grouchy,' she started up again. 'Or unkind. I snarl at people. I judge them. I'm turning into someone who doesn't like young people. Or any people for that matter. I tut. I can't stand people who tut.'

'It's not a crime to be annoyed sometimes,' Niall suggested.

'No. But a kid on a scooter. A fat person. I don't even know them, they're harmless, and they rile me, just by being there. I swore at one the other day. It's not how it should be.'

'It's not really about should,' said Niall. 'You were having a bad day. You swore at someone. You probably apologised? Not great, but not a disaster. Rather than dwelling on it, you could think about how it made you feel. Reaction to other people's not a bad place to start. If you want to have a bash at understanding some stuff, that is.'

Nina considered telling him that the person she'd told to piss off was about four; a chubby, white-socked leg propelling a silver scooter, hustled away from the nasty, angry, mad lady by a soothing (fat) mother. She wondered

4

how he'd react. 'It made me feel guilty. And pathetic. I just thought, *Get a grip, Nina*,' she said instead. 'I was rude to you too. When I first arrived, I mean. I'm sorry. I don't like rude people.'

She'd growled even before she sat down on the grey wing chair (she'd expected a couch). 'I'm only here because they made me come.' She wasn't sure that was true.

'First ground rule. Only be here if you want to be. If you leave now I won't charge you.'

When she hadn't left, he'd asked what she knew about therapy. There were broadly two types, she'd said. Serious, important stuff to help people past terrible things – rape or bereavement or one of those mental distortions that make you think you're too ugly or brittle for anyone to care about you. And New Age, navel-gazing bollocks dreamed up by the bored middle classes to prod imaginary neuroses.

'So you're expecting what from these sessions?' He didn't ask her which category she fell into.

'Psychobabble, probably, no offence. I'm not really sure. I thought it might be interesting.'

'It's always interesting. And, I promise, no jargon.'

He didn't ask about 'they', the mysterious forces that had nudged her to his drab therapy room. She liked him a bit more for that.

*

'So how was the shrink?' Nina's son asked when she got home. 'You did at least go?'

'I've told you. He's not a shrink. He's a therapist.

Completely different. He's going to help me understand things, like he's my primary school teacher. He didn't say what things. And I've got homework. I'm to spend this week being nice to people.'

Jonah looked horrified. 'Not including me, I hope.'

'I'm already nice to you. I let you borrow my car.'

'Only so I don't drink.'

'That may be one of my reasons. Hard as it may be for you to accept, we didn't talk about you. I'm to be kinder to strangers. Apparently, if I'm nice to other people, it'll help me be nice to me too. That's the theory anyway.' Nina was sure she could hear her eyes clicking as they rolled.

'No more picking fights with children then,' said Jonah. 'By the way, Kate's coming over later. We're going to have another look at that flat, the one over in Herne Hill.'

'Lovely.'

*

After they'd gone (taking her car), Nina stood in front of the mirror, smiling encouragingly. 'That's a very smart scooter,' she ventured, in the singsong voice people use with small children.

Ridiculous.

Chapter two

Niall had suggested keeping a record of her daily encounters. She arrived at her next appointment brandishing her tiny triumphs. She wanted his approval, although she wasn't sure why.

'*Smiled at five scooters,*' he read. 'How did that go?'

'Fine, mostly. I went for the ones that nearly ran me over. Which was most of them. The parents, or sometimes they were Latvian au pairs, must've thought I was a bit odd, although most of them looked grateful. One of the children told me his name was Spider-Man. I think he was lying.'

'*Held fat person's dog.*' Nina thought she saw a raised eyebrow as Niall read.

'Outside Waitrose. I could see he was worried about leaving it outside so I said I was waiting for someone and could keep an eye on it. It was a peculiar colour, almost orange.'

In total, she had listed eleven small conversations over the course of the week. 'It made a change,' she said to Niall. 'Most of the time I only really talk to Jonah, my son. He lives with me. You'd like him.' She babbled on about Jonah, who'd stayed at home through university to keep her company, and sometimes she didn't know how she'd manage without him. She loved him. She loved his girlfriend, too. Kate. Sparky. Considerate. Not one of those glossy types you saw shrieking over Prosecco. They'd named Jonah after that dreadful song about stopping the cavalry. Her husband liked it; he had terrible taste in music. Not after the song as such. The person who sang it.

'You haven't talked about your husband,' said Niall when he could get a word in.

'No point. Gone,' said Nina. 'See you next week. Jona Lewie, by the way, the singer. Look on YouTube. The song will make you cry.'

*

On her way home, Nina took her usual detour through the park. Nature wasn't as ever-changing as people made out. The midsummer leaves were stuck in a green rut. Pharmacy green. Plastic sparkling water bottle green. Council garden waste bin green. Prosaic, everyday names. None of that fey nonsense dreamt up by whoever did the paint charts Jonah had shown her.

A man sitting on a bench half waved and almost said hello. He seemed to be smiling at her. 'Waitrose?' he asked. Another suburban green. 'You helped me out at Waitrose. A few days ago. You minded my dog?' He pointed at an orange blur running round and round a tree. 'Squirrels,' said the man.

'Oh, of course. I was happy to help.' Nina looked across to where the dog was now standing stock-still, ready to pounce. 'That doesn't look like a fair contest,' she said. 'Does he ever manage to catch anything?'

'He's more enthusiastic than gifted in the hunting department. In most departments really. It's fun to watch though, if you've got time. I can buy you a coffee. To say thank you. I've got to hang round for at least another half hour for Neville to run his legs off, so you'd be doing me a favour.'

Neville. Why did people do that? 'You don't meet many Nevilles,' she said. 'I can only think of Neville Chamberlain. It's interesting, what people call their animals. No one uses Spot or Rover anymore. You could cast an entire Victorian melodrama with the names of the dogs in this park.' She was babbling again.

'Mine's after a rock star. You'll never guess which one. He's got a biography that explains everything. And a webpage. I don't know if you've ever adopted a dog. They give you a whole backstory.'

Over take-away coffee, the man filled Nina in on the improbable history of Neville. His apricot toy poodle mother had fallen into uncertain company. Luckily there was a market for attractive woolly puppies, if properly presented. Someone had thought it would be fun to name the entire litter after the members of Slade before putting them up for adoption. Neville (after the lead singer, real name Neville Holder) had been absorbed into an artists' collective. He was rumoured to have served occasionally as a life model. The paintings were abstract, so it was hard to tell. Then the artist that was fondest of the dog had moved away. Neville's career as a muse ended and he found himself on the books of an upmarket boarding and rehoming centre.

'Is any of that even remotely true?' Nina asked.

'Elements of truth, I imagine. He's definitely a creative. He wrote his own message for the website. I'll show you.' He scrolled his phone to a home page made up of photos of winsome dogs. The kennel was called the Hound-dog Hotel. The message on Neville's profile page was in rhyming couplets.

'Couldn't you have gone to Battersea? I bet they don't go in for all that puffery.' She was doing it again. Criticising his choice. He didn't seem to notice.

'I wasn't looking for a dog. I never thought of myself as a dog person. My doctor suggested I got one to help my weight. I mentioned it to a couple of friends and word got around. Someone knew someone at the kennel and the rest, as they say… And here he is. Hello, you. Did the pesky squirrels outwit you again?'

Neville licked his hand and then sat down in front of Nina. He gave a tiny whine and sank his head into her lap. His tail swished across the ground, dislodging small pebbles and twigs from the path.

'Do you remember me?' Nina asked. From the way the dog gazed adoringly at her, she thought he did. He had lovely eyes. She ruffled his curly tangerine head. His father must have been one of those bouncy reddish breeds. An Irish setter perhaps, a small one, or a spaniel. 'You're so handsome. I can't imagine anyone giving you away.'

There was something friendly about wasting time on a park bench with a man who talked too much. People smiled as they walked past, mainly at Neville. Other dogs came to say hello. The owners introduced their pets but never themselves. Nina chalked up two more Prime Ministers, a Gordon and a Boris, and several more characters for a melodrama.

When they got up to leave, they found they were heading for the same gate. Nina learned even more about Neville as they walked. He was strangely fussy about toys, spurning anything rubber or squeaky. He liked table tennis bats. He'd lost his frisbee earlier when it got caught on a breeze and landed in a tree. It was his favourite. They'd need to see about getting a replacement.

Neville's tolerance of small talk wore thin as they turned into a leafy street. He pulled ever more frantically on his lead, before stopping outside a low garden gate and barking, quietly and once.

'This is us,' said the man. The small front garden was barren clay, with a shallow hole to one side. A gang of dandelions lurked in the corner. 'Neville's teaching himself to dig.'

'So I see.'

'I'm hoping his excavation skills will be useful when I get time to sort out the garden. Although judging by how unhelpful he's been with the unpacking, I'm steeling myself for disappointment.'

'You've recently moved in?'

'Last week.'

'I thought I hadn't seen you in the park before. I walk there most days. How are you getting on?'

'Neville's a bit unsettled. He'd only just got used to my old place.'

'I'm round the corner, turn right then second left. Number 13. If you need a packet of sugar.'

'We're neighbours then,' said the man. 'Neville, say goodbye to your nice neighbour and we can see about your dinner.'

Nina was almost home when she realised that they hadn't told each other their names.

Chapter three

'Jonah?' He'd promised to cook.

'Jonah?' Louder this time, shouting up the stairs.

Nina looked at her phone. Nothing. She checked the Transport for London website. Severe delays between Clapham Junction and Barnes, due to an earlier incident. An incident. Who wrote these pieces of non-information?

She'd stopped tripping over the bags for life lined up in the hallway. They'd been there for over a week and lost the element of surprise. Jonah had made a meal of packing them, denouncing the contents to her as he went along. Could she believe she'd bought him this and, also, that he'd actually worn it? That sort of thing.

She'd seen a frisbee amongst all the crap he'd been assembling. It would be another kind gesture for her list to donate it to her new woolly neighbour. After a couple of false starts, she fished a pristine plastic circle from bag number four. The company logo for Jonah's employer was printed on the top, its bold ambition of delivering nothing less than the absolute best etched artfully round the edge in brown.

As she was repacking the bag, a key clicked in the lock and the front door opened slowly. 'Hi, Nina,' Kate said, edging past. 'The charity shop stand-off's still going on, I see. Those bags have bred since I was last here.'

'I'm not giving in.'

'Good.'

'It would take him fifteen minutes, there and back.'

'I know. I did tell him. Is he here? He texted that there were delays.'

'Not yet. Come in, darling, we can start on the wine before he gets here.'

'Excellent.'

They sat at opposite ends of the sofa, facing each other, their backs leaning against the arms, gently throwing the frisbee between them until it fell to the floor.

'I was thinking,' Nina said. 'You could take some kitchen stuff from here. There's that soup-maker I've never used. And normal things too, of course. Plates. The spare sieve.'

'Thank you. It's coming around quickly. The big move.'

'Oh, I don't know about quickly,' said Nina. 'He's nearly twenty-five.'

'You know what I mean. Neither of us has ever lived with anyone before.'

'You're not having second thoughts?'

'No,' said Kate. 'We're both very excited about it.'

'Excited,' said Nina. 'That's what I said when my therapy bloke – you know, that Niall that your landlady recommended – started asking nosy questions about me and Martin. How did I feel when we first got together?'

'Therapists are supposed to be nosy,' Kate said.

'Well, whatever. Apparently "excited" isn't good enough. He wants me to make a list of the reasons Martin adored me. Can you imagine anything more ridiculous?'

'Jonah asked me about his strengths and weaknesses. It was quite early on when he was going for some job or other. I couldn't come up with a single weakness. That's when I knew I was sunk.'

'I can give you a few weaknesses.'

'No, you're fine. It's part of the process of moving in together. Finding out each other's bad points.'

'For better or for worse.'

'Something like that. You should do that list, Nina. The reasons Martin liked you.'

'Adored. Not liked. I might need some more wine for that.'

'I'm serious.'

'I'll think about it,' said Nina. 'Although I'm not sure all this positive self-affirmation solves anything. Most people already have far too high opinions of themselves. Pass the bottle, would you? Thanks. Now tell me about your day.'

They were still on their second glass when Jonah appeared.

'Fucking trains,' he snarled.

'And good evening to you, too, Mr Grumpy.'

'I left work early specially. I was going to cook something amazing.'

'Never mind,' said Nina. 'It's the thought that counts. I can knock up some pasta. Could you pick that up, please, as you're on your feet?' She pointed to where the frisbee had come to rest.

'Is that mine? What's it doing in here?'

'It's the funniest thing. I suddenly needed an emergency frisbee, as you do, and you had helpfully left one cluttering up the hallway. What are the chances? It's lucky you hadn't already taken the stuff to Oxfam, or I'd never have found it.'

'I thought we agreed you wouldn't nose through my stuff.'

'I thought we agreed you'd take it to the charity shop.'

'I've been busy.'

'A corporate frisbee,' said Kate. 'Oxfam will be thrilled.'

'Oxfam will have to manage without,' said Nina. She explained about her afternoon with the new neighbours.

'Retired, I suppose,' said Jonah. 'Or unemployed.'

'Why d'you suppose that?'

'It's Friday. Who walks their dog on a Friday afternoon?'

'You do make assumptions.'

'I wonder who I inherited that from.'

'I'll interrogate him fully about his economic status,' Nina said. 'When I pop round to give the dog his present. Unless you want to do that, Jonah. It's on the way to the charity shop.'

Chapter four

Kate was up early the next day. Nina found her in the kitchen, scraping dried-up bits of last night's carbonara off the pan.

'I'm working this afternoon,' she told Nina. 'I'm going home first to change. I can drop that off if you like.' She nodded at the frisbee, now wedged companionably with a bottle of wine in a Waterstones bag.

'I'll walk with you,' Nina said. 'It's a glorious morning.'

They found Neville sitting in his front garden next to a small pile of earth. He got up, sniffed Nina's knee, and slumped down again.

His owner was arranging a blanket in the back of a blue hatchback car.

'Oh hello,' he said. 'You're out and about early.'

'We're on the way to the station. Nina's got a present for your dog,' said Kate.

'Instead of a bag of sugar,' said Nina.

'Thank you. I'm Colin, by the way.'

'Kate. And you already met Nina.'

'Thank you. Look, Neville, it's our nice new neighbour. With a present for you.' He rolled the frisbee in Neville's general direction. 'It's very kind of you. The wine too. Thank you. I'd offer you a coffee, only we need to get going. I'm working over in Brockwell this morning and the traffic can be a bit of a nightmare. You'll find us in the park around five, though. We can try out Neville's new toy then.'

They chatted for a bit about traffic and the weather until Nina and Kate waved them off, Neville barking his farewells. 'I wonder what he does, on a Saturday, that he can take his dog,' said Nina as the car turned the corner. 'Jonah will be cross that I didn't ask.'

'You'll get another chance later,' Kate said. 'When you meet him in the park. He practically invited you along. Are you coming as far as the station, or do you need to get home?'

*

They crossed the bridge and wandered arm in arm along the high street towards the tube. The shops were opening for the day. They were largely impractical. You could buy any number of designer perfumes or giant glossy houseplants but nothing actively useful.

'Would you think of getting a dog?' Kate asked.

'Jonah always wanted me to. He said he'd help look after it. He probably meant it, but you know Jonah.'

'It would be company.'

'Hard work, though. Always needing feeding and entertaining.'

'A bit like Jonah then.'

'Jonah is more practical as a housemate. He's tall for starters. I've not had to climb a stepladder since he was about fifteen.'

'I'm hoping he'll do some decorating at the new place. I've been giving him paint charts to look at.'

'Yes, I saw. Farrow & Ball. Very fancy. There's a lot to think about. Making your first home together.' She wanted to offer some advice, but whoever decided where to position bus stops had chosen the narrowest bit of pavement. Probably someone who never travelled by bus. It was impossible to walk and chat. 'I'll say goodbye here. See you soon.'

She watched as Kate was swallowed up into the crowd of people getting off buses. Saturday morning and already busy. So many people with somewhere they needed to be.

*

Nina retraced her steps as far as the café by the bridge. It was built into the arches next to a row of picturesque boathouses. Cheerful rowers rubbed shoulders with serious boatbuilders. London seagulls and pigeons squabbled over crumbs. The sun was already high, the tables sheltered from the worst of it by the trees that grew lazily from the riverbank. She messaged Jonah in case he wanted to join her.

The people at the café tables were the same people she'd see on her wanders through the park. Or at least the same sort of people. Everyone looked content. The family at the next table were laughing about the silly thing that Arthur had done that morning. Nina couldn't work out if Arthur was the boy or the golden retriever. Two women and a man bounced jauntily dressed babies, swapping them over from time to time in a complicated game of pass the infant. Joggers clattered by. Three dachshunds arrived with their young owners. She recognised these from the park. Confident little dogs with housemaids' names – Ethel, Dora and Mabel.

'Glad you could come,' she greeted Jonah. She'd known he would. They'd used up the bacon and eggs in last night's emergency pasta, and she and Kate had toasted the end of the sourdough loaf for their breakfast. 'Can I get you something? Then you can stay with your bike.'

He was in a better mood this morning. When they were settled with coffee and pastries, Nina updated him on her discussion with Kate about taking some stuff from the house. It could be a long-term loan, she said, if he felt awkward. He didn't, he said. She should know that he never minded accepting things. (Nina did know that, now she came to think about it.) Even old things. It was good to recycle. Although as she was offering, what they really needed was bits of furniture. Only if she could spare anything. He'd made a list for her to look at.

'So, what about frisbee man?' asked Jonah when they'd finished. Nina had stood her ground on the kitchen chairs and conceded a small red sofa.

'What about him?'

'It's not like you. A total stranger. You never talk to strangers. And suddenly you're giving him my stuff.'

'One small piece of plastic that you never wanted and never used. You were already giving away your stuff.'

'That's not the point.'

'I'm not sure I know what the point is.'

'This person. This man.' He made man sound like

a rare wild animal. 'Do you even know anything about him?'

'Let me see,' Nina said. 'My interrogation didn't get very far because, despite your assumptions, he was going to work. His name's Colin. He's well educated. He knew who Chamberlain was.'

'Chamberlain?'

'Yes. The dog's called Neville, which made us think of Chamberlain. He's taken a shine to me. He was all over me this morning and showed no interest in Kate. The dog, I mean.'

'He might be a weirdo. The man.' Jonah watched too many real-life crime films.

'Thank you for your concern.'

'I'm only looking out for you.'

Nina could look out for herself. Years of practice. She said as much. 'Although I'm much more interested in why you think someone who was being friendly towards me must automatically be weird.'

Jonah had a particularly deliberate tone he used when explaining things to Nina. She still hoped he'd grow out of it. He spelled out how odd it was that a middle-aged man on his own would suddenly get a dog. Also, it was odd that someone would randomly start talking to someone in the park. In London. You had to be vigilant. You read about it all the time, on social media.

'Middle-aged women, like you, Mum, are vulnerable.'

'That all seems rather flimsy,' said Nina. 'It wouldn't stand up in court. Apart from the middle-aged bit. I'll grant you that. It wasn't random. We'd already half met when I minded his dog.'

'You must like him,' Jonah said. 'To go to the trouble of getting him a welcome present. When have you ever welcomed new neighbours?'

'I have no idea yet if I like him. He seems fine. Chatty. Not weird. I do like the dog. He's so ridiculous and a very unusual colour, a sort of orange.' She found herself rehearsing highlights from Neville's exotic life history. She showed Jonah the web page. He was charmed. He said it was clever marketing. Exploiting the whole modern human and dog zeitgeist. Pulling at the heartstrings of a certain type of customer. Nina protested that people didn't buy the dogs and Jonah went on at length about the genius tie-in with the boarding kennel part of the venture. Hound-dog Hotel was a brilliant name. Also, the logo was so clever. It took a certain type of flair to add a hyphen and shape it like a bone.

'And there was me thinking it was bollocks,' said Nina. She had no idea how she had ended up with a son who worked in marketing.

'In a way, it is,' said Jonah. 'The whole dog thing is an interesting case study. No one needs a dog, unless they're a farmer, or blind, yet everyone wants one.'

'That's to do with feeling loved,' said Nina. 'Kate asked if I'd get a dog. Now you're moving out.'

'Will you?'

'I doubt it. I might like my freedom too much. And it wouldn't be much use around the house. A poor substitute for my clever, helpful son.'

'Dogs are about status these days,' said Jonah. 'Look at them all. That one over there's got a tartan bow tie. Someone's trying to make an impression.'

'Not everyone is as calculating as you, dear,' said Nina. 'I expect they just thought it would look sweet. The dog looks happy.'

It did look happy. All the dogs at the café looked happy. The people too.

'I've got to go,' said Jonah. 'I'll have to owe you for breakfast. I've only got plastic, no cash.'

'Will you be at home later?'

'Don't know yet. I'll text you.'

*

It was too lovely a morning to go straight home. Nina wished she'd brought a book with her, or a newspaper. More restful than scrolling on a phone. She fancied another coffee. There was a long queue snaking out the door. It would mean leaving her table to the whims of the next happy family to stop by. Sometimes it was the smallest practical things that made being alone so complicated.

The terrace was filling up. A polite boy came up to her. 'Would you mind awfully if I took this chair that no one's sitting in?' He was so posh it was almost endearing.

'Be my guest.' Nina watched as he scraped the chair across to where three similar boys were clamouring round a woman. From this distance, she looked a bit like a younger version of Princess Anne.

She'd wanted to ask him about his outfit. He was in those white pyjamas with a thick cotton belt that people wear to do martial arts. The child was only about ten. Talking to strange children was inviting trouble.

Saturday morning activities. Taking it in turns with

other parents to ferry offspring to play inconvenient sports. Nina had always looked forward to swimming lessons. Indoors, and the instructor did all the work while the mums and occasional dads chatted. The smell of chlorine and damp children in the car on the route home, dropping off Ashok then Lukas then Freddie, always in the same order. Most weeks, a stray boy or two would come back to their house for lunch. Martin cooked at the weekend. He'd been adventurous and often successful with ingredients.

Chapter five

Two of the bags had gone from the hallway. She did a quick scout to see if they had made their way to the bins or back to Jonah's room, but no sign. Probably two was all he could safely manage on his bike. She could just about lift the remaining four. They'd be heavy, especially in this heat. She'd need to make two trips.

In the bathroom, she picked up Jonah's towel from the floor. He'd left the top off the toothpaste again. Martin used to do that too. Maybe all men did. Jonah's toothbrush had a new bristly head. It stood proudly on the shelf, flanked by Nina's electric one and the green plastic one Kate used when she stayed over. A single toothbrush bathroom was going to look very forlorn.

It was too early for lunch. She checked her email and sure enough her mother had sent a cheerful message listing the highlights of her week. These included admiring the pictures of the flat that Jonah had sent her. 'I've invited them to come and stay with me for a week later in the summer,' wrote Annette. 'After they've settled in. I don't suppose they'll have any money left for a holiday and we always have great fun together.'

There was no invitation to Nina to come along too. She wouldn't have gone, but even so. 'That will be lovely for J & K,' she wrote back. 'They're going to be exhausted. They have so many plans to decorate. We're all learning a lot about colour schemes. Nothing can simply be called "green" anymore, as you can see from the enclosed.' She attached a photo of the paint chart. 'These colours include "churlish", "arsenic" and "card room". I bet you can't guess which is which.'

She thought about telling her mother about Niall's idea of detailing Martin's reasons for marrying her, but she wasn't sure she was ready for the answer.

It was easier, Nina found, to list all the reasons she'd adored Martin. (Her mother would have views on that too.) A few of them had worn off over the years they had been together, of course. Stupid, trivial things. Really there was only one reason that mattered. He was just so thoroughly Martin. He had such confidence that everything would be fine. It was infectious. Anyone would have fallen for him. Although they hadn't. Her mother never liked him. Even Jonah had said that devastating thing when he was about fourteen. 'I know it's sad and it will always be sad, but in a way it's easier not having Dad. He was so loud and, also, he always wanted me to be best, even at football and art and stuff where I was rubbish.'

It was true. Martin had been competitive about unimportant things. When it came to women, he was much more sure of himself. He hadn't wanted the prettiest or the coolest or the most popular. He wanted Nina. She'd never asked him why. They weren't that kind of couple, forever analysing and questioning.

He always laughed a lot when they were together. They both did. That was one for the list. Good sense of humour. It was the main trait people looked for in a soulmate. A massive cliché. That didn't mean it wasn't important.

*

Nina was beginning to think about food when she heard noises in the hallway.

'Oh, hello again,' she greeted Jonah. 'We do still have the side gate. You don't have to wheel that through the house.'

'Sorry.' He didn't look it.

'Are you back, back? Or just dropping your nice oily bike off via our lovely white kitchen?'

'Change of plan. I was going for a bike ride, only it's too hot.'

'If you're going to be here this afternoon, I can help you get organised. We could take the rest of the bags to the charity shop. Thanks for getting rid of the first two. That was a big help.'

'Anything to make you happy, Mother dear.'

'Or to stop me nagging.'

'That too. Can we have some lunch first? I'm starving.'

Over Greek salad, Jonah updated Nina about the flat. 'Kate's going over there on Monday or Tuesday to check a few measurements. You could tag along.'

'You're not going with her?'

'I'll be at work.'

'It's a big responsibility. Setting up home together. I'm not sure you should be leaving everything to Kate.'

'A few measurements is hardly leaving everything to her. I've already seen the place twice.'

'You don't seem that enthusiastic. Every time you talk about it, you always go on about practical things. Making sure furniture will fit. Painting walls. Everything's about the flat. It's never about you and Kate.'

'What about me and Kate?'

'It's a big change. It won't be like living with me.'

'Obviously.'

'Kate says she's excited about it.'

'She is.'

'She says you're looking forward to finding out more about each other.'

'That sounds like Kate. This salad could do with a few more olives.'

'You know where the fridge is. You need to be sure you're doing it for the right reasons. I worry about you.'

'So you've said. Pretty much every day since I told you. We know what we're doing, Mum. We're both sick of shunting between houses. This way, we can wake up in the same place every morning.'

'Is that it?'

'Is what it?'

'You can wake up together.'

'Yes. What else is there to worry about?' He sounded so sure. 'If it all falls apart, I can always come back here. There's a six-month break clause on the lease.'

'Hotel Nina.'

'Don't give me that. You like having me here.'

'Yes, and I enjoy your charming company. I'm not the only one. I gather from Granny that you're going to spend the summer down there.'

'Not the summer. A few days.'

'You never mentioned it.'

'Why would I?'

'No reason. I was a bit surprised, that's all. Finally getting your independence after all these years, and the first thing you do is invite yourself to go and stay with Granny. Who, as you know, indulges you even more than I do.'

'She invited us. And you know how hard it is to say "no" to Granny.'

'Did you want to say "no"? I thought not. Maybe you should have done. Moving in with someone isn't a matter of dumping your belongings and then going off on a jaunt. You'll have to get used to it being you and Kate and four walls. All day, every day. Not just when you wake up in the morning. That's the easy bit.'

'It's going to be bliss. That mad landlady of Kate's; all those lodgers wandering in and out for a few weeks or months. It's exhausting.'

'If it's peace and quiet you're after, Kate could move in here.'

'I know. We don't want to do that. Also, I'm not the only one with my own life to live.'

'You're hardly cramping my style.' Nina wasn't sure she had a style to cramp.

'Go and see the flat, Mum. You're going to be a frequent and quite possibly our favourite visitor and Kate thinks you'll give better advice than me on making sure it's up to scratch, you know, with your high domestic standards.'

He looked pointedly around the kitchen. It was a bit shabby round the edges, but it was clean. Cleanish. 'It's a lot of work keeping a place going,' Nina said. 'You'll both need to do your share.'

'Do I feel a lecture coming on?'

'I'm not lecturing. All I'm saying is that running a home is boring.'

'We know that. We're not kids.'

'You need to be sure it's for the right reasons.'

'So you said. You're always looking for reasons. It's not complicated. Kate wants us to move in together and I want to be with Kate. So that's what we're doing. It'll be fine.' Again, he sounded so sure.

Chapter six

Jonah couldn't or wouldn't get the day off work so Nina went with Kate to see the flat. They met at the nearest station. Thunderstorms had driven the heat away. 'It's a bit of a trek, or we can get a bus,' said Kate.

'Let's walk,' Nina said. 'It will help me get my bearings.'

The immediate area was busy, with interesting-looking shops tucked into the nooks and crannies of the railway arches. As they headed up the main road, things got quieter. They turned into a street of tall houses with steep front steps. A hopelessly young man with a shiny face and a large bunch of keys greeted them.

To Nina, the set-up looked much like any other slightly botched conversion – a grand house with a hallway full of pizza menus and minicab cards. Foxes had been at the bin bags. The street looked cared-for, geraniums and busy lizzies draping from windowsills; one of those streets that had come up in the world. There was a pub on the corner with a menu on a chalkboard.

'It's a few flights up, I'm afraid,' the boy agent said when he'd fiddled with locks and they were safely inside. The staircase was steep and wide, with a Mary Poppins banister.

'You'll have a job getting your stuff up here,' Nina said. 'Are you sure you wouldn't do better to get a removal company?'

'I suggested that, but Jonah's got it all worked out. Look at these brilliant windows. So much light.'

'Cold in winter,' Nina said.

'It's all double-glazed,' said the agent. 'And there's a new combi boiler in the kitchen. Throws out a lot of heat.'

'You don't need to convince me,' said Nina. He'd addressed his comments to her. 'I'm not the one who's going to be living here. It's charming. In a way. This is a lovely, airy room. It won't matter to Kate and Jonah that the kitchen and bathroom are so tiny. You can put up with anything when you're young. And I can buy you some pots of paint, Kate, as a housewarming present.'

'Yes please! The landlord offered to redecorate but we said no, we'd do it. You can choose the colours. Jonah's hopeless. He'll go for something pale to make the most of the light. With those massive windows, we could play with something dramatic,' said Kate.

'What is it with men and paint? My therapist, Niall, he's painted his walls that insipid yellow that looks like a spot that needs squeezing.'

'Jonah says you roll your eyes less about the therapist now,' said Kate. 'I hope you didn't mind me suggesting it?'

'I got over it. Mind you, I still told Niall I'd been forced into it.' Nina laughed. 'He's quite shrewd, I don't think he believed me. I expect I'll bail out before we get into anything heavy. The little things, the smiling at toddlers stuff, I'm quite enjoying all of that.'

'Jonah was cross,' said Kate. 'He said it was a terrible idea. Therapists in general. He thought they'd start labelling you.'

'Ah yes, menopausal empty nester. Lonely, unmerry widow. I'm keeping a lid on all that. You read so much about therapy stirring up demons.'

'It hasn't though? Stirred up demons?'

'No. Not yet anyway. Maybe he won't find any.'

*

After Martin fell, Nina had got the bathroom changed. They stayed in the house, Nina and Jonah, and she gave up work. The workmen put a heated towel rail where the shower used to be. Every so often, when Jonah was out, Nina would sit leaning against the rail, nuzzling the cosy blue towels – sapphire, the label said – and she'd howl. Then Kate had let herself in one day to leave something for Jonah, and found her.

'You miss him, don't you?' Kate had said as Nina subsided.

'He's not gone yet... Oh, I see, you mean Martin. It's been so long, I don't completely remember him. I miss the idea of him and the maleness, you know, the way men smell sort of solid and tell you so many boring things and forgive you. Hairy legs in the bed. Martin was always happy. And noisy – he filled the house. He adored Jonah.'

'Everyone does,' said Kate. 'I'd liked to have met Martin; I like noisy men. It'll be quiet here without Jonah, although you can always borrow him back. You'll be OK, Nina.'

'I feel bad for Jonah,' said Nina. 'He'd have had more fun with Martin around.'

'Jonah's fine,' said Kate. 'He just wants to know you'll be OK. We both do.'

'Oh, I'm always OK,' said Nina. 'I'm still terrified, even so. Please don't tell Jonah that. He's been babysitting me quite long enough.'

They'd talked for a long time, Nina plucking at a towel, blue Egyptian cotton threads dropping onto the tiled floor. She never had asked Martin why he was so particular about towel colours; it seemed such a stupid thing to care about. She supposed it was something to do with having been sent away to boarding school.

*

'What do you think?' Kate asked. They'd found a café down the road from the flat. Sticky floors and formica tables. 'This place must have been here for years.'

'I like these old cafés,' said Nina. 'There's something solid about them.'

'I meant about the flat. Did you like it?'

'Honestly? Or tactfully?'

'You could try both.'

'As I told the agent. It's charming.'

'You make it sound as if charming's a bad thing.'

'I counted the stairs on the way down. Seventy-two, plus the front steps.'

'Good exercise.'

'The main room is gorgeous,' Nina pressed on. 'Or will be when it's painted and cleaned. But everything else is miniature. You're going to spend all your time in that one room. You'll be living on top of each other.'

'That is kind of the point.'

'That novelty can wear off,' said Nina. 'Sometimes it's good to have somewhere to hide at home, when the other person has friends over, or is in a bad mood.'

'We'll have to hope no one's ever in a mood,' said Kate. 'We thought we'd put a sofa bed in the second bedroom, so that can double as a sulking room if we need one. It's our first place, Nina. It's not forever and it's our chance to see if it works.'

'I know. I wish it was a bit more suitable.'

'You take what you can get, these days,' said Kate.

Nina hoped she was talking about the flat. 'Jonah says it was your idea,' she said.

'It was both of our ideas. We didn't have a big talk about it. We'd probably have done it sooner if things had been different.'

'You mean if I'd been different?'

'Yes. Partly. In a good way. You've made it so easy for us. I'm very at home at your house.'

'I enjoy having you there,' said Nina. 'You'd be more than welcome to move in properly.'

'I know. But we've decided, Nina. This is what me and Jonah want.'

Chapter seven

A few days later, Nina was waiting for a bus when a familiar plump figure came by. He looked incomplete without his dog. 'Colin,' she said. 'Where's your faithful friend?'

'Oh hi, Nina. He's at home. I'm doing tough love, building up the time I can leave him on his own without coming back to a disaster zone. We managed a whole hour yesterday without major incident.'

'That's quite a tie.' It must be nice to be so badly missed.

'It's mainly fine. Except if I need to go anywhere. It's only since we moved house. The vet says he'll settle down when he realises that I always come back.'

'Well, if you ever need a babysitter in the meantime,' said Nina.

'Really?'

'Yes, really. He can keep me company. Jonah's moving out, as you know, and he's been nagging me to get a dog. It would be a trial run.'

'Well, if you're sure, I'm actually a bit stuck later this afternoon. I know it's short notice. It will only be for a couple of hours.'

'No time like the present,' said Nina. 'This looks like my bus. I'll be back about two. Number 13, come any time.'

*

Nina laughed when Colin turned up on her doorstep armed with Neville, a yellow duvet cover, dog treats and a plastic bag containing two chewed and slimy table tennis bats. 'He's very well equipped,' she said. She noticed that he hadn't brought the frisbee.

'The sheet is to go on your sofa, save you the hairs,' he said. 'They're not supposed to shed, not the poodle bit. This one didn't get the memo.' He let Neville off the lead as they stepped into the house. 'We went for a long walk at lunchtime so he should be tired.'

'You look very smart,' said Nina. 'Where are you off to?' She hadn't liked to ask earlier in case it was something medical, but no one put on a tie to go and see a doctor.

'Creative focus group,' said Colin. 'It's a posh name for spending the afternoon with small children. I make computer animations for adventure series where people can make their child the hero and come up with the plot, within reason. There are some well-heeled parents bringing little Felix and Arabella along to discuss concepts.'

Nina could see the appeal. 'My husband made Jonah a special version of *The Tiger Who Came to Tea*, with a boy instead of a girl, called Jonah, obviously. I've still got it somewhere.'

'It's the same kind of thing, except the kids get to create the stories. Six episodes, so everyone is locked in.

Are you sure this is OK?' He nodded towards Neville, who was busy licking the bottom of the kitchen cabinets. 'Not too much of an imposition?'

'It's a complete imposition,' she said. 'Although Neville looks like he's making himself useful.'

'I'll only be gone a couple of hours. Three at most. He'll headbutt the door if he wants out. He's better in the living room. He'll never settle in here if he thinks there's food.'

'The living room it is then.' Neville was unperturbed as Colin left the house.

The afternoon was less entertaining than she'd hoped. Neville watched silently while Nina arranged his sheet on the sofa and then jumped up and lay down with a sigh. She sat next to him, gently winding his curls round her finger, until he fell asleep, dreaming dreams that featured tiny growls and smelly farts. It meant she could read her book in peace.

Neville woke up only when Kate and Jonah appeared, greeting them with a lavish dance around the living room, then barging open the French doors and charging into the garden.

'Good of him to fertilise your roses,' Jonah said, watching as Neville squatted. 'I can clear that up if you like.'

'Oh, leave it,' Nina said. 'It's not as if anyone's going to tread in it.'

'Have you had fun?' Kate asked. 'He's lovely. So cuddly.' Neville had come back into the house. He squeezed himself back onto the sofa where Kate had plonked herself next to Nina, not bothered by the stray hairs on the yellow sheet. Both women had one arm around him. 'If he was a cat, he'd be purring.'

'Not one shred of fun,' Nina said. 'Slept like a baby. Company all the same. You might be on to something, Jonah, with your guff about people and dogs.'

'I'm usually right,' Jonah said, sounding like his father. He disappeared into the kitchen to make tea.

Colin arrived shortly afterwards. 'Right on cue,' Nina said. 'There's fresh tea in the pot. Meet the family. This, as you will have gathered, is Jonah, and you already know Kate.'

'Hi,' said Jonah. 'I've heard lots about you. Also about Neville. I've been telling Mum she should get a dog.'

'I've heard lots about you too. I can see that Neville has taken a shine to you.'

'He's certainly very friendly,' said Jonah. He was dunking a biscuit into his tea and Neville had taken this as a sign of a new best friend. 'He's less orange than Mum made out. I was thinking Tango.'

'There's a definite tinge,' said Nina. 'He's been a considerate house guest, Colin. Quiet. At least until these two got home. How did you get on?'

She fetched a mug for Colin, who settled into a long explanation about his afternoon's focus group. He thought Nina would be amused by the earnest mother who had wanted to cast her child as an aid worker while the child wanted to be a fairy princess. The modern type that got to boss everyone around and didn't have to marry a soppy prince. Jonah interrupted so often with questions about business models and ethics that she soon lost interest. She was pleased to see them getting along so well.

'He passed muster then,' she said to Jonah as Colin and Neville departed, leaving the yellow sheet 'for next time'.

'He's OK,' said Jonah. 'That's a clever business he's set up.'

'Is it? I always thought children could make up stories without much help. They can probably do the computer bit too.'

'The parents don't know that. He's tapped into the guilt market.'

'The what market?'

'Guilt. You know. Parents thinking they need to do more for their children.'

'Strangely enough, Jonah, I do know all about that. I didn't know it had a special name. Still, I'm glad you approve. You did give him the third degree. Asking if he was police-checked. That was quite rude.'

'He didn't seem to mind. I feel more confident for knowing that he's been vetted. Also for meeting him.'

'I wonder if he feels better about you, too. I must ask him when I see him.'

Chapter eight

Moving day had been fixed for the first Sunday in August. As she waved him off, Jonah promised to come back soon and sort out the rest of his room. Nina knew how elastic 'soon' could be. She could at least tackle the laundry. It would take her mind off how empty the house was.

They'd given Jonah the best bedroom. The view over the little garden, bursting with lavender and honeysuckle and so many bees that Nina could hear them even from up here. Plain painted walls. Wooden shutters for days when the sun poured.

He'd stripped the bed. That was thoughtful. The plain steel-grey duvet cover was tastefully masculine. Its matching pillowcases smelled slightly stale.

Once upon a time, Nina must have bought the final superhero duvet set that Jonah would ever use. She tried to remember when. Growing up was so drawn out. It was impossible to keep track of all the first and last times for anything. Milestones passed without anyone noticing.

Chucking out the bunk beds. That had been a moment. There'd been heated discussion about getting them in the first place.

'That ladder,' she'd fretted. 'It's so dangerous. He's only eight.'

'He's a sensible boy,' Martin had said.

'What if he falls?'

'No one is going to fall,' Martin had said.

More arguments years later when Jonah decided that bunk beds were embarrassing and childish and had to go.

'That's a good idea,' she'd said. 'We can get twin beds if you like. Then you can still have a friend to stay any time you want.'

Sleepovers. The same rationale Martin had used when the bunk beds had first arrived, in bits, with badly drawn diagrams to explain how they fitted together. It was a miracle everyone had survived them.

'Twin beds are tragic,' Jonah had said. 'They're for old people. Don't you know anything?'

The double bed had killed off sleepovers. Or maybe he'd already outgrown them. More than a decade went by before any of Jonah's friends spent the night in his room. Then Kate. No discussion this time. No arguments. A silent expectation that Nina would welcome this calm new girlfriend into their home. 'She's not moving in, Mum,' Jonah had explained patiently. 'That would be weird. She might stay from time to time. Also, that green toothbrush in the bathroom, that's Kate's.'

*

It was no longer a child's room. A faint smell of aftershave mingled with the scents of an English summer's day. One

42

picture on the wall, spectacular Yosemite granite in its black-and-white Ansel Adams glory.

Clearly Jonah hadn't put away all his childish things just yet. Two lopsided model helicopters from his military history phase rested dustily on a high corner shelf. The smaller one had been deployed on numerous missions, from the bedroom window to the garden, where Martin would catch it before it crash-landed. He'd never missed. Its garish fleet-mate was made of Lego. Martin had christened it the Patchwork Apache. He'd rescued it from a mishap of lost bricks with a surgical strike on Jonah's Lego aviary. Flamingos, parrots and kingfishers had sacrificed bright wings to create a magnificent machine. They'd never been confident that it would fly, so hadn't tried.

Jonah had gone off helicopters when he was ten after his grandmother explained to him about pacifism. Martin was filling his head with far too much war nonsense, her mother had told Nina. If Martin minded this latest intervention, he'd never said. By then, he'd stopped commenting on anything Nina's mother did.

Jonah's attention had turned to space. This was so much more impressive. All those men (and a few women) with rockets. More enduring too. Jonah and Nina had long since painted over the shiny stars and planets that Martin had painstakingly stuck on the ceiling as a surprise for Jonah's eleventh birthday. It had been harder than they'd expected to obliterate the light. Dribs and drabs of the Milky Way shone through.

'We could get someone in to do it properly,' Nina had offered.

'I like it,' Jonah had said. 'We should leave it. Dad would be happy that I can see his stars.'

The walls had been redone many times, by professionals, the colour changing over the years, through the neon punk and black goth eras and settling on something with a stupid name that was basically white. Nina always asked the decorators to leave one strip of wall untouched. Martin had added height marks, every six months, until they stopped somewhere around Nina's chin. Jonah was adamant. He wanted to keep the marks to help him remember. It was important to remember how big he'd been when Dad had died, already nearly grown up.

Or how little. Nina thought that was a better way of looking at it. If they drew a new line now, she'd need to stretch up to reach it.

The room was cluttered but still seemed empty. Some of the furniture was gone. The carpet was oddly dappled. Bleak pale islands where a bookcase and a chest of drawers had been lifted, fringed by lines of ingrained dust.

He'd left a large cardboard box in a corner, with an unnecessarily convoluted note – 'Stuff to sort out later, do not throw out, Mum, also no snooping, I know you want to, but don't, OK.' Jonah's inadequate long-term filing system. 'It's the digital age,' he'd said, 'and we're saving the planet yet there's still all this paper shit. I need to go through it so I don't bin anything important. You can help me. My old school reports are in there somewhere. You'll like reliving those.'

The box had lost its sharp edges since it first arrived in the house bearing, according to the picture on the label, a fat cathode TV. Rummaging through the top wasn't really snooping. A couple of layers in, she found a little bundle of birthday cards. Splendid wholesome boys and gilt lettering. 'To My Grandson'. Inside, messages of love and encouragement in insipid italic fonts. Nina knew before opening them that they were from his other granny. Her own mother would never have bought anything so cloying.

Nina and Martin had known the hazards of small families. They'd worked hard to make sure that Jonah didn't feel left out, filling the house, and often the bottom bunk, with friends. Martin embarked on complicated collaborations with Jonah, running races in the park, building a den in the garden, researching the next big world sporting event, persevering with Lego models even though neither of them really had the knack.

All this teamwork was usually enough, although not always. Martin had complained to the school about a 'bloody tactless' class project on 'Everyone we love'. Most of the other kids were tangled up with aunties and uncles, cousins, grandparents, dogs, half-brothers, stepsisters, cats, people in faraway countries, ordinary brothers and sisters who were annoying and pinched their stuff but were someone to play with. There were new babies and hamsters and weddings and the occasional disaster area – a cousin in prison ('Hardly suitable for a school project,' Martin had said), an auntie who'd been on a TV game show and only won £10 ('A salutary lesson,' Martin had said).

Jonah had complained too. By nine, he'd perfected the art of escalating grievances. Two grannies were better than nothing. It still wasn't fair. Everyone else's family was bigger. There weren't enough people for anything exciting to happen. Also, they didn't ever see one of the grannies, so she didn't really count. Also, he only had the same mum and dad he'd started out with. Also, they didn't even have any pets, not even a goldfish.

'You don't need lots of people to make things exciting,' Martin had told Jonah. 'Not when you have an Action Dad, like me.'

As it turned out, he was right (he usually was). The evening Martin fell was the most excitement there had been for years in the quiet leafy street, ever since that famous actor had almost moved into number 8.

Nina and Martin had been going out for the evening. Jonah was away on a school trip to the Isle of Wight to mark the end of primary school. The water had been running a long time before it occurred to Nina that the loud singing in the bathroom had stopped.

A neighbour had heard screams and rung 999. The ambulance used its siren. Jonah was sorry to have missed it. He'd have helped, he'd told Nina, over and over again for days and days until she wanted to scream. If he hadn't been away on the stupid school trip, he'd have helped. Also, did she think Dad would be cross that he hadn't helped?

Nina hadn't helped either. The ambulance people hadn't let her go with them. The police had come too and left a young officer behind. She called Nina 'love'.

'Is there anyone I can call, love? The hospital will do their best, love. Where are your children, love? Can someone look after the children?'

'My husband,' Nina had said. 'You'd better call my husband. Use my mobile, here.'

'Love, your husband's had an accident. He's at the hospital. Is there someone I can call? A friend? Or another relative?'

'Mum,' Nina had said. 'Please call Mum. She'll know what to do. Please get my mum.'

Annette had indeed known what to do. She told the policewoman to put the phone on speaker so they could both talk to Nina. She confirmed that there was only one child, and he was away from home.

'So please drive my daughter to the hospital. Make sure she takes her house key and money for a taxi. I will get the first train up in the morning.'

In the days that followed, there was a death to register, organs to be donated, a funeral to arrange, people to be told, lawyers contacted, a grandson to be looked after. Annette bustled everything into shape. She cleaned up the bathroom where Martin had fallen. She arranged for the headteacher of the school to drive her to the Isle of Wight to collect her grandson. Jonah had been excited by that. He'd told Nina that the headteacher had a seriously nice car and, also, he was the only boy in the whole school ever to have ridden in it.

For the first few weeks, until long after the funeral, Annette had stayed at the house. Not in the 'guest room', occasionally used to shelter friends of Martin's who were over the limit to drive home, but in Jonah's bottom bunk.

'You need your rest, Nina,' Annette had said. 'This way, if he needs to talk to someone in the night, I can be there. I can explain things.'

'How?' Nina remembered asking. Or maybe, 'Why?'
Too many questions.

*

After the accident, Nina and Annette had become
email friends. This was Annette's doing. She had started
emailing almost every day – little bits of news from
Cornwall, questions for Jonah ('Is Harry Potter as exciting
as everyone makes out?'), invitations to come and stay
('I asked around and there are lots of places where Jonah
could do some more surfing lessons'). Cornish summer
holidays became the norm and sometimes Christmas too.

Annette had tried to coax Nina out of giving up work.
'Jonah's going to be at school all day. You need something
to get you out of the house.'

Then she'd tried to talk her into moving to Cornwall.
'We could both look after Jonah, and he loves the sea.'

Nina had said no to everything.

As Jonah got older, he and Annette had taken to
Facebook while Nina stuck firmly to email. It was easier than
talking. Her mother was an entertaining correspondent.
They swapped book reviews and caustic commentary on the
state of the world. Annette offered only oblique suggestions,
but the subtext was the same: move house, take an interest,
pull yourself together. Cornwall was looking wonderful
now that spring/summer/autumn/winter (even winter!)
was here. The local drama society was a bit cack-handed, but
great fun, even if, like Annette, you were strictly a backstage
type of girl. (Nina found 'girl' a particularly irritating
word.) There was a witchcraft museum across the county,

at Boscastle. 'We're so lucky to be alive today!' Annette wrote, the exclamation mark deadening any sympathy with the sentiment. 'Back then, women like us, alone and opinionated, would have been easy targets.'

Not like us. Like her, Nina had thought on reading the email. *I'm not alone. I've got Jonah.*

The ease of Nina and Annette's email friendship didn't translate to real life. The wry, lively online version of her mother had little in common with the cajoling, controlling person who turned up at appointed rendezvous. After some chat about the journey and the weather, a passive-aggressive comment on a new coat or haircut, Annette's desire to fashion Nina's widowhood into a lifestyle would take over. Nina needed to stop wallowing. There was Jonah to think of.

Nina started suggesting shorter and less frequent meetings. The train service was good these days, she told Annette. If they both set off early, they could meet for lunch somewhere halfway. Exeter, perhaps. Of course, Annette was welcome to come and stay in Twickenham, any time, but Nina knew that she was busy. It could be difficult to get away.

*

'We're supposed to talk about mothers, aren't we?' Nina had asked Niall at their most recent meeting.

'Are we?'

'Evidently. Isn't therapy all about people's mothers? Except when it's about sex? Or Oedipus, which is sex and mothers – the best of both worlds.'

'Is it?'

'Please don't tell me that you are a qualified therapist and you don't know about Oedipus.'

'Nina, if this is your way of telling me you want to talk about your mother, then we can talk about your mother. You're the boss.'

'I'd rather talk about Martin's mother. If that's OK with you.'

*

Martin hadn't been kind to his mother. He'd called her maddening, maudlin, meddling Maud. He'd make a funny humming noise when her name was mentioned. The trouble had started earlier but came to a head with the marriage. According to Martin, her objections had been (1) not in a church, (2) the baby, due four months after the hastily arranged wedding. She'd sat stony-faced through the ceremony.

When Jonah was born, Maud had rung to say she thought she'd better mention that she was going to be away for a couple of weeks around the time they might be thinking of the christening. Martin told her there wasn't going to be a christening.

'We should make an effort with your mum,' Nina had said to Martin, on and off over the years. Her objections to the wedding had been ridiculous, but she was that generation and she was in the North. Attitudes were a bit different up there. 'You know that Jonah would love to see more of his other granny. I don't want him growing up thinking it's OK for men to forget their mothers.'

Martin would change the subject.

Maud had met Jonah for only the fourth or fifth time in his life at the funeral. The birthday cards had started after that. Never any personal message, just 'Happy Birthday from Grandma Maud' and whatever doggerel the card company had printed.

'Maud's a funny name,' Jonah had said one year. 'It makes her sound very long-ago.'

Nina hadn't known that he'd kept the cards. She was glad.

Chapter nine

Sometimes Nina tried to imagine how life would have been if she had taken any notice of Annette. Not so much moving to Cornwall, which had always seemed too light and too damp. When they visited for the summer holidays, Nina had always been struck by the memorial benches that cluttered the coastline. People had loved these views all their lives, many of those lives outrageously short. Young dead men (and a few girls) brought to grief.

But carrying on working, keeping a toehold in an outside world that didn't revolve around Jonah. She did sometimes wonder about that.

'I'm sure I set you a bad example,' she'd said to Jonah one morning, years ago. He had finished university a few weeks before and was job-hunting.

'Not at all,' he'd said. 'Me out all day, you sitting around watching daytime telly. It's perfect aversion therapy. You've made me want to work. I couldn't do it, spend so much time hanging around the house. I need people.'

'Your father was like that,' said Nina. 'Always people around. And you know I don't watch daytime TV.'

'I've never understood, though. I mean, when I was still a kid, I can see that not going back to work made sense. I liked knowing you were here. But not when I stopped needing you.'

'You'll always need me. Someone to boast about you. Someone to drive you mad. Someone to wear a stupid hat to your wedding.'

'Not forgetting the home cooking and free ironing. That's what people assume if I tell them I still live at home. The ones that haven't met you, that is.'

'D'you know, I don't think I've ironed anything since your dad died,' said Nina. 'Those planet-wrecking, chemically made school shirts were a godsend.'

'You ironed Dad's shirts?'

'Once or twice. He was the same as you. He liked doing it himself. It made him feel powerful, making those sharp creases. Anyway, until you get a job, you won't understand how annoying working can be.'

'Oh, I've got a pretty good idea on that,' said Jonah. 'All those years making soya lattes haven't gone to waste.'

'An office job, I mean, with teams and a hierarchy, nine to five. Annual appraisals. Not larking about as a barista for a few hours to earn beer money.'

'Don't be such a snob. It was bloody hard work. Skilled, too.'

'Yes, but offices are terrible. Even if the work's OK, the people will drive you crazy. They get obsessed by job titles and things that make no difference to anything. I had one of those attention-seeking types in my little group. Everything revolved around her. When Martin died, I just knew she'd be the one to organise the collection, and a garish sympathy card – high-gloss poppies as if we were commemorating a war.'

'Wasn't she being kind?' Jonah said. 'Showing support?'

'She was enjoying herself. She brought a small troop from my office to the funeral too. An invasion. None of them had even met Martin. When I was deciding not to go back to work, she was part of the reason.'

'It's all coming out now,' said Jonah. 'I need a job. I'm not like you. People don't get on my nerves so much.'

'When's the interview again?'

'Thursday. The email's hilarious. They will be evaluating my people skills and my can-do attitude through an approved competency matrix. I've arranged to meet up with someone I knew a bit at uni who works there, so I can find out what that means in real life.'

*

Once he'd got the job, he started wearing shirts more often than T-shirts, even at weekends. Nina supposed that was better than growing into a middle-aged man whose clothes signalled how interesting they were – the Stones tour they'd seen live in Berlin or the marathon they'd run in Belfast. It made her feel old to see him dressing like his father. Peeping in his wardrobe, she saw that he'd left a couple of shirts behind; stripy with contrasting collars and happily out of fashion now. Nina toyed briefly with the idea of ironing one of them, just to get that Sunday smell of hot cotton and steam.

The days had never felt empty enough to do anything non-essential in the house. She couldn't remember when she had got so adept at watching time drift by. She could plan an entire day around one of the tiny chores that other people did on Saturdays – getting new watch batteries, having shoes reheeled, renewing the TV licence. All those things that kept running out. Twice a year, she would go and meet with her accountant (who was really Martin's accountant). A dead Martin was worth a lot of money; she needed help to keep track.

Even so, she'd have to find extra things to do now that Jonah had gone. He was quite time-consuming, always making plans that she had to accommodate or mitigate. He'd given her lots of warning. 'Mum?' he'd said. It must have been around Easter because she'd been picking daffodils from the garden. 'Can I ask you something?'

Nina had weathered the years of questions. Why was Dad dead? Why couldn't they get a dog? Why couldn't Jonah have a computer in his room, all his friends did? (All his friends had dads too, or stepdads, or every-other-weekend dads.) Now Jonah was twenty-four, his questions were less predictable and more reasonable. At least on the surface.

'You know Kate?' Jonah had continued.

'With the green toothbrush, and often in my kitchen in the mornings. That Kate?'

'We want to get a place together. Rent a flat. Brockwell or Dulwich or somewhere.'

'Oh,' said Nina. 'Are you here this evening? Only the

fridge is a bit dismal so we might have to get a takeaway, or I might just have egg on toast.'

'Is that it? About me and Kate, I mean.'

'What's there to say?' Nina had said. 'You and Kate. You'll enjoy a flat.'

'You don't mind?'

'It's not up to me. But, no, Jonah, it'll take some getting used to, but no, darling, of course I don't mind.'

Later, mashing tepid egg into cold toast, she'd thought how well she'd reacted. Taking it in her stride. It was what she did.

*

Kate had rung the next day. 'Jonah says he told you. Are you sure you don't mind?'

'Hi, Kate. Just suppose I did mind – and I don't – I don't suppose it would make any difference, do you?' Nina was firm.

'We don't want you to be lonely, that's all,' said Kate.

'Whatever makes you think I'm lonely?' said Nina.

'You must be,' said Kate.

'Must I?' said Nina.

'I mean, I would be. In your position.'

'In my position? What is this, have you taken up mind reading?'

'Nina, I know you, remember. You don't go to work. You don't have friends. You don't go out. Everything's Jonah. And me, obviously.'

Nina had been irritated. 'Well, maybe I want a break from that. Jonah, you, being all young and excited. Maybe

I'm tired of it.' She'd stopped herself. 'Look, Kate darling,' she remembered saying, 'I'm not trying to be nasty. I'm pleased for you. It's your turn to be happy.'

Did people take turns at being happy? Nina wondered now. It sounded like one of the questions Niall would ask her. She'd had her turn at being happy. She'd been good at it. Then the singing from the bathroom had stopped. The music had stopped.

Chapter ten

'He's been gone for four days,' she told Niall. 'I haven't heard a peep out of him, unless you count a text message, which I don't.'

'And how do you feel about that?'

'About what? The move, or the text, or the no other communication, not even a thank you for the housewarming present. You do need to be more precise with your interrogations.'

'Any of it. Or all of it,' said Niall. 'This is your space, Nina. You choose what we talk about.'

'Ah, yes. Talking therapy. The answer to all the world's problems.'

'You are still not persuaded of its value,' said Niall.

'No,' said Nina. 'Are you?'

'And yet, you keep coming back,' said Niall. 'I wonder why that is?'

Nina wondered that too. 'It makes them happy,' she said. 'Jonah and Kate. Well, Kate anyway. Jonah doesn't really approve.'

'It makes Kate happy? Is that important to you?'

'It's all questions today, isn't it?' said Nina.

'Why don't you humour me?' Niall said. 'I know that's another question. We can start gently. Tell me one thing you feel about something you have mentioned so far today.'

'I bought them a housewarming present. A vacuum cleaner. It's called Animal because everything has to have a name. It was expensive. I wanted to get them something boring and necessary that they'd resent spending money on, that they'd also use. Even Jonah is fundamentally quite clean.'

'And you're waiting for an acknowledgment?'

'He ought to say thank you. It's good manners. And it's an excuse to get in touch. I haven't spoken to either of them for four whole days.'

'I'm interested that you are counting the days.'

'They're important days,' said Nina. 'My first days on my own since forever. Please don't ask me how that makes me feel, because I don't know. I don't want to know.'

'It is good that you recognise change,' said Niall. 'You can learn to own it, if you're prepared to try.'

'You want me to own being on my own?' She'd like him better if he didn't talk in slogans.

'You can roll your eyes, Nina, that's a healthy reaction, although perhaps not the most constructive. How would it be if I asked you to tell me what being on your own means to you?'

There was a lot she wanted to say. She didn't know what was stopping her. She'd been alone before, sometimes for days on end as brief school trips gave way to larky holidays and some short-lived, ill-advised environmental volunteering in the wet wilds of Scotland in Jonah's first summer break from university. 'Camping. Rain. Midges. Fucking awful,' he'd said by way of explanation when he appeared back home after one night. She'd been so pleased to see him that she'd forgotten the lecture about the money she'd spent for his working holiday, the importance of not giving up if something was difficult or uncomfortable.

'A bit of me is hoping he might come back,' she said. 'I adore Kate. I'm lucky he fell for someone like her. Then I catch myself thinking that if it doesn't work out, he might live with me again.'

'And you'd like that?'

'At one level, yes, but of course not. Grown men shouldn't live with their mothers. It turns them into serial killers.'

'So it's a question of what people should or shouldn't do?' Niall asked. 'What about what they want to do?'

'Jonah wants to live with Kate. And not with me. What I want doesn't really come into it, which is as well, because I don't know.'

'I can help you find out what you want,' said Niall. 'If you'll let me. Perhaps between now and next time, you could make me one of our lists. Five things you can do that don't need Jonah.'

'Is that the old gratitude theory again?'

'Very good, Nina. You've admitted it's important, with what you said about Jonah and your gift.'

'Thanking someone for the thoughtful present is good manners,' said Nina. 'It's not the same as being grateful. I promise I'll think about it. As you asked so nicely.'

*

Outside, it was one of those still, grey days that could be any time between March and November. The bus home pottered through the uninspiring streets. She'd thought of four of the five things before it had even gone two stops. Pop into a shop. Catch a bus. Check her phone (nothing). Pick up a toy flung by a toddler in a buggy. None of them things she particularly wanted to do, although the way the child stopped screaming as soon as she handed over the grimy velveteen crocodile was cheering. Really, Niall was losing his grip. If he meant her to count things she was free to do now she wasn't picking up after her own child, he really should have said so.

Colin and Neville would be in the park. They'd turned up a few hours after Jonah drove off on Sunday, enticing her out for an early evening walk. 'Neville thought you might like company,' Colin had said. 'He gets his outing anyway, so if you don't want to come it's no skin off his nose. Or, rather, his snout.' Nina found this pedantic way of talking irritating, but she'd gone along anyway. Neville looked even more orange in the late light of an English summer's day. They'd taken the frisbee, which made for an energetic walk. Rather than fetching it – 'He thinks retrieval is someone else's job,' Colin had said – Neville would give chase, then stop and wait with his plastic prey for them to catch him up. If they were too slow, he'd yowl.

Between throws, Colin had told Nina a lot more about his weekly routine. Wednesdays were always working-at-home days, one anchor in the week to make sure that at least some of the creative design got done. That meant a walk with Neville in the middle of the day.

Following the path from the gate towards the riverside exit, Nina could see that Neville had company. He was rolling in the long grass near the old walnut tree, with a brown dog pouncing and egging him on. After a minute or so, the dogs switched roles, Neville abandoning his post briefly to come leaping up at her, his friend in hot pursuit. 'Neville! Down,' came the familiar voice. 'Sorry about that,' said Colin. 'He hasn't passed his not-jumping-up module yet.'

'He looks like he's having fun,' she said. The dogs had resumed their game. 'Do you remember that kids' rhyme, you know the one about the quick brown dog jumping over a lazy fox?'

'It's the other way round, isn't it?' he said. 'The fox jumps over the dog. The concept of a lazy fox is rather less plausible.'

'Less so than a brown fox? Not that any of it adds up. Foxes and dogs, foxes bad, dogs good, not to mention big, bad wolves. There's enough to worry about keeping people on track without imposing human characteristics on animals. So does this extra dog have an owner, or have you been out and found a brother or sister for Neville?'

'He's mine.' A woman walked towards them from the direction of the toilets.

'Nina, this is Linda,' said Colin. 'Another of the lunchtime dog walkers.'

'Hi, Nina,' said Linda. 'Did he behave himself?' This was aimed at Colin.

'Don't take this the wrong way but I'm not sure he even noticed you'd gone,' said Colin.

'He's pleased to see you now, though,' said Nina. The brown dog had trotted over and was rubbing itself round Linda's trouser legs, like a cat.

'He's trying to get the burrs from the grass off his coat,' said Linda. 'Meet Muddy.'

'As in Waters?' asked Nina.

'My husband likes to tell people that,' said Linda. 'Our famous blues-singing dog. My son chose the name because Muddy rolls in mud given half a chance. I can't see your dog?'

Stupidly, Nina felt embarrassed. 'I'm more of an observer,' she said. 'I've never been in a position to take on the responsibility, what with everything else that needs doing. I like them being around, especially in this park. They're interesting to watch, if that doesn't sound too stalky.' She was burbling. 'What I mean is, I don't have my own dog. Colin sometimes lends me Neville.'

'That sounds like the best of both worlds,' said Linda. 'Muddy's great, aren't you, boy, yes you are, but he's a lot of work. I resisted for ages. Gus – that's my son – wore me down in the end, he always does, and to be fair he's done his bit. Now he's leaving home, we might have to get a dog walker.'

'My son's just left home, too,' said Nina. *Get a grip*, she thought. This random woman didn't want to hear about Jonah.

'You know how weird it is then,' said Linda. 'Partly we're looking forward to it, no more negotiating round a teenager, and of course we're excited for him, heading off to Oxford. I can't believe he's eighteen already. Or that eighteen is old enough. He only ever eats fruit because I make him.'

'Mine's older,' said Nina. 'I'm still not convinced he's properly grown up. They say boys never do. Do you think Colin needs a hand?' She nodded over to where Colin, holding a lead, was trying to coax Neville out of the long grass. 'Neville,' she called. 'Come to Auntie Nina.'

She was briefly flattered when Neville bounded over. He swerved away just as she reached for his collar.

'He's gone on strike,' said Colin. 'I forgot to bring any bribes.'

'I've got some,' said Linda. 'Assuming you mean treats.'

'Thank you,' said Colin. 'You're a life saver. I've got a Zoom call at two and need to get home.'

'I can bring him if you like,' said Linda. Neville was standing a few feet away staring at them, ready to run at the slightest hint of an approach. 'Me and Muddy need to stay out for another while yet.'

'Or I can drop him off on my way home,' said Nina. 'I'm not in any rush and the park's so lovely.' *It is lovely*, she thought. This late in the summer, it had lost that try-hard atmosphere when everything was so busy blossoming and flourishing there was barely time to breathe.

'If you're sure you don't mind,' said Colin. 'Neville.' He put on the low, firm voice people use to impress their pets. 'If you don't come now, this minute, I am leaving you behind. I mean it. Bye, Neville.'

Neville watched him walk away, then turned and threw himself back into the long grass.

'Poor Colin,' said Linda. 'He adores that dog, but it's completely wilful; it takes no notice of anything he says.'

'You know them quite well then,' said Nina.

'We met through our dogs,' said Linda. 'Muddy made a beeline for Neville a couple of months ago, not long after they moved locally, and we've coordinated our walks when we can. It's great; they wear each other out as you can see.'

'I can indeed,' said Nina as the two dogs tore past, chasing each other in ever decreasing circles until they stopped at their feet.

'Gotcha,' said Linda, clipping a lead onto Neville. 'Join us? We can walk for a bit if you like.'

'I would like,' said Nina. 'Do you want me to take him?'

She realised that she had never walked a dog on a lead before. It felt strangely powerful. She could set Neville free or keep him close and there was nothing he could do about it. Muddy seemed content to trot along beside them, hanging back occasionally to sniff a tree or another dog, but always coming back if Linda called.

Part way round their second circuit of the park Neville started pulling on his lead in the direction of the gate. He looked at Nina and dabbed at her leg with his front paw.

'Someone's ready for home,' she said. 'This is my gate too, so if it's out of your way I can take him.'

'If you're sure,' said Linda. 'We should do this again. If you're not too busy. Tell Colin bye and we'll see him on Friday night.'

Friday night. More than just dog-walking friends then.

Chapter eleven

Colin had left his front door ajar. Neville shoved it open with his head and scuttled Nina into an overly tiled kitchen. He gulped water from his bowl.

'I'll just be a mo,' Colin called from an adjacent room. 'Just finishing up.' She eavesdropped as he concluded his discussion. He was all business. The deadlines were easily achievable, everything was on track, he very much looked forward to showing everyone his work on Friday week.

'The prodigal returns,' he said, joining Nina and Neville in the kitchen. 'Time for a brew?'

'I don't want to disturb your work,' Nina said.

'Another half hour won't hurt. I have mainly procrastination on this afternoon's schedule. Thank you for bringing this young man home.'

'Other way round,' said Nina. 'He brought me home.'

'Other way round. Like the fox and dog. I looked it up. The fox does the jumping.'

'Really?' She wasn't interested, but it was sweet that he'd bothered to look.

'Apparently so. I looked up the differences between foxes and dogs and the way we anthropomorphise them as well. It's amazing how much procrastinating you can do if you put your mind to it. Milk? Sugar? Biscuit? No, not you, Neville.' He cleared a place on the scuffed wooden table and put down a tray with a proper teapot, cups and saucers, a milk jug and a flowery bowl of sugar lumps with tiny tongs. 'Would you like to help yourself? The biscuits are in that tin. Home-made by Waitrose. Then I can see to this one.' He rubbed the dog's neck.

'He's in a bit of a state,' said Nina. 'That grass he was rolling in was pretty sticky.'

'Very ragamuffiny.' He did have a strange way of talking. 'Nothing that a good comb through won't sort out.' He picked up a double-sided hairbrush that was sitting on the draining board and started gently working his way through Neville's matted coat. Orange fur and an assortment of plant life floated into the air, landing mainly on the floor, although she watched as a stray hair from an upwards stroke pirouetted into the milk jug. If Neville was her dog Nina would have taken him into the garden to be groomed.

'Your tea things are lovely,' she said. 'You don't often see a Brown Betty anymore.'

'It's really old,' said Colin. 'Our flat was very modern so we got a lot of old stuff to temper it. This table is from the 1930s.'

She didn't like to ask who 'we' were. 'It's a funny name for a teapot,' she said. 'No one knows who Betty was. The brown is from the colour of the earth they use, the original clay or some sort of glaze.'

'Same as Linda and Muddy then, naming him after the earth.'

'I suppose so. She said cheerio,' Nina remembered, 'and something about Friday night.'

'She can make it. That's good,' said Colin. She hoped he'd elaborate, but he started talking about Muddy and the jolly japes – he used that awful phrase – the two dogs had on their shared walks.

'They turned quite demure after you'd gone,' said Nina. 'Linda and I were able to have a good conversation about our sons.' In truth, Linda had done most of the talking. Gus was a serious-minded boy. His teenage rebellion took the form of disapproving of everything his parents thought, let alone did, and haranguing them endlessly about why they were wrong. He went on a lot of marches. Linda and her husband, Dmitry, were forever tripping over placards. 'She's glad he's going, just to get some peace and quiet, or so she says,' Nina continued. 'She'll feel differently when he's actually gone.'

'I've met Gus,' said Colin. 'He takes Muddy out sometimes. He's not a very restful sort of person. He'll be there on Friday, so you'll see what I mean.'

'Friday?' said Nina.

'The dog walkers' pub quiz. Didn't Linda tell you? It's that pub tucked away behind the station. You should come along. Now that you're a bona fide dog walker, that is.'

'I'll think about it,' she said. 'Thank you.' It might be fun. She'd probably go. Unless Jonah called in, of course; he'd said he'd pop back over the weekend.

Tea really did taste better from a proper teapot. She accepted the offer of a second cup and they chatted for over an hour, mostly about Colin's plans for the house and the strange things people think they need to make a home. His china plates had been his parents'. And the sugar bowl. People shouldn't just chuck stuff out when people died.

As she was leaving, Colin asked her if she'd give him an honest opinion on something. That was the worst question to ask anyone. It was always so hard to know what to say. Fortunately, he was only asking about the tiles in the kitchen.

'When I was looking at the house before buying, it looked fun,' he said. 'A beige house, your standard blank canvas, and then this kitchen. Now I'm living with it, I'm not so sure.'

'They're certainly bright,' she said. 'And numerous. They make quite a statement.' Three of the walls were covered almost to ceiling height with a dizzying arrangement of yellow, red, brown and turquoise. 'They might be OK if you hung some pictures over some of them,' she said.

'Or if I got someone in to rip them all out and start again,' he said.

'There is always that option,' said Nina.

*

She was still thinking about redecorating when she got home. Apart from the bathroom, just that once, and Jonah's room, she hadn't bothered much. Everything was a serviceable white. A cheerful pair of brothers, Wlodek and Jerzy, had been on hand every three or four years to refresh anything too tired. 'A new start,' she said out loud. It sounded so easy when you only had to say the words.

Chapter twelve

On Thursday morning, she cracked. Jonah's phone went to voicemail. She sent a text.

'You're alive then?' she said, as he called back. Half an hour wasn't bad. She must have pitched her message about right. Insistent but not too anxious.

'Why wouldn't I be?'

'Oh, you know. Global apocalypse. Bubonic plague. Pointless, trivial accident.'

'I am very much alive and so is Kate. You worry too much. We'd have rung, only it's been mad getting the flat sorted out. I'm at work now so can't talk long.'

'One tiny phone call. Hello, Mum. It's chaos. I miss your cooking. Thank you for the lovely present. How hard can it be?'

'You could have rung me, if you'd wanted to know how we were getting on.' There was a defensive whine in his voice.

'I will always want to know how you're getting on,' she said. 'And I will always worry about stupid accidents.'

'Well, don't,' said Jonah. 'Lightning doesn't strike twice.'

That wasn't true. You only had to look at the news or poke around a churchyard.

'Don't let's argue, Jonah,' she said. 'It is good to hear your voice. Are you all unpacked now?'

'More or less.'

'And you're coming to sort out the rest of your stuff this weekend? Like we agreed.'

'Well...' There was a silence.

'Well, what? I thought we'd agreed.'

'It's just, Kate...' he started.

'So it's Kate's fault.'

'If you let me finish, Mum.' The patience-of-a-saint tone he always used to explain things she wouldn't entirely want to hear. 'Kate's been pulled into the team at the O2 for Saturday's gig.'

'Let me guess. It's bring-your-boyfriend-to-work day.'

'Partner. Not boyfriend. We're not fourteen. Also, don't be ridiculous. She gets a guest ticket. You know it's my favourite band and the tickets sold out months ago.'

She couldn't keep track of Jonah's favourite bands. 'Remind me of the name,' she asked. She'd have to google them later. 'Surely they all have their own lighting crews?'

'They bring in local techies to help rather than fly everyone in from the States. She's there all weekend so if I came it would just be me, and a rush, so we wondered instead if we could come across one evening in the week.'

She could hardly say no. After months of lighting dreary corporate events and shopping centre installations, it would be good for Kate to do something more exciting.

'Also, Mum,' Jonah said, 'don't take this the wrong way, but do you still have the receipt for the hoover?

Not to worry if not, it's very handy and lightweight and thank you, only there is one already in the flat, it's cordless which is brilliant, and if you did have the receipt and it was from John Lewis or somewhere then there are other things we need more and it seems a shame for it just to sit in a cupboard taking up space and also Kate said it was better just to tell you and you wouldn't mind and would rather know.'

'So many words in such a short time,' she said when he paused. 'You could be a racing commentator. Or a rap artist. Or do I mean grime artist?'

'Kate said I should ask.'

'I expect I can find the receipt somewhere,' she said. The binmen didn't come until Friday. It might still be in the recycling. 'Why don't you make a list of what it is you need and we can see what we can sort out. Now, shall we say Tuesday for you and Kate to come over?'

'That'd be great. See you then.'

*

Her own bright-orange vacuum cleaner had seen better days. Its smirky face was wearing away, rather like her own, and it was selective about what it would lift. Some marketing genius decided that machines should be given human names and personalities, and now they behaved as unreliably as people. Something lighter and pet-friendly might come in handy. Jonah and Kate could have a gift voucher. Or, more likely, Jonah would enter their wish list straight into the John Lewis website and mock-casually open the page at the check-out icon, waiting for her to offer to pay on her credit card. Many of his baffling gadgets had found their way into the house like that.

Tuesday was only five days away. He'd come straight from work, expecting to be fed (to be fair, she had said she'd cook something celebratory). There'd be no time to clear his room or do anything useful, but she could talk to him about redecorating. Give him a deadline. She'd already tidied up a corner of the attic, ready to welcome anything he wasn't sure he was ready to throw away.

Wlodek's number was still in her phone. A young voice answered. Yes, they were still very much in business and Nina was on their system as a valued loyal customer. Nina imagined a database of customers by category – Valued and Loyal, Awkward, Crap at Paying, Litigious. The girl could send Dad or Jerzy round to chat about what Nina might want doing. There was a window on Monday if that was any good?

Dad. Wlodek had shown her pictures of his family, fair-haired with open, wide faces. He talked about them a lot. It was one of the reasons she liked him. The daughter, the eldest, would be grown up by now and, it seemed, working in the family business. She didn't have even the slightest hint of an accent, but of course children didn't talk like their parents and she'd lived here most of her life.

Chapter thirteen

The pub had a large conservatory, opening up onto a small patio area where three people were smoking. Most of the quizzers had left their dogs at home, but Neville was there, sleeping on a rug by Colin's feet, curled up with a white puffball who Colin said was called Mildred 'as in George and'. He whispered that poor George had crossed the rainbow bridge, only yesterday. Incredibly sad and everyone was heartbroken. He waved sympathetically at Mildred's family at the next table – a couple about her age and an older woman. They waved back and raised glasses. They didn't look like people whose dog had died only hours ago. Perhaps they were putting on a show.

Altogether there were about twenty people arranged in teams around pale tables. Nina hadn't been in this pub since it changed hands and evidently moved upmarket. It wouldn't be brilliant in the winter. For a chilly August evening, it was pitch-perfect, proud glossy plants, arty books and bright ceramics breaking the starkness of the blond wood and gleaming glass.

A scrawny boy in a Coal Not Dole T-shirt called them to attention. His hair looked like it might have been a mohican before it grew out.

'That shirt's going back a bit,' Nina whispered to Linda, who'd beckoned her to sit next to her.

'No cause is ever too old,' said Linda, 'not in our house. That's Gus. Colin might have mentioned that he runs the quiz.'

'When Mum has stopped talking,' said Gus, 'welcome to round one. That's round one of questions, not drinks, although just a reminder that this is a pub, so drinks are encouraged. In moderation – and if you're driving, then, next time, walk.' He thumped the table. 'The round one questions are specially curated with Mildred and Muddy, who sends his apologies, and Neville and Peter and Wendy in mind.' Nina could see Peter and Wendy in the garden, playing a growly game of tug of war with a pink towelling rope, loosely supervised by one of the smokers. They were tough, purposeful animals, some kind of terrier, not at all suited to their fey names.

'Question one,' Gus continued. 'Who invented the pooper-scooper and, for a bonus point, in what year? Question two. What was the first city in the world to introduce dog poo laws and, for a bonus point, in what year?' This went on for another five questions.

'Who knew there was so much to learn about dogshit?' the man opposite asked when Gus announced a break for people to go to the bar. This was Linda's husband, the fourth member of their team. He sounded American. 'I'm Dima, short for Dmitry,' he'd said when Nina arrived. 'I'd get up, only as you can see…' His wheelchair was a bit too high for the table.

'Faeces are endlessly fascinating,' said Colin. 'At least to Neville. One of his very favourite games is to find another dog's excrement and roll in it. They don't mention that in the adopt-a-dog brochures.'

'Most people do pick up, though,' said Linda. 'Thanks to the poo laws. There used to be nothing worse than treading in mess, especially in the summer.'

'I dodged a bullet there,' said Dima. 'I can't tread in anything and I can't reach the ground to gather Muddy's offerings. I guess that makes me the lucky one.'

Gus clanged a glass. 'Right, ladies, gents, people who don't identify as either, or anything, are you ready for some answers?' The pooper-scooper was from the 1950s, which no one believed until they looked it up on Wikipedia. 'It was a very bad invention,' said Gus. 'Everything you collect goes straight to landfill. If you want to know more about greener methods of reducing your dog's carbon, and indeed methane and nitrogen, paw print, then catch me at the end of the quiz. Now, to round two.'

The remaining rounds covered more conventional fare, each theme focused on a decade. She scored points for her team naming the original members of Duran Duran. Colin knew all the technology questions, and between the four of them they covered off most of politics and movies. At the start of the final round, they were in equal lead with Mildred's family, but then it was 1970s sport. Niki Lauda. Martina Navratilova. Three people none of them had heard of. A gymnast they said was Russian and Gus said was from Belarus. 'Not the same thing at all, not even, as the song goes, "Back in the USSR".' He awarded the win to the George Memorial team.

'Did you enjoy it?' Linda asked Nina as one of the bereaved victors claimed their prize, a packet of Bonio and a bottle of Prosecco.

'Very much. Gus is quite the quizmaster. Very informative.'

'Hectoring,' said Dima. 'Didactic. The pub love him because he gets people talking about issues and they stay and argue over more drinks. It can be a bit much, especially when he brings politics into everything.'

'He'd get on with my mother,' said Nina. 'She's a great one for causes and campaigns.'

Mildred's family came over to collect her. There were embarrassed mutterings about how sorry they were about poor George. Neville woke up and was outraged to find his fluffy friend being spirited away. He started barking in a way that drew looks from other tables. 'I'm going to have to take him home,' said Colin. 'Walk with us, Nina?'

'You're welcome to stay, Nina,' Linda said. 'Gus will most likely disappear off to meet his friends once he's finished evangelising. We'll get something to eat. They do a mean fish and chips.'

'If you're sure you don't mind. I don't want to intrude.'

'Not at all. I'd like you to stay.' Nina thought she heard something pleading in the tone. 'And you'll come back, won't you, Colin, once you've settled his nibs?'

'I can't see his nibs tolerating that,' said Colin. 'He had a home-alone afternoon and it didn't go well.'

Nina had hardly spoken to him all evening. 'I tracked down Jonah,' she said. 'They're coming to dinner on Tuesday. Join us if you'd like, and Neville too, of course.'

'Poor Colin,' Linda said, watching the yapping dog lead him out of the pub. 'Neville's adorable, but he's only ever lived with women. He has no idea that Colin is supposed to be in charge. Not that Colin seems to have worked that out either.'

'He's a lovely dog,' Nina said. 'I babysat him a few days ago. He was no trouble. I spoke to him the way I used to talk to Jonah when he was little.'

'My point exactly. Neville needs to be in a family where a woman calls the shots.'

'We could do a trade,' said Dima. 'Our household is three males and three females, Nina, and the females are most definitely in charge.'

'Take no notice of him, Nina,' Linda said. 'I'm going to order. Fish and chips for you? And another glass of wine?'

'Thank you. Yes please. I only met Linda for the first time this week,' she said to Dima. 'I didn't realise you had other children?'

'We don't. Two cats, females, two adults, one nearly adult and one dog. The she-cats rule the roost.'

'It sounds like a busy household,' said Nina. 'It's just me now; my son moved out at the weekend.'

'No animals?'

'None. Unless you count the foxes or the wasps, which seem to be rampant this year. I must have a nest.'

'And no husband? Is that too direct?'

'People never ask,' Nina said. 'Direct is refreshing. He died. A long time ago now, although it often feels like it happened last week. Time's very bendy like that. And now can I ask you a direct question?'

'Accident. Eight years ago. I fell off my bike.'

'Actually, I wasn't going to ask about the wheelchair.'

'Also refreshing. People ask and don't know what to do with the answer.'

'I didn't think it was any of my business. I was interested in your name. It's very Russian but you sound American, and you don't look Russian.'

Dima appeared amused. 'I left my Cossack hat at home. Not much call for it in August.'

'You know what I mean. You don't have those typical Slavic features. Cheekbones.' He was shaking his head at her. 'I'm digging a hole for myself, aren't I?'

'It's lucky Gus has gone home,' Dima said. 'He'd be off on one about judging books by covers, although he'd call it much worse.'

'Gus would call what worse?' said Linda, returning with the drinks.

'Nina is just questioning my heritage,' said Dima.

'I'm sorry,' said Nina. She couldn't read his tone. 'I didn't mean anything. I find it fascinating, how names do and don't affect expectations. Like those dogs earlier, Peter and Wendy.'

'We were talking about me,' Dima said. 'I've got Russian ancestry, four generations back. I've never been there and have the same level of ignorance about it as the next US born and raised guy. The original family surname was Smirnov, which caused its own assumptions. My dad fixed that by taking my mom's name. He was teetotal and couldn't deal with the irony.'

'How about you?' Linda asked. 'Nina could be Russian. Or musical. Nina Simone.'

'Stolidly British since forever. Jonah looked into it in great detail when Brexit happened in case we could wangle any other nationality. Nina's one of those names with lots of meanings. When I was about twelve, I decided it was after Columbus's ship. I rather liked the idea of sallying forth and exploring the world.'

'And do you?' asked Dima. 'Are you a great explorer? Do you have stupendous adventures right here in Twickenham?'

He was mocking her. She was sure of it. 'None of the above,' she said. 'One way and another, my husband dying was adventure enough. Thanks to insurance, it meant I didn't have to work, and I've been quite busy enough bringing up Jonah.'

'I wouldn't like that,' Linda said. 'Not working.'

'Note that she didn't say she wouldn't like being a widow.'

Nina thought it best to ignore that. 'I assumed you didn't work,' she said to Linda. 'There I go, assuming again. Colin said you were one of the regular lunchtime dog walkers.' The coarse grey plait and drapey scarf had made Nina wonder if she was an artist.

'I'm a university professor. Law. Mainly research and I do a lot of it from home. It doesn't really matter when I put the hours in, and getting out at lunchtime keeps me sane.'

'Whereas it drives me mad,' said Dima. 'Getting out anywhere is a huge palaver. You should feel honoured that I've made the effort, Nina. I am also a lawyer, as I am sure you were planning to ask. Commercial property planning law. Acting always for the big guys, much to our son's, and I suspect sometimes my wife's, chagrin.'

'Is Gus studying law? Following the family footsteps?' It was something to say. It wasn't relaxing dealing with Dima. She hoped the food would arrive quickly so she could eat and leave.

'History and Politics,' said Linda. 'It depends on his A-level results next week. He's done brilliantly all the way through and he found the admissions test easy, so we are confident.'

'Those are subjects I can at least understand what they're about,' said Nina. 'Jonah did Marketing. He talks in riddles.'

'Snake oil,' Dima said.

'I don't follow.'

'Marketing. It's all about manipulating people into wasting money on fake products.'

'Not entirely,' Nina said. 'You don't always know what you need until someone points it out to you.' She often wished Jonah was doing something more tangible, but she wasn't going to have a stranger criticise him.

The food arrived. Linda rootled around at the back of the wheelchair and produced a broad tray that fitted neatly across the arms to make a tabletop. It was nicer than a TV-dinner tray that you'd use when you couldn't be bothered to do anything. Even so it was somehow demeaning. Like a toddler's highchair. Maybe Dima didn't see it like that. Nina noticed that all through the meal, they both talked to her or, in Dima's case, talked at her. They never spoke directly to each other, not even to ask if they'd pass the salt.

Chapter fourteen

'Thank you, Nina, that was a real treat,' said Kate, stacking the last of the dinner plates into the dishwasher. 'We've been living on takeaways since the move.'

'There's dessert, too,' Nina said. 'Courtesy of Colin.' She lifted a deep blue tureen from the freezer.

'It's only ice cream,' said Colin. 'But it's home-made.'

Nina tried not to think of the dog brush on his kitchen draining board or the hair floating in his milk jug. 'I've got some fruit salad as well,' she said. 'Not very home-made, although I did pick some blackberries along the towpath this morning and shoved them in. They seem to come earlier every year, the blackberries.'

For a few moments, Nina's kitchen fell silent, bar the low humming of the fridge and the clang of spoons on dark grey bowls.

'I can tell you do a lot of cooking, Colin,' Kate said. 'This is delicious.'

'I like food. You can probably tell. I used to do more before I got Neville. He likes to help, which is charming, if largely counterproductive.'

'Speaking of Neville,' said Jonah. 'He's very quiet. Should someone go and check?'

'Good idea,' Nina said. 'You could stick your head in on your way to the stairs. You know, the ones that go up to your room that you are going to sort out this evening.'

Nina wasn't sure how Jonah managed to disturb a sleeping dog. He only had to have a quick look through an open door where they'd left him dreaming on the sofa. She watched Neville pad into the kitchen and head straight for the dishwasher, licking plates until Kate, who was nearest, slammed it shut. He was probably allowed to do that at home.

Neville moved to the French doors, closed against the drizzle, and started barking. 'Does he want out?' asked Nina.

'I don't think so. He's probably shouting at foxes. They have some lively discussions. I find it's better for peace and quiet to keep him away from the windows in the evenings.'

'Coffee in the living room in that case,' Nina said. 'Go and grab a pew, Colin, and take Neville with you. I'll bring the coffee through in a minute.'

'None for me, thanks,' said Kate. 'I'll nip upstairs and see if Jonah needs a hand.'

Nina thought about fishing the espresso maker and its dinky cups from the back of the cupboard. She'd been brought up to make an effort for guests. Maybe not that much effort. 'This is a mugs, not a cup and saucer, household, as you can see. Not that I didn't have huge teapot envy at yours,' she said to Colin as she plonked a tray down on the coffee table. She loved these mugs. Solid, bright colours that lit up any mood. 'Help yourself to milk and sugar.' She watched as he heaped three spoons into the royal blue mug, stirring vigorously.

The room didn't look quite right without the small sofa Jonah had purloined for his rented flat. Nina had moved other furniture around to fill the gap. Now she had company, an actual guest, she could see that the new arrangement didn't entirely work. To reach the coffee table, both people would need to sit on the remaining sofa, one end of which was covered in Neville's special sheet. Neville himself was on the floor by Colin's feet.

'Actually, I'd better not drink this,' Nina said, retreating to an armchair. It would be too awkward squeezing in next to Colin. He took up a lot of space. 'I have enough trouble sleeping as it is.'

'Neville and I should toddle home soon, leave you all in peace.'

'I wasn't hinting,' Nina said. 'There's no rush. Jonah will be down in a bit asking if he can take my car to go home with whatever clobber they've decided is essential. And Neville seems happy, not like the other night at the pub.'

'That wasn't his finest hour. Normally he lasts a bit longer on quiz night. Linda said you had a nice evening after we'd gone.'

'I stayed until about nine. I hardly ever eat out, except with Kate or Jonah. It made a change, and it was kind of her to include me.'

'Linda's great,' Colin said. 'Very sociable. Dima's a bit tricky at first. Did you find that?'

Nina wondered why he was asking. 'Did they say anything?' she said. 'I got the impression he didn't like me very much, or approve of me, it was more that. It might just be his way, of course. He's very forthright.'

'Very,' said Colin. 'According to Linda, it's his Russian heritage or his American upbringing or his lawyerly education.'

'I found him a little intense. They both are. Clever. It can't have been easy for them, adjusting after his accident. I don't know what we'd have done if that had been Martin. He'd have been so angry. Although he'd be much angrier about being dead, so it's all relative.'

If she wasn't careful, she'd find herself rabbiting on about Martin. She didn't know Colin well enough for all of that, not yet anyway. She changed the subject. 'I had a builder round yesterday,' she said. 'Someone I've known for ages. His son was one of Jonah's friends at school. I could give you his number. For your kitchen tiles. That's what gave me the idea, talking about your plans for your house. They do gardens, too, if you're interested.'

*

Jerzy had turned up while she was having breakfast, greeting her as an old friend. 'Nina! Is long time! And house, it look like is long time too!' It had been good to see him. She gave him coffee (in the red mug) and showed him Jonah's room. He asked her puzzling questions about what she wanted to do with all that space now that Jonah had gone.

'He complicated everything,' she told Colin now. 'Once their kids had moved out, Jerzy and his wife sold up. Downsized.'

'That doesn't sound like very good business negotiation,' said Colin. 'You'd think he'd do better telling you to remodel the whole house.'

'He did that too. He's coming back on Friday to talk me through some ideas. A big plan, he calls it, which I assume means expensive. He got me thinking, though. Do I really want to rattle around a three-bedroom house on my own?'

'You could get a dog,' Colin said, gently rubbing Neville's belly with his foot.

'So Jonah and Kate keep telling me. I can see the advantages. Neville's lovely. I'm not sure I can be bothered with the responsibility. Borrowing yours seems like a good compromise.'

Jonah and Kate emerged from upstairs, empty-handed. 'We have a plan, Mum,' Jonah said.

'That sounds ominous. Colin and I were just talking about plans.'

'It's a good plan. For my things. We've labelled everything. A for attic, D for dump and H for home.'

Home, she thought. This had always been Jonah's home. 'That sounds very organised. Congratulations. And have you worked out how your property is magically going to find its way to A, D and H?'

'The "H" bit, so far.' He looked quite pleased with himself. 'We could put it in the car now so it's out of your way. Save you carrying everything. It's not much, and then you can drive when you come to lunch, on Saturday.'

'Who said anything about lunch on Saturday?'

'I did. Just now. Kate and me are inviting you to lunch on Saturday. Also, we wondered, as you don't use it much, if we could borrow the car for a few days after. You know we're going to Granny's on Sunday and the trains aren't running. Engineering works.'

'I'll have to let you know about the car,' said Nina. 'I might need it next week. Saturday would be lovely, thank you, so why don't you bring your stuff downstairs and we can see if it will all fit. Is it all neatly boxed up? No, I thought not.'

'Bin bags will be fine,' said Jonah. 'I'll just grab some.' He went into the kitchen, Neville trotting optimistically at his heels.

'Is there a lot to go to the dump?' Colin asked Kate. 'I've booked a slot on Friday, as it happens, so could cram some more in.'

'I can't have you doing that,' Nina said. 'Jonah can make his own arrangements.'

'What own arrangements?' Jonah appeared at the door, brandishing a black plastic roll. 'You'll need to get some more bags next time you're ordering a delivery,' he said. 'Luckily there's enough here for now.'

'Colin was offering to take stuff to the dump for you.'

'Brilliant, Colin, that would be brilliant. I owe you one.'

'And I was just explaining to Kate why that wouldn't be possible.' Nina was firm.

'Do you want to come upstairs and see what there is?' Jonah said.

'Did you hear what I said? Colin can't take your things.'

'Sure he can. It's only a few bits and pieces. Most of the stuff is going in the attic. I'll help you shift it next time I'm over, Mum. D'you want to take a look, Colin?'

Colin started to get up, then seemed to think better of it. No wonder he looked embarrassed, Nina thought. She often worried that Jonah was too used to getting his own way. 'It's up to you. Don't feel under any obligation,' she said to Colin.

'It can't do any harm to do an assessment,' Colin said. 'Survey the task in hand. Lead the way, Jonah.' The stairs creaked as he followed Jonah up.

Kate stretched on the sofa, putting her feet on Neville's sheet. 'Is Neville still in the kitchen?' she asked. 'That silence is a bit suspicious.'

'I'll check.' Nina found him under the table, chewing the oven glove. She'd bought it on impulse on her last visit to Kew, drawn by its beautiful colours – navy, orange and a mustardy shade – and the slightly stylised design of the flowers. Using it made her think about the promise of spring. 'Are you going to give that back?' She pulled on the free end. Neville growled half-heartedly, his tail flicking, and retreated further under the table.

'He's happy,' she told Kate, returning to the living room. 'Destroying my property. Now, how did you get on at the weekend?'

'The O2? We were absolutely the hired help, but it was great to see such a big operation. The lighting designers are geniuses, easily as creative as the band.'

'Ah yes. The Appropriate Adults. The name seems a bit tasteless to me. Still, what do I know? I read a review. Something about capturing the modern zeitgeist – can you have an unmodern zeitgeist, I wonder? – with a startling fusion of metal, bluegrass and uptown funk.'

'I didn't see much and we wore ear protectors. Jonah enjoyed it and it's given him bragging rights.'

'Surely Jonah doesn't need any more of those?'

Kate looked puzzled. 'What makes you say that?' she asked.

'Jonah,' Nina said. 'Obviously I'm biased, I'm his mother. From where I stand, he's got everything. Tall, handsome, bright, job with prospects, the flat, friends, his delightful, sensible, not-a-pushover girlfriend. That's you, by the way.'

'I figured that out.'

'A mother who will always look after him,' Nina said.

'He appreciates that,' said Kate. 'We both do.'

'It is good that you're not a pushover, though. I do worry a bit occasionally that he takes people for granted. Like he just assumed that Colin would help with the room clearance.'

'Colin did offer,' Kate said.

'Or me, with the car. Or helping himself to my furniture.'

'What's brought this on?' said Kate. 'If something's not convenient, you only have to say no. Like with the car. We can easily hire one. Or there is a replacement bus for the trains. It's a faff and will take a bit longer. It's perfectly do-able, though.'

'I don't like saying no to Jonah.'

'Well, luckily I don't mind it,' said Kate. 'Now, should we go upstairs and see what's taking those two so long? They're probably embroiled in some retro computer game by now.'

They found Colin and Jonah sitting on the floor upstairs, carefully dismantling the Lego helicopter into colour-coded piles. Nina wondered why. She supposed it was a good sign, that Jonah was so casually destroying

Martin's inept handiwork. Thirteen years was plenty of time to mourn, and it didn't mean he'd completely forgotten his father.

Chapter fifteen

After clearing up the next morning, Nina went for a walk. She hadn't been to the park on her own for days now. Mindfulness. That was supposed to be what you did if you walked in nature by yourself. Everything had to have a purpose. Life was simpler when you could just go outside for the sake of it.

Quite a few of the regular dogs were out on their daily prowl and a lot of extra children frittering the end of their school holidays in a way Nina found reassuring. She stopped to watch a girl of about twelve throw a ball into the river for an enthusiastic golden retriever. She'd never seen a smilier dog. The girl was a good thrower. Maybe she played cricket; a lot of girls did these days. She was with two friends who sat on a bench, giggling over a phone and adding the occasional commentary. 'Great throw, Immy. Great fetch, Herbie.' They looked like they could stay there all day.

Nina felt something touch her leg and looked down to see forlorn eyes gazing up at her. A brown tail wagged tentatively as the dog gave a snivelly whine. 'Muddy?' She wasn't sure. The tail moved faster. 'What are you doing here?' Looking up and down the towpath, she couldn't see any sign of Linda or Gus, so she headed back into the park. Muddy padded too close beside her, almost tripping her up.

She'd come out without her phone. Colin would have Linda's number. After about twenty minutes looking round the park, she headed to his house, welcomed by ever louder barking from Neville, who was on sentry duty in the front garden. 'Greetings!' Colin said. He looked like he'd only recently got up. He was wearing ill-advised shorts and worse socks. 'How kind of you to bring something to entertain Neville,' Colin continued. 'Look how excited he is to have a visitor.' Neville had sprung into action, chasing Muddy up and down the narrow staircase.

'Hi, Colin. It's a relief to find you in. I didn't know what else to do. I found Muddy, as you can see. I think he's lost and I've got no way of contacting Linda.' She explained how Muddy had sought her out. 'He's probably fine and then I'll feel stupid. He did seem to be on his own and I thought you could phone. I don't have her number.'

'No problemo.' That was irritating. 'Take the weight off while I find out what's what.' He ushered her into the kitchen. The table was empty apart from half a peanut butter sandwich and a banana skin on a rather lovely emerald-green plate. It looked like a lazy kind of breakfast.

'Righty ho, no it's no trouble,' she heard as he finished his call. 'Seems you were mainly right, Nina, after a fashion. Muddy was with Dima and Gus until they argued. Dima and Gus, I mean, not the dog; he's always very mellow. Gus stomped off; Linda doesn't know where to, but Muddy will have followed him for a bit and then given up.'

'And Dima?'

'It's tricky for him with Muddy. The lead and his wheels don't mix. He waited for a while, then went home. Apparently it's happened before and the dog makes his own way back. Linda's at an outpatients' appointment. She can pick him up later, or she did ask if one of us was at a loose end, if we could drop him back home. It's on the other side of the park.'

'I suppose I could do that,' Nina said. She didn't have any other plans. 'Can I borrow one of Neville's leads?'

'You can borrow Neville as well, if you like. You'd be doing me a favour.'

The dogs were still capering on the staircase with a boisterous energy that was less charming indoors. 'I'd love to, but I'm not confident I can deal with the pair of them. We could all go?'

Colin seemed to consider this for just long enough for Nina to think he was genuinely tempted before an elaborate headshake and lots of words about his work deadline. 'Sorry, sunshine,' he said to Neville, holding onto his collar as Nina clipped a lead onto Muddy and dawdled at the front door.

'Oh dear,' she said, 'he does look outraged. He's making me feel guilty. I'll make it up to you, Neville, I promise.'

'See you later,' Colin said. 'You know the place I mean? Linda and Dima are flat one on the left. I'll let them know you're on your way.'

*

'It's Nina, the great explorer!' Dima greeted her at the front door. 'You found your way OK? Muddy's a good navigator. He could have saved you a lot of trouble.'

'It was no trouble,' Nina said. As soon as she let him off the lead, the dog crept past Dima and scuttled indoors.

'Of course, you did strictly speaking create trouble for me too. Taking away an animal, without the owner's consent.'

'I thought he was lost. He told me he was lost.'

'He told you? Is that zoolingualism? Or a form of witchcraft?'

'Empathy,' said Nina. 'He looked sad and a bit frightened. I couldn't see Linda or Gus, so I decided to help him.'

'You didn't look for me, I notice.'

'No. You told me that you don't walk Muddy.' She didn't want to sound defensive. 'The normal response when someone does you a favour is to say thank you.' Now she was sounding rude.

'You're quite right. Thank you, Nina,' Dima said. 'Will you stay and say hello to Linda? She's on her way back.' He turned his chair away from her and wheeled along a wide, tiled hallway. Nina followed him into an open-plan kitchen and reception room. A tabby cat slept on one of the fat turquoise sofas. 'Make yourself at home. Although I'd recommend you use the other sofa. Hillary there is not one for sharing.'

'Hillary?'

'I told you the cats were the first ladies in this household. That's Hillary. Michelle will be asleep on one of the beds. I believe, this being Britain, this is the point at which I offer you a cup of tea.'

'I'm fine, thank you.' She needed the loo but didn't like to ask.

'If you don't mind, in that case, I will leave you to it. Case the joint. Help yourself to reading matter.' The walls were lined with low bookcases. 'Muddy has taken himself off to Linda's study. If he comes back in here, he's allowed on the furniture. Same rule, cats and dog alike. A democratic household.'

Was this how men looked after guests? Colin had left her alone in his kitchen and now Dima was trusting her with this much grander affair. Other than the sofas and the bookcases, the room was sparsely furnished. Everything looked expensive. There was one other chair, a rich brown leather recliner, a pair of crutches propped against the seat. An oil painting above the fireplace showed a sweeping landscape with so much sky she thought it could only be American. The kitchen worktops were different heights, giving that end of the room the gappy look of a child in thrall to the tooth fairy.

*

'Good! I'm glad you're still here.' She hadn't heard Linda arrive. 'I told Dima to keep you entertained. He never takes any notice of me.'

'I didn't want to disturb his work,' Nina said. 'I'm sorry about the confusion over Muddy. I really did think he was lost.'

'It was Dima's fault,' said Linda. 'He insisted on taking

him out. Said it wasn't fair that the dog should miss out on my account. So strictly speaking, my fault, in Dima's head. He manages perfectly well when it suits him. Gus just went along for something to do, but they argued, so Gus pissed off to his mate's. He and Dima always argue.'

'That must make life difficult.'

'Families. There's always someone at home making someone's life difficult.'

'Not at my home. Not anymore.' Nina felt a sudden pang. She missed squabbling with Jonah.

'A room of one's own,' Linda was saying. 'Or rather, a whole house of one's own. Sometimes I think that would be bliss. Anyway, Muddy doesn't like Dima when he's in his wheelchair, so when he saw you, he'll have thought he'd defect to your pack. He's quite crafty.'

Or discerning, Nina thought. 'Aren't dogs all about loyalty?' she asked.

'It's the wheels. Muddy freaked out after the accident. It got so bad for a while, we thought we'd have to rehome him. Dima was the one who said no to that. There'd already been enough disruption for Gus without taking his pet away.'

'He never got used to it?'

'You mean Muddy? No. If Dima's in his chair and there's no one else at home, the poor dog skulks in my study until me or Gus calls him. He'll be there now.'

'He did disappear into the back somewhere,' Nina said.

'As did Dima, by the looks of it. He did at least offer you tea? Did he also show you where the cloakroom is? That door just by the porch, on your left.'

When Nina came back into the room, the kitchen sink and one of the countertops had got taller. Everything matched again. 'This is all very space age,' she said.

'We got a lot of advice,' said Linda. 'Specialist designers. Magic buttons everywhere.' She demonstrated, sending the sink up and down and up again in a smooth, silent glide.

'We could have done with something like that,' Nina said. 'Martin was so tall. He always grumbled that doing anything in the kitchen gave him backache. Not that it stopped him. Jonah takes after him, at least in being tall and grumbling.'

'They make standard kitchens to suit what they call average human height, which they say is about five foot five or six. Because obviously the only men who peel potatoes are Napoleon-sized.'

'In a way it's quite thoughtful,' Nina said. 'Usually men design things to fit other men.'

'Yes. I am sure generations of women are grateful to have been chained to just the right size of kitchen sink.'

'It's very clever, though,' Nina said. 'Sensible.' The open-plan room with no awkward door to swing in your face. No bending down to reach power sockets at floor level. The matching grab rail and towel rail in the cloakroom, in expensive chrome rather than wipe-down hospital plastic. 'They should design all homes like this.'

'People are waking up to that now,' Linda said. 'We were lucky. We were already living here. Ground-floor flat, room to swing a wheelchair. Life could carry on almost as before. We didn't have to make many changes.'

Nina had sometimes thought about what would have

happened if Martin had survived his fall, damaged in some way, but alive. She'd dreamt up all sorts of practical scenarios. Selling the house and moving to a flat (not as grand as Linda's). Employing good-natured helpers. Jonah helping choose the whizziest gadgets. Anything that would allow her and Martin to spend their nights sleeping in the same bed. Jonah to keep his dad.

'Your flat is really lovely,' she said. 'So much light. And that painting is beautiful.'

'It's one of Dima's,' Linda said. 'He's one of those annoyingly talented people who are good at things. Art. Music. Sport, before. His job.' She didn't look particularly happy about all these accomplishments.

'I'd love to be able to paint as well as that,' Nina said. 'It's so interesting, how some people know what to do with the different colours and textures.'

'You should get Dima to tell you all about it,' Linda said.

They drank their tea on the turquoise sofas, joined first by Muddy, then the second cat (another tabby) and then by Dima. Nina watched how easily he used his crutches to support him as he hoisted himself into the armchair. He must have strong arms. She asked about the painting. He preferred American landscapes, Dima said, the hugeness. Britain had its moments, especially the west, or so he'd heard. Mull. Cornwall. He'd never been. His whole face changed when he talked about the light and ways of making his paintbrush dance. When he asked if she'd join their team at the pub quiz again, a week on Friday, she said yes.

Chapter sixteen

'I know I shouldn't have laughed. He did look comical. Like Elizabeth I. Here, I'll show you.' Nina pulled up a photo on her phone. Neville's tangerine curls were perfectly framed in a stiff high-necked collar. 'I told Colin it was a ruff. He was too busy being agitated and feeling guilty to appreciate the joke.'

'To be fair to him, it is also a pretty lame joke,' Jonah said.

'Poor Neville,' said Kate. 'What happened to him?'

'He rolled onto some broken glass. Nothing serious thankfully. He's got stitches so the vet's given him one of those cones. Anyway, the point is, Colin was at the vet and not the dump yesterday, so your clobber is still in your old room, Jonah.' There. She'd said it. His old room. Not his room. This was his home now.

In weekend traffic, it had taken Nina less than an hour to drive across London. The flat looked better than when she and Kate had viewed it a few weeks earlier. Nina wouldn't have chosen navy for the walls. ('Pitch blue,' Kate said.) The sunlight picked up flecks of dust and blotches where the paintwork was a bit uneven. Fraying purple and orange curtains lapped beneath the windowsill, falling a few inches short of the floor.

'Please tell me you disapprove of the curtains,' said Jonah.

'They're certainly lively. Quite 70s. They could do with shortening, or lengthening.'

'Kate chose them,' said Jonah. 'We want bright colours. We were debating which ones, then these arrived, uninvited.'

'They were in the charity shop,' said Kate. 'He hates them. He told me off for spending money on them.'

'Our first domestic argument,' Jonah said, wrapping an arm round Kate's waist.

Nina commented that the distressed floorboards must mean downstairs could hear every footstep. 'We thought that,' said Jonah. 'We wondered if we could borrow a rug. The one in the spare room would go well, and it's not as if anyone's ever in there.'

'Much as I hate saying no to you, Jonah, I am going to have to think about that.' She'd decided to give into him less easily. 'Now, can I be nosy and get the grand tour before we eat?'

There wasn't much to see. She made the same admiring comments she'd made before. Cosy. Charming. Light. The tiny bedrooms were separated by a stud wall that looked to have been added long after the house was built. Not much storage space. The IKEA wardrobe neatly boxed up in the corner would partly solve that. If it ever got built, of course. The kitchen and bathroom were in the eaves, with strange sloping ceilings and inappropriate windows. Nina wasn't convinced that the ferns and spider plants on the bathroom windowsill were an adequate substitute for a blind.

Two people could stand in the kitchen provided neither of them moved to run a tap or get something out of the oven or fridge. Nina went through the motions nonetheless. 'Something smells good,' she said. 'Can I help with anything?' They made noises about there not being much to do and her being their guest so she must sit down and relax.

'Although if you did want to be useful, you could set the table,' Jonah said, handing her an assortment of cutlery, mostly forks, from the drainer. She recognised two of them from the set she and Martin had bought in France and never used, saving them for best. She didn't remember Jonah asking if he could take those.

The food was excellent. Nina thought she hid her surprise well. Light Middle Eastern spices and a lot of spinach. 'You do seem to be settling in,' she said. 'Very homely. Apart from the curtains. I'm with Jonah on those. If I'm allowed to take sides.'

'We wouldn't dare stop you,' said Jonah. 'You're too fond of saying what's on your mind.'

If only he knew. 'You're not the only ones playing house,' she said. 'That's the wrong phrase. Nesting. That's not right either. Sorting a place out.'

'Colin, you mean,' said Kate. 'Has he done anything about his garden yet?'

'Actually no, and yes,' Nina said. 'He's got garden people coming in a couple of weeks. I'm minding Neville while they work. I'm quite looking forward to it. I meant our house. My house. Jerzy was round again yesterday.'

'Jerzy, as in Lukas's dad?' Jonah asked.

'The very same. Lukas is off doing a PhD somewhere cold – Uppsala, I think Jerzy said. Or Trondheim. I'm sure you could track him down if you wanted to. It's a shame to let old friendships drift.'

'Pots and kettles, Mother dearest.'

Nina had friends once. Before widowhood and single parenthood edged everything else out. 'Learn from my mistakes,' she said. 'Anyway, Jerzy is still very much in London and running his building company and we came up with a plan for the house. I wanted to talk to you about it before agreeing.'

Painting was only painting over the past, Jerzy had said. He had beautiful plan for Nina to make new future. The house would be more welcoming to guests and easier to sell because one stone killed both birds. (Why would anyone want to stone birds to death?) Nina's bedroom, the one she'd shared with Martin, was at the front of the house and dark. It was big enough to add an ensuite shower room. Jonah's old room got the daylight and the views over the garden. Nina could wake up to sunshine every morning (except when it rained). 'You and Kate could have your own bathroom if you stopped over. None of that waiting for me to spend far too long in the shower, and I might sleep better away from the traffic.'

'It's hardly a busy road,' Jonah said.

'No. But car alarms. People talking on their way home from a late night. Deliveroos. It can get quite noisy.'

'All those years and you've only just noticed now? Or were you secretly wishing I'd leave so you could take my room back?' That whine. She had no idea who he'd inherited that from. 'I'm barely out the door.'

'That's why this is the best time to do something. If I do something,' Nina said. 'Otherwise it's all change now and then more change a few months down the line.'

'Trading me for a new toilet. Thanks, Mum.'

'I'm still thinking about the ensuite,' she said, 'and Jerzy needs to check how feasible it is. Pipes. I do need to ring the changes. Do something radical. It's too much, otherwise, Jonah.'

'It's my room,' said Jonah. 'My memories. I don't understand the sudden rush.'

'I do,' said Kate.

'Well, maybe the two of you can talk it over later. I should probably start to make tracks anyway. There are the car keys. Your stuff is still in the boot; I couldn't face bringing everything up the stairs.'

'I can walk with you to the station,' Kate offered. 'It will get me out of doing the washing-up, won't it, Jonah?'

'You will drive safely, Jonah? And give my love to Granny. Message me when you get there or you know I'll worry.'

'OK.'

'Thank you for lunch. You must give me the recipe. We can talk again about the house, so don't even think about it while you're on your holiday.'

'OK.' He'd take a few days to come round. He could cook a chickpea tagine and (maybe) put together flatpack furniture, but he was really still a child. Her child and completely gorgeous and adorable, nearly all of the time.

'Are you really in a rush to get home?' Kate asked as they reached street level. 'The stairs are less dizzying when you've made a few trips.' Nina had found herself clinging to the banister, watching her feet negotiate each single step. The worn carpet on a few of them was as shiny as a dachshund's coat.

'The park's only about ten minutes away,' Kate continued. 'It's the other side of the station. It's worth seeing. I've already been swimming in the lido. We could do that together one day, if you like, before the summer's completely gone. Are you thinking about selling the house?'

'I didn't say that.'

'Didn't you? That's what I heard. In all the years I've known you, you've never had a guest to stay, apart from me and I wasn't exactly a guest, more an imposition. So the second bathroom for visitors doesn't add up.'

'We had a procession of waifs and strays staying over when Martin was alive. It was fun. He'd cook them bacon and eggs for breakfast, even the vegetarian ones.' Like so much else with Martin, his hospitality had been more generous than thoughtful. 'I might have all sorts of plans. I just haven't thought of them yet. I should have been more tactful with Jonah, though I didn't think he'd care. He's taken everything he wanted.'

'He'll be fine,' Kate said. 'I was the same when I left home for the first time.'

'You were eighteen.'

'Nineteen. My sisters were fighting over who'd get my bedroom before I even got my A-level results.'

'Who won?'

'Neither of them. Dad was offered a job in Edinburgh, so they moved up there a few weeks after I went off to uni.'

'Jonah can't really think I wanted him out,' Nina said. 'He knows how much I wheedled to try and get you to both live with me, rather than renting Mrs Rochester's attic.'

'I'm not sure that analogy does me any favours. Mad and locked up.'

'Until she burned the house down,' said Nina, 'which was very convenient for everyone. Happy endings all round. I need to think about the future. In the short term, without Jonah there to kind of dilute them, I can't be living with all those reminders. I need to make the house look different. And it would be nice to open the curtains to the garden every morning.'

'I'll talk to him,' Kate said. 'He misses him too, you know. His dad.'

'Martin would have expected nothing less,' said Nina. 'He'd have wanted to be missed. That's some view.' London's showier highlights stretched into the distance. 'Seeing that makes it hard to imagine living anywhere else. I haven't decided anything yet, Kate. You will make sure he understands that?'

They looped around the park. Nearer the lido, the sounds changed – happy human shrieks and less birdsong. A miniature train that Kate had told her about turned out not to run on Saturdays. Nina was pleased. She liked the grass and the trees and the dogs. All this extra entertainment was distracting.

'Thank you for coming to see us,' Kate said as they reached the gate. 'And thank you for the car! The station's just up there. I hope you get home OK.'

'I'll be fine. Enjoy Cornwall.'

The journey home was more involved than it should have been. Disruption due to earlier operating difficulties meant no westbound service on the district line. Nina thought of her car, parked on a strange street, fully charged so that Jonah and Kate wouldn't find themselves stranded on the M5. The overground trains would be running from Waterloo. On the escalator up from the tube, she stood behind a large girl in tiny shorts over carefully laddered tights. Not a girl who would end up chained to a kitchen sink. Nina hadn't been this close to someone else's buttocks since Martin died. It was hard not to stare.

Chapter seventeen

Most of the UK was enjoying some lovely sunny weather, the cheery BBC announcer reminded her before every news bulletin. Except for the South West. A deep depression and clouds rolling in from the Atlantic. Did clouds physically roll or was that a trick of the light? Jonah and Kate appeared undaunted. Every day, a few photos would arrive on WhatsApp – anoraks, wet hair, white-tipped grey seas in the background. *Mum looks well,* Nina thought, zooming in on a picture of Annette and Jonah, paddling arm in arm and laughing. The caption was the same on all the images. 'Having a wonderful time! Wish you were here! J, K and G xxxx'. It wasn't true, of course, but at least they were staying in touch.

'G?' Colin asked.

'For Granny.'

'Of course. That's one thing about not having children. I get to keep my own name. Although I am "uncle". They're in Australia, so it's a rarely used label.'

'I didn't know you had family in Australia?'

'We've only recently met, Nina. Extended family history hasn't made it onto the agenda yet. My sister went on a working holiday, met someone – his name is Bruce, how stereotypical can you get – and that's where she stayed. I have three nieces I barely know, although there is some talk of the eldest getting a working visa at some point now she's finishing uni.'

'That's terrible,' Nina said. 'Family so far away.'

'Further than Cornwall certainly,' said Colin. 'Judy and I stay in touch and the plan is for me to get out there for her fiftieth, in February, assuming I can make arrangements for him.' He scratched Neville's chest.

'He's looking a little doleful,' Nina said. 'Not his normal bouncy self.'

'He's embarrassed by the collar.'

'Ruff!' she couldn't resist. Neville glared at her.

'Don't tease him. It's only for another day or two.'

'He knows I'm his friend, don't you, Neville? So, Australia. That's exciting. I always fancied seeing the Barrier Reef one day.'

'That's about 2,000 miles away. They're in Perth, in the west. It's very sunny, even by Australian standards, and extremely far from anywhere else.'

'Sounds perfect. February's ages off, so plenty of time to sort something out for Neville. Presumably his alma mater would take him, the Heartbreak Hotel?'

'Hound-dog Hotel. I'm sure they would. I worry about the psychological impact of abandoning him again.'

'Psychological impact? He's a dog, Colin, he'll get over it. And you wouldn't be gone for long.'

'Three weeks is what we're thinking. As you say, it's a long way off. Thanks for dropping by. Neville and I need to do some work now. We're going for a drink later if you'd like to join us? The White Swan.'

He was sending her away. She'd dropped in on the off chance on her way back from an appointment with Niall. Lots of questions about the empty house and how she felt about getting it remodelled had left her feeling reluctant to go home. Of course she'd known Colin might be busy. It was stupid to be disappointed.

Chapter eighteen

Quiz night came round again. Possibly the last one for a while since Gus had, as predicted, smashed his A-levels. People weren't exactly queuing up to take over as question master. Nina was putting on lipstick when she heard her car wiggle into the narrow driveway.

'Surprise!' Kate jumped out of the passenger seat, smiling broadly.

'I thought you weren't coming home until the weekend,' Nina said.

'It's Friday,' Jonah said, unloading black bin bags from the boot. 'The weekend starts here. TGIF.'

'I wasn't expecting you until Sunday. You didn't call.' He'd sent a couple more photos that morning. Kate feeding an ice cream cone to a fat gull. Annette and Kate standing on either side of a Betty Stogs beer sign.

'It's a surprise.'

'Yes. So Kate said. But why?'

'Do I need a reason to surprise my mother?' Jonah said. 'We've brought real pasties. They'll still be warm, Granny gave us this thermal food cosy thing. You'd never know they've spent seven hours in the car.'

'It's lovely to see you, of course. I'm going out, so it will have to be a quick hi, bye. We can arrange something else soon.'

'You never go out.' His expression was one she hadn't seen before. Confused. Crestfallen. Disbelieving. Disapproving. It was most unattractive.

'Only to the pub,' she said.

'That's OK then. Nothing special. I'll just take this lot inside.'

'What is all that? Did you collect me some nice seaweed from the beach, perhaps, so I can make an invigorating bath scrub, or some iodine-rich superfood soup?'

'It's our laundry,' Jonah said. 'We knew you wouldn't mind. If you do it here, it can dry outside and you can bring it back at the weekend. Or we can collect it. Although probably easier for you if you've taken the car back. D'you want us to leave it here?'

She'd need to go to the car wash, Nina thought. A seven-hour drive hadn't shaken off the sand or bird poo. 'I would like my car back please, Jonah, thank you. And I am supposed to be going out, as I said.'

'But we want to tell you about our holiday,' Jonah said.

'And I've arranged to see my friends. You should have let me know you were coming.'

'Don't worry, Nina,' Kate said. 'We don't want you changing your plans on account of us. We've had a long drive, though, and I can't speak for Jonah, but I'm starving. Would you mind if we hung around here for a bit, ate the pasties? We could run the washing machine and then all you'd need to do is put the stuff out on the line in the morning.'

For a moment, Nina was torn. It wasn't every day that people were looking forward to seeing her. They hadn't said so as such but she'd made the quiz team complete. Four brains definitely better than three. But how often did Jonah go out of his way to surprise her? 'Let me make a couple of phone calls,' she said. 'I daresay they can manage without me. Now, unless you also stole a cool box from Granny and filled it with Cornish ale, I'm guessing there is nothing to wash those pasties down. I don't have anything in the house, so someone will need to pop to the Co-op.'

'I'd be happy with tea,' Kate said. 'We've been quite free with the beer these last few days. I'll stick the kettle on.'

Nina took her phone upstairs to be out of earshot. She watched from her bedroom window as Jonah unloaded the car. His T-shirt rode up slightly as he lifted a case from the boot. From this distance, it looked as if he might be getting a tiny bit flabby. She rang Linda first. 'We were looking forward to seeing you. Let's go for a drink in the week instead. I can do Tuesday. Or Wednesday. Or Thursday. So really there is no excuse.' Then she rang Colin and found herself agreeing that he would drop Neville off on his way round to the pub.

'All sorted,' she said, coming back downstairs. The washing machine was churning and foaming. Someone had added too much powder. She'd need to run a second rinse cycle. 'We have extra company. Neville disgraced himself at the last pub quiz, so Colin is leaving him with us. I imagine he'll enjoy a bit of pasty.'

'You seem to spend a lot of time looking after Neville,'

Jonah said. 'I hope Colin isn't taking you for granted.' Nina thought of several replies to that, none that would contribute to a pleasant evening. She kept quiet.

It was warm enough to eat in the garden, which made life easier. When she opened the ugly black plastic food box, oniony steam wafted upwards. The greaseproof paper inside was warm to the touch. Nina had emptied a bag of salad into a bowl, to at least pretend to be healthy she told them, and put a roll of kitchen towel on the table. She found ketchup at the back of the cupboard and was busy overriding Jonah's objections to this not being authentically Cornish when the doorbell rang. 'Perfect timing,' she said as Neville leapt at her and then sat at her feet, wagging his tail so energetically his whole body moved. 'You look liberated,' she said, tickling the clean fur where his cone had been.

'This morning,' Colin said. 'He went a bit puppyish straight after. He's calmed down now.'

'Jonah and Kate are in the garden. Do you want to come and say hello?'

'I'll just wave,' Colin said, following Nina through the house, Neville pushing past. He wasn't noticeably calm. 'I promised Gus I'd get to the pub early to help him set up.'

'Colin!' said Jonah.

'Neville!' said Kate.

The men did that slightly awkward half back slap that Nina had noticed before while Kate made a fuss of Neville. 'Can you join us for a quick drink?' she asked Colin. 'It's only tea, which technically is still drink.'

'No thanks. I need to get going. I'll see you later, Nina, about ten if that's OK?'

113

'That's fine,' Nina said. 'Good luck with the quiz.'

'It won't be the same without you,' Colin said. 'Bye, you, please behave yourself.' He patted Neville on the head and left via the side gate.

'How was your holiday?' Nina asked when he'd gone. 'It looked wet. This pasty smells revolting. I might make some cheese on toast if anyone is tempted.'

'It is a bit horrible,' Kate said. 'They tasted delicious the other day. Maybe they don't travel.'

'Never mind. It's the thought that counts.' An ill-judged thought that had cost her an evening she'd been looking forward to, but well-intentioned.

'I don't know what you are complaining about,' said Jonah. 'My pasty's great. Neville thinks so too.' He tore off a corner to throw to the dog, then wiped his greasy fingers on his T-shirt.

'I'll fix up the cheese on toast,' Kate said. 'You can tell Nina what you and Annette got up to.'

'That sounds ominous,' Nina said. 'Have you and Granny been scheming?'

'Would we?' Jonah asked.

'I have no idea what goes on between the two of you sometimes,' Nina said. 'I'm sure you have lots of secrets.'

'Millions,' said Jonah.

'She's well? The photos looked like you were enjoying yourselves.'

'She seems very well,' Jonah said. 'She's given up her car, though. Says it's to do her green bit. She had us drive all over to visit places she hasn't been for ages. Lots of walks near nice pubs, although it was raining so we did more pub than walk.'

'I didn't know she'd stopped driving,' said Nina. 'It must make it tricky.'

'I don't think so. She's got lots of people at her beck and call. It's funny really. There she is living somewhere small and here we all are in London and she's got far more friends than all of us put together. She's joined a kind of social club, based at one of the hotels.'

'She certainly keeps busy,' Nina said. 'Her emails are always full of news.'

'When did you last see her?' Jonah said.

'I'm not sure. A couple of months back?'

'It was a year,' Kate said, coming from the kitchen with a trayful of cheese on toast.

'That can't be right.'

'Almost a year then.'

Nina thought back. The shops had been full of V-neck kids' jumpers and novelty stationery. Start of the new school term. 'Is it really that long?' she said. 'Still, it's not as if we're not in contact. We email all the time.'

'I didn't realise either. Not until Granny mentioned it.'

'Didn't you and Granny have more interesting things to talk about?'

'Lots,' Jonah said. 'She probably minds a bit, to say anything. She doesn't normally talk about you at all, beyond how's your mother, fine, that's good, all that stuff people say without thinking about it. So me and Kate had an idea. Well, it was more Kate's idea. We told Granny it was mine because she takes most notice of me.'

Nina was wondering when Jonah would get to the point, if he had one, when Kate took over. 'When did you have a holiday, Nina?' she asked.

'I don't like the sound of that.' Nina had a horrible vision of the four of them at Gatwick waiting for an easyJet flight to Spain or, worse, of her and her mother crammed into a shared cabin on a cruise to see the Northern Lights. 'Please tell me you haven't arranged any kind of treat.'

'We wouldn't dare,' Jonah said. 'Although we had fun imagining what you'd hate most. There are some festivals that involve tents, and murder mystery weekends where you have to dress up.'

'Granny wouldn't like that any more than I would,' Nina said.

'You'd be surprised,' said Jonah. 'She's partial to a bit of drama.'

'You don't need to worry, Nina,' Kate said. 'You're not committed to anything. We did some gentle googling and found a lovely spa hotel near Exeter. Annette says she'd like to stay over somewhere – your day trips are quite tiring – and you could hang out together.'

'Hang out?'

'It just means faffing about with no particular plans,' Jonah said helpfully.

'I know what it means,' Nina said. 'I'm struggling to imagine Granny and me on a weekend away.'

'You never know until you try,' Kate said. 'The hotel looks gorgeous. I'll send you a link. Think about it, Nina. You might surprise yourself and enjoy it.'

'I'll think about it,' Nina promised. She'd cross that bridge later. There was a good chance that her mother was indulging Jonah's attempts to bring the family closer and wouldn't want to go.

After Jonah and Kate had left in a cab (paid for by Nina), she cleared up. Neville looked on in disgust as she put most of the uneaten pasties into the food recycling. It was only nine o'clock. An hour or more to kill before Colin came back to collect his dog and regale her with stories of the evening she had missed, the fun people had had without her.

Chapter nineteen

There'd been enough rain at the weekend to get the forecasters excited. Yellow warnings. Surface water. A sympathetic smile from the handsome TV weather presenter, tucked up in his cosy studio, for anyone who had outdoor plans. That must be a strange job. Two minutes in front of a camera a couple of times a day, and who knew what they did the rest of the time. Jonah's laundry was dry and neatly folded. Nina's kitchen still smelled of too-hot cotton from the ancient tumble drier.

They'd set boundaries when Jonah was still living at home. It had been his idea. He wasn't paying rent, but he was an adult and apparently that meant taking on selected chores. It was never his turn to clean the bathroom or unload the dishwasher. They'd taken it in turns to cook and do the grocery order. It brought a pleasing variety to their eating habits. They agreed a laundry rule that they didn't do each other's. Nina broke this all the time. It was how she'd first found out about Kate. Cinema tickets in his jeans pocket. He'd told her he was going to watch the cricket somewhere with friends (one of the Sky Sports pubs, depends where we can get in) and come home after she'd gone to bed.

The ticket was for the Curzon, not the local one, and for something she hadn't heard of. The title didn't quite make sense. Something about love. The words didn't flow; someone struggling to translate the essence of the original French or Arabic or Russian. The ticket was for the 1.50pm showing, so even something highly worthy and harrowing would have been over by teatime. She hadn't said anything but had been glad of the tip-off. It gave her time to get used to the idea of a girlfriend.

He'd always had friends, of course. Nina's phone still contained long-neglected entries: Ashok Mum Kovila, Lukas Dad Jerzy. Their boys were often to be found hunched over computer consoles in her living room while Nina fed them socially acceptable snacks. Later, there'd been the occasional girl, mumbling, temporary and pretty. Girls with storybook names; a Polly and then an Aurora (what were her parents thinking?), who'd been around for months until she'd disappeared to university in the North – Manchester or Newcastle – and hadn't been mentioned again. By his early twenties, his friends had been mainly anonymous and plural (I'm going out tonight, meeting friends, might be late) or on Fridays the people from his office in town. They did boring things involving sport and alcohol and comedy clubs. And then there was Kate. Nina couldn't believe her luck.

*

'Thank you so much, Nina,' Kate said now as Nina arrived at the flat with the clean washing. 'We'd never have asked you if we'd known it was going to piss it down all weekend.'

'Wouldn't you?' said Nina.

'Jonah might have,' Kate said. 'Are you coming up? He's at work. I'm not due anywhere until this afternoon. I can show you that hotel we were talking about.'

The flat looked more lived-in and also scruffier than the last time Nina had been there. Kate shifted a pile of stuff from the table to the sofa and fired up her laptop. The hotel website was peppered with aspirational language – elegant, boutique, wonderland. Nina conceded that it looked lovely and not stuck out in the middle of nowhere. There would be plenty of distractions. 'You really think this is a good idea?' Nina asked Kate.

'It's up to you,' Kate said.

'Don't give me that. I can't see that Jonah would have suggested somewhere as suitable as this, so my guess is that you and my mother have been talking.'

'People go away with their mothers all the time,' Kate said.

'No one I know.'

'You don't know that many people. Promise you won't tell Annette I told you this, but she asked me to ask you.'

'So this is her doing?'

'It's not anyone's doing,' Kate said. 'Don't overcomplicate things. You haven't seen your mum for a year. A little city break might be fun.'

'I'll ask her,' Nina said.

'Do that,' said Kate. 'Think how you'd feel if you didn't see Jonah for a year.'

'That's different.'

'If you say so, Nina.'

*

The difference is Kate, Nina told Niall when she saw him later that day.

'Run that past me again,' Niall said.

'My mother didn't like my husband when he was alive and liked him even less when he was dead. Whereas I like Kate.'

'That's alright then,' Niall said.

'Are you being facetious? Only I don't believe therapists are allowed to do that.'

'It seems to me, and this is only a theory, that you blame your husband for your distance from your mother.'

'No,' Nina said. 'I blame her.'

'Maybe you could have a go at not blaming anyone? Does everything have to be someone's fault?'

Nina thought most things did. She'd studied Julius Caesar at school. The fault in our stars. It was her fault that Martin had died. She'd never told anyone the full story.

She'd taken the week off work while Jonah was on his school trip. That way, if he was nervous (he wasn't) or homesick ('It's brilliant, Mum, heaps better than our house and also they've got the sea,' was the only phone call), she'd be able to talk to him straightaway or even drive down to collect him. On day two, Martin had arrived home unexpectedly at lunchtime, bearing bright flowers.

'I went to the shop by the station, you know the one, and said I wanted every gerbera in the joint.' He looked pleased with himself. 'Happy anniversary. I've booked dinner specially.' It wasn't their anniversary, but he said it was the anniversary of their third date so that counted. He'd thought she looked so sad that morning, her baby boy all grown up, all the way to eleven; only a precious few months before his voice would break.

She'd planned to watch Wimbledon; it was the days when Britain had an actual hope. Martin had said no, let's spend the whole afternoon in bed, like they used to. They'd looked at photo albums and nuzzled a bit and talked and talked, and at one point he got up to make her a cup of tea. At about six, she stirred herself to have a shower. 'Damn,' she said, returning damp to the bedroom wrapped in a bright blue towel. 'We forgot to have sex.' She sat beside him. 'We could maybe skip dessert in the restaurant and come back early.' She licked her finger and slid it between his lips. He put his hand under the towel. 'Or we could be very quick and noisy with the house to ourselves.'

As it turned out, they weren't that quick. They were quite noisy, especially Nina. Martin said that he'd have to spend dinner thinking about how to deal with such wanton behaviour. She'd made him all sticky and now he'd have to rush his shower. The table was booked for seven.

She'd heard the water run and his unashamed bass tones belt out the Carpenters. He was on top of the world. Then a thud and then nothing except running water.

Chapter twenty

'It's just us,' Linda said. 'Gus is off to Oxford next week and he and Dima have gone for a curry. Bonding. Or so Gus says. Dima thinks he's going to butter him up for money.'

'I've never noticed this pub before,' Nina said. 'It's cosy.'

'It was always my favourite,' said Linda. 'It's difficult for Dima. The wheelchair is so big. So it's a treat to be here with you.'

'I suppose it does take up a lot of space,' Nina said. 'More than a bar stool anyway.'

'Dima's always taken up too much space,' said Linda. 'Even before his accident. Never marry a man with hobbies. Or ambition.'

'That ship's already sailed,' Nina said.

'There's always a next time.'

'Not for me,' said Nina.

'How long's it been?'

'Too long.' Martin had been dead almost as long as they'd been together. 'But also not long enough.'

'You're lucky,' Linda said.

'How do you figure that out? The merry widow life is not all it's cracked up to be.'

'You married the right person. Most people don't. You must have noticed.'

'I wanted to be married to Martin more than I've ever wanted anything,' said Nina. 'That's never gone away.'

'There's never been anyone else?'

'No. As you said, I married the right person. There was only one of him.'

'Whereas Dima was a catch,' Linda said. 'It was like winning a contest I didn't know I'd entered. Next time around, I'm going to go for someone less dazzling.'

'Next time? You're not saying that you and Dima...?'

'No,' Linda said. 'It doesn't stop me imagining what it would be like. It's going to be strange it just being us in the house. Empty nesters already.'

'Not totally empty,' Nina said. Not empty the way her house was. Everything exactly where she'd left it when she came downstairs in the morning. 'You've got each other. And the cats. And Muddy.'

'And Muddy. You should get yourself a dog, Nina. They're massively annoying and inconvenient. Keep you occupied.'

'I'm already occupied enough,' Nina said.

'Doing what? Colin and I were trying to work it out the other day.'

'Nice to know that you and Colin talk about me.' Nina was more flattered than annoyed, which surprised her.

'Not as a general rule,' Linda said. 'Normally, it's Colin's latest plans. But it came up the other day. He was wondering about asking you another Neville favour and wanted to know if I thought you'd be too busy. Hasn't he spoken to you yet?'

'I haven't seen him for a few days.'

'He has a proposition for you. Not my place to say. You should get a job, Nina. Then you wouldn't be at his disposal.'

'I don't need a job,' Nina said. 'One of the few actual perks of being a widow, or very specifically being Martin's widow. Most people are screwed financially but he'd made provisions, as they say. We used to joke that I'd murder him for the proceeds.'

'It's not just the money,' Linda said. 'Meeting people. Using your brain. Feeling important. I'd hate not to work.'

'I liked it well enough,' Nina said. 'When Jonah was little, it was a life saver spending time with adults, not that some of them weren't childish in their own ways. I could never be doing with team building or development goals or any of that nonsense, though. People were always bringing in cake.'

'Cake is good. Although hazardous. I was reading about someone who sued their employer for aggravating their disordered eating by encouraging cake in the workplace.'

'My point exactly,' Nina said. 'If I'd been like you, doing something I really cared about, then it would be different. I'd drifted into project management because I was organised and slightly nosy and they were good about flexible hours for school holidays. It wasn't tempting enough to drift back in when they lost patience with my bereavement leave.'

'Volunteering then,' Linda said. 'People would bite your hand off.'

'I did that for a while,' Nina said. 'In the early days. At the library.' It had been depressing. Reshelving stories about women pluckily finding romance after 300 pages of tedious wrong turns, and men finding murderers or fighting wars.

'Hobbies? You are clearly creative. Dima says you are interested in his art. And Colin said you know all about ceramics.'

They really had been talking about her. 'I studied ceramics back in the day. It's not practical. You need access to a kiln. I tried papiermâché for a while. That was nice and messy, although quite boring. Jonah used to hide my creations from his friends.'

'Surely you must want to do something?' Linda said.

Nina wasn't sure she did. 'You should meet my mother,' she said. 'She's forever nagging me to take up interests. She doesn't understand that the world is interesting enough on its own.'

'I'd miss people if I wasn't doing anything,' Linda said.

'Martin was like that. Peopley jobs and lots of team sports.'

'A bit like Colin then.'

'I can't imagine Colin playing sport,' Nina said.

'I meant his work. All those focus groups. And the quiz. You know that was his idea? And he's out every night with some project or other. Says it's his duty as a newly single man to get involved in local life.'

'Sounds like you're keeping tabs,' Nina said. She thought Linda blushed. It may have been the wine.

'It's the lawyer in me,' Linda said. 'I like knowing where everyone fits in.'

'I didn't know he was newly single. He doesn't give that impression. More of a freewheeler.'

'Five years. She was called Susannah. It ended amicably. Now he says he's of no fixed abode on the relationships front.'

'That sounds like Colin. Did you ask what he meant?'

'Naturally. He's not looking for anyone new and is busy with work and with Neville. If the right lady – can you believe he said lady, he's so old-fashioned – if the right lady comes along, he'll worry about things then.'

'You have been probing.'

'Call it due diligence. Or nosiness. Gus is always telling me I need to respect people's privacy.'

'Gus must be excited. Not long now.'

'He's going to change the world,' Linda said. 'He actually said that. Such a cliché. I'm just relieved he's turning out OK. It's not been easy for him with Dima's accident.'

'He'd have been about the same age as Jonah was?'

'Ten,' Linda said. 'Explaining that his dad was broken to a ten-year-old took some doing. They had to get used to each other again.'

'Whereas Jonah had to get used to not having his dad at all.'

'I don't mean to be insensitive,' Linda said. 'Losing Martin altogether must have been harder than what happened to us.'

'It's not a competition.'

'Dima was so prosaic about it. Upbeat.'

'That's good, isn't it?'

'I can see that now. It meant I wasn't allowed to be upset. My husband had changed and I had to get on with it.'

Dima's legs didn't work very well, but Nina thought he must be very much the same person he'd always been. Martin was like that too. You knew what you were getting into when you threw your lot in with someone who was so fully themselves. Getting yourself out again when they'd gone for good, that was the tricky part. She wasn't sure why anyone would bother with that.

Chapter twenty-one

Nina bumped into Neville in the park a few days later. He was chasing fallen leaves that were scuttling across the path. He paused briefly to lick her hand, then went back to the serious task of investigating the golden autumn casualties.

'Well. Look who it is. Where have you been hiding?' Colin was wearing what appeared to be a new jacket. It didn't suit him.

'Not hiding,' Nina said. 'I'm still in the park every day. We've obviously been on different schedules.'

'That's autumn for you,' Colin said. 'The business end of the year. Not a moment to myself. I've got Christmas commissions already. Do you want to hear about them?'

She was too polite to decline. Elves, Santa, snow people (you weren't allowed to allocate a gender these days) and joy were all mentioned more than once. A lost Christmas puppy. Nina had seen enough of Colin's work to know that his talent was in how he wove tired themes together into charming and fresh animations. For someone who talked such a lot, he was surprisingly good at listening to what people wanted.

'You won't be too busy for the quiz on Friday?' She'd circled the date in her diary. The only fixed appointment in a blank week.

'It's mandatory,' Colin said. 'The last one before young Gus enters the dreaming spires. They said that last time too. He really is off now. Leaves on Sunday.'

'Yes, Linda was telling me about it,' said Nina. 'They'll miss him.'

'We're going to help each other out with the dogs,' Colin said. 'Take it in turns to walk them both.'

'I'd be happy to do my share,' Nina said. Strictly speaking, she didn't have a share. 'Linda said you had a favour to ask me. If it's dog-sitting, you only have to say the word.'

'Thanks. I'm still juggling dates. Nothing confirmed yet. I'll let you know.'

'I'm always happy to look after Neville,' Nina said. 'Muddy too, for that matter.'

'Appreciate that. We've got to shoot now. Will we see you on Friday?'

'Yes. Great,' Nina said. He was always in a hurry these days.

She watched as Colin and Neville ambled colourfully towards the gate. It was never truly clear which of them was in charge. Neville tugged on his lead in whichever direction he fancied. He looked happy to wait as Colin stopped to chat to first one, then another, walker. Not too busy for casual chitchat. Linda had been right. Colin wasn't everyone. Not everyone made friends so easily. Not everyone would think a duckling-yellow nylon puffer jacket was a good idea.

Autumn was always difficult. Everything dying. In a blaze of colour but still dying. People pretended otherwise, rushing around buying new school shoes and signing up for evening classes. The celebration days reeked of death. Hallowe'en with its ghosts and, worse, bonfire night. Burning a man for trying to blow up other men. A strange notion of fun.

*

When she got home, Nina found an email from Jerzy. All systems go for the new bathroom (please send deposit to confirm). There would be a big mess and the water would be turned off for some of the time. She might want to arrange to stay somewhere else at least for the first couple of days.

Would going away with her mother really be so bad? The key was to think of it as a treat. A mini break in an interesting city. Not a chore born out of guilt and inconvenience. Nina worked hard to persuade herself while she checked availability at the hotel. She drafted many versions of an email to her mother, settling after false starts about quality time and planets aligning on a simple although untrue statement that she'd love to spend a day or two exploring Exeter together. She pressed send and waited.

Chapter twenty-two

Six months later, Nina would look back on the Exeter trip with disbelief. Sixty-five hours (she'd counted) together. Annette striding confidently through unfamiliar streets. They didn't have fun exactly, but it had been pleasant enough. The weather was kind and it was a beautiful part of the world.

Nina had discussed the trip in advance with Niall. He'd not been much help. (He was very poor at providing answers.) 'Only you can decide if it's the right time for whatever it is you want to tackle.' That was the problem. She didn't know what she wanted to tackle. How to forge a different relationship with her mother. Less careful. More like it had been back before marriage and bereavements got in the way.

Once the date was agreed and the hotel booked – separate rooms please, Nina, don't let's push our luck – her mother had taken over the itinerary, packing it out with diversions. Her energy was exhausting. Nina quickly realised that having a lot of plans got rid of the opportunity for any conversation. She wondered if Annette had done this on purpose. Discussion was all about what time they should call a taxi for the theatre and whether Dawlish or Teignmouth looked nicer for a little jaunt to the seaside on the way to or from Totnes, or whether they could walk from one to the other given the weather and the tides and in those shoes. The theatre was that rarity, a comedy that was funny. It had been a long time since Nina and her mother laughed together about the same things.

They had lots to say about the places and people they saw. Totnes was less interesting than they'd hoped. Pretty, of course, with some fine old buildings and rather too many fudge shops. Disappointingly, the hippy-dippy trappings they'd expected from the Twinned With Narnia sign (they saw a photo, not the real thing) were no worse than anywhere else. It was hard to pass as genuinely alternative with WHSmith and Boots on the main shopping streets, her mother said over crumbly scones in an olde tea shoppe. Its menu was elaborate italics and ink drawings of roses. The business had been established in 2014. It will be olde one day, her mother said, there's no need to get agitated. You do fret about the most unimportant things.

They said their goodbyes at the station on Thursday morning. 'This has been lovely, darling. Give my love to Jonah and Kate.' Nina watched from the platform as her mother lifted her case into the overhead rack. She waved as the train pulled away. A child waved back. Nina's mother already had her nose in her book and didn't look up.

*

The builders were packing up for the day when Nina got home. The worst of the work was over, Jerzy told her.

Apart from the dust, Nina could see that it had been a success. Not the ensuite she'd wanted. The plumbing was too complicated. Still, a downstairs shower and loo that fitted the dead space perfectly. A room with no history.

Chapter twenty-three

'It's a new basket,' Colin said, 'with an old blanket. So he has somewhere else to sit, as well as the sofa.' The yellow duvet cover lived permanently in Nina's living room now. 'It will make him feel at home.'

'I think he already feels quite at home,' Nina said. Neville had greeted her joyously and was busy liberating shoes from the rack in the hallway.

'It's good of you to take him.' Colin moved the ironing board and plonked the dog basket in the corner of the kitchen.

'It is, isn't it?' said Nina. She still didn't think it was strictly necessary. How disruptive could it be having people digging up the garden? She didn't want Colin to change his mind, so she kept quiet.

'The main thing he likes is company,' Colin said. 'He's got drawbacks as a colleague, it's true. He enjoys watching me work and, of course, comes to most of my workshops. He's a very good icebreaker. People will always talk to dogs.'

'I like company too,' Nina said. 'We'll have a wonderful time. Your plan is to collect him in the evenings? Or I can drop him off?'

'I can pick him up. I'm using one of those workspace places for the week, you know the freelance networking hub arrangements.'

'Not really,' Nina said. 'I was always a "go to the office, see the same people every day, do some work, eat some biscuits, go home again" person. I had a desk and my own mouse mat.'

'Living the dream,' said Colin. 'Anyway, I've booked the space until 5.30pm so I can call in for his nibs on the way back. He can have his dinner at home.'

'Are you listening, Neville? No food in this house.'

'You must come for your dinner too, one evening,' Colin said.

'Thank you,' Nina said.

*

A full-time dog, even if only in the daytime, was different to covering the odd walk or spare afternoon. Neville followed her around the house, mimicking her movements. If she sat down, he sat down. This was fine. If she got up to potter or wash up her coffee cup, then he'd be up too. This was less fine. He helped her unload the washing machine, gathering up socks and putting them in his basket. He was reluctant to give them back and she had to speak to him quite sternly.

'You've been here plenty of times before,' she told him. 'I have no idea why you are so fidgety.' She talked to him a lot. Certainly more than she'd talked to her mother on their mini break. He only knew a few words; a 'rich, functional vocabulary,' Colin had said – walk, biscuit (pronounced bikkit), sit, down, no, NO! He seemed to like listening as she explained what she was doing or told him how sad she was and had been for a long time now.

Colin claimed that Neville had conquered his fear of abandonment and could safely be left alone for up to three hours. This wasn't true. The first afternoon, she decided it would be easier not to bring him while she queued in the post office. She got home to a trail of feathers. She was briefly confused; maybe a bird had flown in, although she'd left only the small bathroom window open and it would need to be very agile, even for a bird.

'He stole one of my pillows,' she told Colin at picking-up time. 'He made sure it was quite dead before storing it in his basket.' The hoover refused to eat the feathers and she'd had a sneezy time picking bits out of the filter.

'Feathering his nest,' Colin said. 'Quite the little capitalist. I'll buy you a new one. We can take it out of his pocket money.'

'I only mention it because it's a sign of distress,' Nina said. 'According to Google.'

'He doesn't look very distressed. Quite the opposite. But if you want, I can get someone else to mind him this week?'

'I wouldn't hear of it.'

'That's really what I got the basket for. If you tell him to go to bed when you go out, he'll settle down nicely. At least that's what he does at home. Sorry, I should have told you that at the start.'

'We know now,' Nina said. 'And don't worry about the pillow. It was overdue for replacement.' Some of the feathers had been quite yellow. They'd stuck together in hard clumps. Sweat, she supposed – those hot flushes a couple of years back – and tears, of course.

'If you're sure,' Colin said. 'I'll take his nibs home now. Same time tomorrow morning for drop-off?'

'I can collect him in the mornings if you like,' Nina said. 'We can go to the park first thing.'

*

The walks were the best bit of the day. It was quite different being out with a dog. Everyone said hello or at least smiled, usually at Neville, occasionally at her too. Some of them asked after Colin. Nina spoke differently to Neville when they were out and about. She adopted the brisk two-word cadence everyone else used – 'this way', 'good boy'. No asking him his opinion or explaining what she was feeling or doing. People might have thought she was peculiar.

It was funny weather. It was one of those years when the autumn didn't work properly. The leaves changed too slowly, in tiny relays, and the wind took them before they could get too pleased with themselves. It rained a lot in the nights. Beautiful reds and oranges sank into depressed sludgy piles. Neville got muddy and took full advantage of Nina's new downstairs shower. Jonah had told her she was mad going to all that expense for a second bathroom when she was living on her own and also never had anyone to stay. Watching the warm water change from brown to clear as she rinsed Neville's matted fur, she felt vindicated. 'You'd have been treading mud all through the house otherwise,' she told him. They spent the late afternoons companionably (and damply) on the sofa waiting for Colin to come and take him away again.

She'd hoped to time the morning walks to coincide with Linda and Muddy. Mostly they didn't manage it. Linda's students had returned from their long summers doing whatever students did these days – work minimum-wage jobs and drink beer if they were anything like Jonah. It meant she needed to be at the university more often and earlier in the day until the normal patterns of term kicked in. They got the chance to chat only once, while the dogs played a game that looked a little like Grandmother's Footsteps.

'The flat smells different,' Linda said. 'Boyless. It's funny really. We thought we'd notice the quiet and no more grim, dirgy music. It's more a general lack of something in the air.'

'How's he getting on?'

'Fine, I think, you never really know with Gus. His Instagram's quiet, which means he's busy doing stuff or knows I'm looking. He rang Dima to see if he knew anything about Marx, which means he's doing some work. He thought Dima would have fresh insights, with his Russian roots.'

'Are there any fresh insights to be had on Marx?' Nina asked. 'If you're eighteen and go on marches, that is.'

'If there are, then Dima's the wrong person to ask,' Linda said. 'Fifty-eight and never been on a march in his life.'

Dima was older than Nina thought. There was barely any grey in his wavy hair. 'He must miss having Gus around.'

'He misses having someone else to argue with. It's only me now and we're past the stage of arguing.'

'When Jonah moved out, I missed the low-level bickering more than anything else,' Nina said. 'Little grumbles about who'd clogged up the shower or put the empty marmalade jar back in the cupboard.' That must have been her she'd realised now, as it was still happening.

'You and Jonah get on well,' Linda said. 'Not that I've seen you together, but Colin says you're a great advert for mothers and sons.'

'That's kind of him,' Nina said. 'Although Colin's only seen us together a few times himself.'

'He's very astute, though,' Linda said. 'He gets people. He's interested in them. I wish Dima was a bit more like him.'

Nina wasn't sure how to reply. She didn't have much experience of people criticising their partners to her. No patience with it either. Linda still had her husband. He painted wonderful pictures. He didn't complain. He asked lots of questions, which made Nina think Linda was wrong about him not being interested in people. He'd already found out quite a lot about her.

*

She kept Neville for longer one evening so that Colin could have free rein in his kitchen to prepare supper. It was dark when she set off on the short walk to Colin's house. Neville barked at pumpkin faces lit up in windows, days and days before Hallowe'en. They'd be slimy and brown by the time the actual date came around.

The kitchen smelled of herbs. Dill and parsley plants stood on the counter, in those pots you buy in the supermarket that die as soon as you get them home. A new jar of dried oregano. It looked like Colin had gone to a lot of trouble, but he said no. He liked cooking and was trying out a new recipe.

He'd set the table with a clashing mix of modern cutlery and old-fashioned crockery. More stuff from his parents' house, he said. Heirlooms, if things with no value that came from people who weren't rich counted as heirlooms. Nothing matched, except the table mats, which were dark blue paisley-patterned cork. A lot of dye had gone into making those. Nina thought they must have been a present.

Neville went straight to his bowl, then his basket. 'You've worn him out,' Colin said. 'Which is good because it means we'll be able to eat in peace. Can I tell you about the garden?'

'Only if you're not asking about plants. Mine was trial and error and I'm still not sure what we did right. Or wrong for that matter.'

'Zoning. I wanted to ask your opinion.'

'Zoning?'

'Yes. Part for me and part for Neville. He can use his section to bury my belongings and I can do what I want with the rest.'

'He's quite diggy. Although only at home, I noticed, not in the park.' Nina had made the mistake of leaving Neville unattended in her garden on his first morning. 'I can see the attraction, but I'm not sure how you'd police it.'

'He's very bright. I can teach him to respect boundaries.'

Neville was adorable. Affectionate. Obliging when small children asked their mums to ask Nina if they could stroke him. He wasn't noticeably bright. 'That might get quite frustrating,' she said. 'If it was me, I'd just accept that the garden belongs to everyone and sort of work around it. That's what we did when Jonah was little.'

'Jonah wasn't digging to Australia and pooing on the doorstep.'

'He had his moments.'

'He did?'

'Normal small child stuff. Then bigger child stuff. My lips are sealed. I think if you want a designer garden, you need to not have a child, or a dog, or neighbours with cats.'

'Bit late for that now.'

She couldn't read his tone.

*

The food was sensational. Greek chicken, beautifully marinaded. He'd made incongruous naans too and explained how easy that was to do (it sounded quite messy to Nina). He'd used a lower-sugar recipe. He didn't think you could tell. It was slightly spongy. Perfect for dunking. Neville got up when things came out of the oven. Colin offered him a hunk of the chewy bread, which he declined by spitting it out on the floor.

'You've had a nice time with Neville this week,' Colin said. 'He's been enjoying himself too.'

'You can tell that, can you? He's good company.'

'I can always tell what mood Neville's in. I plan to retrain as a dog whisperer when AI takes over my business. Even untrained I know I'm right because Linda told me.'

Friendship seemed to involve endless rounds of Chinese whispers. 'She's been hard to pin down this week, what with the new term and everything. We managed to walk the dogs together the other day. She said you're still working up to asking me a favour. I wish you'd spit it out, then if I need to say no, there's time to ask someone else.'

'A hypothetical favour.'

'That's fine then. If it's only hypothetical, I'll agree to anything. Provided it's legal and not morally dubious.'

'It's about Neville.'

'I'd guessed that,' Nina said. 'I can't see anything else I could usefully do for you. Are you going to enlighten me?'

'I've managed to get organised for my Australia trip. You remember I was hoping to go for my sister's birthday?'

'That doesn't sound very hypothetical.'

'It's not,' Colin agreed. 'Flights booked. Sister and family primed. The kennels are full though, only for the last ten days, and I was wondering if you could be a last resort. If there's no room anywhere else.'

Ten days. 'I don't think of myself as a last resort sort of person.'

He misunderstood. 'Of course. It was presumptuous of me. Linda said I shouldn't take you for granted. I'm sure we'll find somewhere else. Forget I mentioned it.'

'I'm flattered you asked. I'd prefer to have been Neville's first resort, obviously.'

'Are you saying you'll take him?'

'Yes.'

'I'm not going until the end of January.'

'Plenty of time to sort everything out, then.' People huffed about what a dismal month January was – cold, dark, broke and making pointless resolutions. Nina rather liked the sense that no one was expected to enjoy themselves.

By the end of the evening, she knew a lot more about Colin's Australian family. His brother-in-law didn't like flying and never came to England. Colin and his sister saw each other every couple of years, taking it in turns to make the trip. Judy had brought the kids with her once, but it was tricky with school, and expensive. They were still teenagers. They wouldn't go to the shops with their mother, let alone the other side of the world.

'Do you mind that they're so far away?' Nina asked.

'Why would I? They're still my family. I probably wouldn't see much more of them if they were here. We were never in each other's pockets.'

He must mind at some level. Family mattered. He still had plates from his childhood home. Jonah moving out of reach was Nina's third biggest dread, after him dying, like his father, or falling for someone new, who wasn't Kate. Someone she disliked as much as her own mother had taken against Martin.

Chapter twenty-four

Jonah rang to tell her it would soon be Christmas. 'That depends on what you mean by soon,' she said. 'We haven't even had bonfire night yet. Is it "soon" as in you want to break the news to me gently that you and Kate are going to go and spend it with orphaned elephants and you hope I don't mind?'

'Why would we want to do that?' asked Jonah. 'Elephants can look after themselves. Do you know there's too many of them now? We're having Christmas at home. This home, I mean, with the lovely curtains and draughty windows. Not your home with a fully functioning boiler and a brand-new second bathroom that only the dog uses. Also, we want you to join us. I thought if I asked you now, that gives a few weeks to wear you down into agreeing after you say no.'

'What makes you so sure I'll say no?'

'Let me see. Maybe the lived experience of being your adored son for the last twenty-five years gave me a tiny clue.'

'It's nice that you know me so well. Can I think about it?' She knew he'd tricked her. By telling her she'd say no, she had to say yes. They had no business thinking about Christmas already. It was only just November.

'That's just delaying the inevitable. Tell me all the reasons it won't work and I'll tell you why you are wrong.'

He had an answer to all her objections. No, Kate's family weren't a problem. They were Christmas-deniers and were off to somewhere warm, a Canary Island, where they seemed to think they could avoid the worst of the trappings. In a Catholic country. Granny never came for Christmas and Nina never went there anymore, so that was no different to other years. Nina said every year that she was going to volunteer for Crisis (more convenient than elephants), but she never did. Hard as she might find it to believe, he and Kate liked Nina and wanted to spend time with her.

Then the real reason. 'Also, I invited other Granny. Dad's mum. It was Kate's idea. She said yes.'

'Why?'

'I didn't ask her. Maybe she wants to see what we're all like these days. Maybe she fancies a trip to the bright lights. Maybe she's lonely.'

'No, I mean why did Kate suggest it? How is it any of her business?'

'You'd have to ask Kate. How about you don't? How about we all have a lovely family time and no one gets all analytical.'

'Martin, your dad, didn't want anything to do with his mother.'

'You never told me why.'

'I never knew why. Not really.' He'd been angry. Too angry for too long and too angry to talk about it. He'd shut Nina down any time she'd asked.

'Whatever it was, it will have been stupid,' Jonah said. 'This stuff always is. So this is the year to move on.'

Move on. Another of those worthy phrases that made no sense. 'It's quite the gesture. After all this time. No meetings and then Christmas. Christmas is a big deal.'

'Not for us it's not. Not anymore. This will make a change. A proper family Christmas.'

The year Martin died, Annette had invited them to Cornwall for Christmas. She set up ingenious treasure trails and garish pantomimes. Then there was the excitement of seeing the waves whipped up by the December winds. 'Dad won't mind missing this,' Jonah had said. 'He always liked best putting batteries in the new toys and there aren't any this year that need them. And he wouldn't want to be at Granny's house. He only liked being in charge.'

Nina remembered thinking how wrong Jonah was. Martin would be outraged at the way the world was muddling through without him to organise it. He'd have had trouble admitting that Jonah was enjoying himself so much at his grandmother's house.

Christmas in Cornwall was a fixture for a few years until the year Jonah refused point blank to leave his mates and Annette tactfully decided to go on a river cruise instead and got the taste for big communal Christmases (preferably on dry land). Since then, it had just been Jonah and Nina. They treated it like a normal day. It had suited her well and now Jonah had decided to introduce some unwelcome drama.

They'd never spent Christmas, or any extended time, with Martin's mother. He'd kept contact to a minimum, said he'd have cut her off completely if it wasn't for the inheritance (Nina thought he was joking about that, admittedly in bad taste). Then he died and she couldn't bear the idea of dealing with anyone else's grief. Hers and Jonah's were already too much.

She hadn't seen Maud for years and hadn't thought about her much, not until she found the birthday cards when they were clearing out Jonah's room. Even then, she hadn't realised how important his other granny was to Jonah. 'I promise I'll think about your offer,' she said. 'You need to give me time to get used to the idea.'

'You can let me know, then. We're putting other Granny in the spare room and you can have our room. We'll sleep on the sofa. You can stay as long as you like.'

'That's kind, darling. As we are planning weeks ahead, I should let you know that I will have to be home by February. For fostering duties. Our mutual orange friend.'

'A dog in winter.'

'Meaning?'

'That's what Dad always used to say, when I wanted a pet. Don't you remember? "The thing is, Jonah, a dog's all very well in the summer holidays when you are here to play with it. It will need lots of walks and to be outside a lot, and it's hard to keep up with a dog in winter."'

'I don't think I knew that was how he got out of it,' said Nina. 'I didn't want the mess and he didn't want the heartbreak, if you got a dog and it died. Ironic really. Anyway, Neville's coming for a couple of weeks in the new year. He can lie in front of a roaring fire while I drink whisky and do *The Times* crossword.'

'Better get the chimney opened up, then.'

'Yes. And start buying whisky. And reading *The Times*.'

'You'll have fun,' said Jonah. 'Dad was wrong about dogs. And he was wrong about Granny too. It's OK to say it.' She wasn't quite clear which granny he meant.

A dog in winter. Nina could hear Martin wearing Jonah down. It was a lion really, in the proper phrase, from the film. Peter O'Toole, treacherous and angry, madly in love with Katharine Hepburn. She didn't remember much about it, except it was set at Christmas. She thought there'd been a happy ending.

Chapter twenty-five

'So, how was it?' It was the day after Boxing Day. Colin and Neville appeared on Nina's doorstep. They brought cheese. 'Leftovers. We're going to walk into Richmond. Coming?'

The sky and river were grey, underfoot slippery with mushed-up leaves. They walked slowly, dodging kids with new scooters (as if there weren't already enough of those) and watching Neville have second thoughts about jumping into the Thames. 'It's funny there aren't any puppies,' Nina said. 'Maybe people don't get them for Christmas anymore. You don't see those "a dog is not just for Christmas" ads like you used to.'

They compared notes. If she'd not been at Jonah's, she'd have liked to have gone to Colin's 'fugitives from festivities' event. He held a drop-in open house for anyone who wanted a break from family or was having a solitary Christmas. Colin had been surprised how many had turned up. Everyone had brought cheese, some of it nastily studded with cranberries to make it Christmassy. Some of it vegan, which they agreed was wrong.

'It sounds fun,' Nina said. 'I'd already promised Jonah, or I'd have dropped in myself.'

'Yes. Your family Christmas with extra helping of mother-in-law. How did you get on?'

'I liked her.'

'You sound surprised. You must have known if you liked her, from before, you know from when Martin... You know what I mean. She wasn't a stranger Jonah and Kate rescued from a soup kitchen.'

'I'd only met her a couple of times. Martin had fallen out with her and wasn't in any rush to fall back in with her. I did try. After he died, it was easier to put her out of my mind. I had enough to worry about.'

*

Nina had decided beforehand to let Christmas wash over her. Go with the flow. When she'd told Niall this, he'd said good, that was healthy. He wondered if Nina would find it difficult or liberating or redemptive.

She arrived at Jonah and Kate's late afternoon on Christmas Eve, bearing too many gifts. Champagne, fruit ('Just because it's Christmas, you don't have to stick to tangerines,' she explained), a cake topped with the surviving members of her gang of chipped ornaments (two Santas, a baby Jesus, a donkey and a figure that was either a shepherd or a wise man but it was hard to tell because most of its clothing had rubbed off over the years) and stockings for Jonah and Kate. She filled these with small things she'd noticed they didn't seem to have in the flat – egg cups, nutcrackers, a tea strainer, birthday cake candles and stuff she saw in Lakeland in Kingston that she had no idea anyone needed.

She bought and wrapped up a scarf for Maud. She also put together a small book of pictures of Martin, spending several tearful afternoons scanning photos from dog-eared albums.

'Hi, Mum,' Jonah said when she arrived. 'I've booked a table at the Indian round the corner for this evening, hope that's OK. Maud's here.'

'So I see. Hello.'

'Hello, Nina.' Maud didn't get up from the sofa, but she smiled.

'I'm not sure what else to say.'

'Well, there are always the fallbacks. We could be very British and talk about the journey or the weather.'

'Not forgetting the terrible choice of Christmas television.'

'Then there's commenting on the younger generation. Jonah says there are lots of things you don't like about the flat. We could talk about those.'

'The navy walls, mainly,' said Nina. 'So dark.'

'You like them really, Mum,' Jonah said. 'You just enjoy criticising.'

'That is not true.'

'It's completely true. It's what mothers do. You can't help yourself.'

'I'm just trying to teach you good taste, darling.'

'Gran likes what we've done with the room, don't you, Gran?' Nina hadn't heard him call her Gran before.

'I'm a guest,' Maud said. 'It's not my place to comment.' She winked at Nina. 'The Christmas tree is rather sweet.'

The tree was about two foot high. Either it was the top of something much taller or it had been snatched from the ground when it was a baby. It was in a red pot on top of a corner table and hung with miniature wooden Santas. Someone, probably Jonah judging by how slapdash it all looked, had sprayed fir cones silver and white and arranged them round the base of the pot. 'We were going to get a proper tree,' Kate said, 'then between the stairs and wanting there to be enough room in here to extend the table, we thought a mini version would be better.'

'It's rather lovely,' Maud said. 'I didn't bother with a tree at all this year, as I was coming here.'

'I'm afraid my tree is still in the attic,' Nina said. She'd got as far as unearthing it from behind the boxes of stuff Jonah hadn't got round to collecting yet, then thought, why? Why go to all the effort of unfolding plastic branches and waiting for the lights to fuse when no one was coming to the house (apart possibly from Neville and it would be just another thing for him to knock over).

'If you want to chuck your clobber in our room,' Jonah said, 'we can head straight out. I've changed the sheets and everything.'

'Thank you, darling. Very hospitable.'

'It's so brilliant you're both here,' Jonah said. He didn't often have such a serious face. 'It'll be like being a kid again; Christmas with my mother and my grandmother to indulge me.'

'Although, to be fair, I am the wrong grandmother.'

'No such thing. Grandmothers are the perfect family member.'

'Oh dear. That means I have a lot to live up to.' Maud had Martin's eyes. They didn't twinkle exactly but looked as if the next thought wouldn't be held back for long. 'It's very kind of you all to share your family Christmas with me.'

'It's your family too,' Jonah said. 'It's a pity my other granny couldn't come. We can work on that for next year.'

Nina wondered when Maud had found out the arrangements. There was never going to be a good time to set up a reunion. Perhaps Christmas made it easier. Jonah would be perfectly capable of springing a surprise. Oh, by the way, Gran, Mum's coming too. He'd have told her when he met her at King's Cross and it was already too late to catch a train back to York.

*

The curry turned out to be a good idea. They ordered lots of sides and shared them. Maud liked the food with the liveliest, freshest flavours – ginger and chilli and tomato. 'Dad told me never to trust someone who ordered a korma,' said Kate. 'That's why I'm with Jonah, I expect. It must run in the family.'

'Martin brought a vindaloo back from the takeaway one night when he was about seventeen. He pretended to like it. I could see he was struggling and a bit later I found most of it in the dog's dish, with the dog barking at it.'

'He grew into them,' said Nina. 'He'd cook truly alarming curries – fistfuls of chillis and goodness knows what else.' *This is do-able*, she thought. *We'll be OK mentioning Martin.*

'You went to Lakeland,' said Jonah on Christmas morning.

'Yes. "Thank you, Mother, for the lovely stocking", I think is the more conventional reaction.'

'Well, yes, thank you. Also thank you for being here. I'm having trouble seeing you in Lakeland.'

'I can't have my only son starting out adult life without jam spoons. I'm a bit worried about Maud. I bought her a scarf. It's old lady colours.'

'She'll tell you if she doesn't like it.' This seemed likely to be true. Maud had proved good company over dinner – outspoken and sharp. Like her son.

'I've got photos of Dad too. Maybe I should just give her those.'

'That's her finishing in the bathroom now,' Jonah said. The bath was emptying loudly, making strange froggy noises. 'It's up to you, but I'd start with the scarf and leave Dad's ghost for later.'

*

The day went smoothly. Maud took herself off to church while Jonah and Kate were sorting out the food. No turkey, happily. Instead, another of Jonah's posh stews simmered on the stove, misting up all the windows until water dripped on the carpet. Then, after (a delicious) lunch, in the sliver of time before it got dark, Kate took Maud for a walk to show her the park and the views over London. They saved main presents for the evening. Everyone was very polite, even Jonah, although Nina could tell he didn't like the shirt Maud had given him. It was checked and he only ever wore stripes, like his father.

In the evening Nina and Kate sat up late. 'This feels wrong,' Nina said, 'sitting with you on your bed while Jonah's banished to the sofa.'

'He'll be playing one of his games. Don't worry about him.'

'I was quite apprehensive about today,' Nina said. 'It's been lovely.'

'It felt like a gamble to us, too. Jonah's wanted to bring you and Maud together for ages and we knew you wouldn't be able to say no to Christmas.'

'I sorted out some pictures for Maud. You can see if you think she'll like them. They're still in the car. Here, I can show you on my phone.'

She'd used one of those online companies. It had taken her ages to decide which pictures to include. Martin in an anorak standing on a hill. Martin in stripy shirtsleeves holding baby Jonah. Martin in a starchy suit holding a champagne glass. Martin lying on his stomach looking cross, surrounded by Lego. Martin in a different anorak in the bow of a cross-Channel ferry. 'He looks so young,' Nina said.

'Young genes,' said Kate. 'Look at Maud.'

'I'm not sure it's the right thing to do. They might upset her.' Nina knew she was being pathetic. She'd give the pictures to Jonah (he'd seen them all before) and he could decide whether to show them to Maud. He'd got to know her well by now.

Chapter twenty-six

Nina had a theory that secretly no one likes new year. Staying up until midnight when you normally go to bed at 10.30pm throws everything out of sync. Worrying about how to get home or staying home, enduring garish television. More bloody fireworks, only a few weeks after the smell of bonfire night and Diwali has gone. Jonah and Kate had taken her car to Scotland and she worried about them on the roads.

'None of which addresses the question I asked you,' Niall said. His consulting room was too hot.

'It wasn't a proper question. Not even grammatical. New beginning. What would a not-new beginning be, I wonder?'

'What question would you like me to ask?'

That was a new trick. Nina rather admired it. 'I think,' she said carefully, 'if I were a therapist, which I would not want to be, I would ask if seeing my mother-in-law made me see things differently.'

'And the answer is yes.'

'You're not allowed to do that. Assume you know what I am thinking.'

'It didn't make you see things differently?'

'Of course it did. The woman's Jonah's grandmother, for heaven's sake. It was a relief to see that she's suitable.'

'Suitable?'

'They like each other. Love each other. It's important. Another person in Jonah's corner.'

'And in your corner, perhaps?'

'It's not about me.'

She waited for Niall to say that it was always about her, at some level. His job was to help her acknowledge that. She'd tell him he was wrong, of course. Sometimes it was all about Jonah.

*

Colin loved new year. Everyone made their plans months in advance, so he was doing Twelfth Night instead, without the cross-dressing unless people wanted to, or Epiphany, without the wise men (although if anyone turned up with frankincense and myrrh, he'd be extremely interested to find out what they smelled like). He'd written all of this, and more, on the back of the invitation that he'd dropped through the door, before knocking and telling her all about it until she agreed to come.

Nina had never minded parties, although she was a little out of practice. She'd been brought up to be good at small talk and honed her skills during her marriage. Martin was an extrovert. The calendar was always jammed with invitations. The trick at any gathering involving standing up was to say hello to the first person you saw who didn't seem to know anyone else. If the stranger was female, it used to be OK to open with a compliment. Goodness knows what the protocol was these days.

In the event, she didn't need to put it to the test since as soon as she arrived Colin announced her to the room. 'This is Nina! Neville's guardian angel.' He did the same with everyone who arrived. Snappy phrases that perhaps caught a tiny bit of someone or, more likely Nina thought, gave away how Colin saw them.

She knew some of the others from dog walking and the quiz. Linda and Dima arrived. A moment or two of awkwardness while people made way for the wheelchair. Nina waved and was about to go across and say hello when Neville bounded in, leaping up and spilling most of Nina's wine over the woman standing beside her. Kerfuffle involving kitchen towel and half-hearted attempts to move Neville back into the kitchen where, according to Colin, he could 'do less damage'. This seemed a vain hope given the amount of food on the table. The woman was relaxed about the whole thing. 'Nothing that a bit of Vanish won't sort out,' she said. 'I'm Lina, by the way.'

'Nina.'

'Ah. Colin said I should look out for you. He said we had more in common than our rhyming names.'

'That sounds like Colin.' They talked for quite a while. Lina, short for Angelina ('and who wants to live up to a glamorous name like that?'), was a curator for historic houses, including the one in the park around the corner. They were always looking for volunteers. If Nina was interested, there were lots of details online, or she could give her a ring.

'Ah. Good stuff.' Colin appeared with a plate of sausage rolls. 'I hoped you two would meet.'

'Neville was most helpful in brokering an introduction. Nothing like pouring your wine over someone to start a conversation.'

'So what do you think of my idea? Volunteering.'

'Your idea?'

'Partially, yes. I was telling Angelina here about you. How interested you were in old stuff. My teapot. Plates. Those sorts of things.'

'I was whining about how hard it is to get more specialised volunteers,' Lina said.

'Yes. And I said I knew just the person! You should try it, Nina. I'd have a go myself if I wasn't so busy.'

Lina had explained that they were expanding the porcelain displays in the restored eighteenth-century house. Posh china had been all the rage, the more exotic the better. There was money to acquire some original pieces and decent quality replicas, but not to create explanatory notes or, better still, have someone on hand to talk to visitors. Nina could imagine doing that, at least the explanatory notes. She'd use plain English and avoid any pretentious phrases. She was about to say more when Linda appeared at Colin's elbow.

'Linda!' Colin looked thrilled. 'Meet Lina! We need a Leah! Then a Lee!'

'Nice to meet you, Leah. Hello, Nina.' Linda was clearly distracted. 'I'm sorry to party poop, Colin. We're going to have to go.'

'So early?'

'It's Dima.'

'Is he OK?' Nina looked across to where Dima was talking to two people who were half crouching so their heads were at similar heights to his. They were laughing.

'Of course he's OK.'

'What, then?'

'He has to go.'

She wasn't making any sense. Nina turned to Lina. 'It was lovely to meet you, Lina, and I promise I will google you. If you'll excuse me, I'm going to have a chat with my friend Linda here and see if I can stop them breaking up the party.' She tugged at Linda's arm and steered her into the porch. When Colin made to follow, Nina waved him away. 'You need to circulate those sausage rolls,' she said. 'Leave these two to me.'

'That man is so stupid sometimes,' Linda said when they were out of earshot.

'Which man?'

'My husband.'

'The clever lawyer and artist?'

'Don't tease me, Nina. I'm not in the mood.'

'Are you not enjoying the party? Dima looks like he's having fun.'

'He's given me a thirty-minute warning. There's no downstairs loo. Dima was confident it wasn't going to be an issue. Now he thinks it might be an issue later. A bathroom issue. It's like dealing with a child.'

'Is that all?'

'Isn't it enough? He can't drive himself because it's been his turn to drink. So he's party pooping. Probably literally.'

This was too much information and also not enough.

Nina thought people with spinal injuries had bags. She'd never investigated it properly. Come to think of it, she'd often seen Dima wheel himself into the disabled toilet at the pub. She had a practical solution. Her still quite new downstairs loo was only round the corner. She'd known it would come in handy one day. 'We can say that I'd like him to pop over and look at a painting, or something,' Nina said as she put her suggestion to Linda. 'You know, a cover story to spare his blushes.'

'Dima doesn't blush,' Linda said.

Fifteen minutes later, Nina, Dima and Neville, who had taken the putting-on of coats as an invitation, were in Nina's hallway debating whether the wheelchair was too wide for the cloakroom door. (Neville's contribution to the discussion was to run up and down the stairs, barking.) 'If we get the angle exactly right, it'll be fine.' He was spot on. Inches to spare.

Linda had stayed at the party.

While Dima did whatever he was doing – she was curious but didn't like to ask – Nina took Neville into the kitchen. She still had half a packet of Bonio from when she'd provided day care for him. She tried to get him to shake paws. His social skills weren't that far advanced.

'Nina!' Dima had an excellent voice for public speaking. 'I need help with the door.' She'd pulled it closed behind him and he couldn't turn round to open it again.

'I'm sorry,' she said. 'I didn't think.'

'Absolutely you thought. Linda would have bundled me home and left me there.' He was reversing into the hallway. She couldn't see his face.

'I'll grab Neville and we can head back into the fray. If you're sorted.'

'Maybe a breather first.'

'Cup of tea?'

'You are so British.'

'I'm sorry.'

'Always apologising. Why do you Brits do that?'

'Centuries of ingrained habit. It's not real. You know that really we're looking down on you.'

'I've lived here for long enough to have figured that out. I don't want tea. But let's not go straight back.'

'I thought you were enjoying it?' Otherwise, why was he here? It would have been easier for him to go home.

'Loving it. I need a rest. Take the weight off my feet.'

'Metaphorically speaking.'

'That's what I like about you, Nina. Most people would think that and not say it.'

'Tiptoeing round the wheelchair.'

'That's exactly what people do. Metaphorically. It's the most obvious thing about me and everyone dances around it.'

'Metaphorically. Although, also rubbish. It's not the most obvious thing about you.' His eyes. A bit like Paul Newman. She'd noticed them. And his exhausting cleverness.

'It's a pain in the butt for people. It gets in the way. You'll see when we get back to Colin's. They'll have started dancing now the guy in the chair isn't there.'

He was a little drunk, Nina noticed. Only a little. 'Somehow I very much doubt that. Not when there's talking to be done.'

'Colin does like to talk, doesn't he? Linda brought him and Neville over yesterday after their walk. I could hear them chuntering on. Me and Gus hid in the other room.'

'Gus hasn't gone back yet?'

'He's saying he'll go back if and when he decides. You've raised a son. Do they all go through an unbearable phase, or is it only ours?'

'I'm sure he's not unbearable.'

'Three weeks with Gus objecting to everything and anything. Trying to impose his superior life choices on us. Turn us into greener, better people.'

'I'm all for greener and better, within reason. Jonah went vegan for about a week. That was trying.'

'You think I'm overreacting?'

'I don't know what you're dealing with. Jonah grew out of the hectoring phase. Mostly. What are you worried about with Gus?'

'Beyond lounging round our flat, not helping out, picking holes in his parents.'

'Isn't that his job? He's a teenage boy.'

'It's beyond all that. When we were hiding from Linda and Colin the other day, he was on and on about my accident.'

'Isn't that a good thing?' *Niall would be proud of me*, she thought. *Get things out in the open.*

'He's concocted a whole theory,' Dima said. 'Subconsciously I did it on purpose to trap Linda into a supportive role when she is cleverer than me, as any idiot can see, and to deter the dog who was showing signs of co-dependence. Or words to that effect.'

'I can see that must be hurtful. You must know it's also nonsense.'

'I had no idea he was so angry.'

'Have you told Linda what he said?'

'What good would that do? You might get it, though. Given your history.'

Her history. 'Jonah was never angry about Martin,' she said. They'd talked and talked about it over the long years. 'I'm not sure what to advise. Are you sure you can't talk to Linda?'

'It's not like she can do anything.'

'And you haven't picked it up again with Gus?'

'I don't know what to say.'

'That's not an excuse.'

'Could you talk to him? He likes you.'

'He's met me twice.'

'And you brought his dog home when he ran away. That makes you a hero in Gus's eyes.'

'As I recall it, Muddy would have come home anyway. I can't be a go-between, Dima. You'll figure something out. You and Linda are intelligent people.'

'I know. It's a curse.'

'Clever enough to know that everyone's family is different. The one bit of advice I might give is that I kept talking to Jonah. Even if he didn't want me to.' For quite a few years, she hadn't really talked to anyone else. She didn't think it was the right time to mention that.

'It's probably easier for women.'

'Now that, Dima, really is nonsense. When you have got off your sexist high horse, I can tell you at tedious length about how I don't talk properly to my mother.'

'Can't wait. But also, sorry, I think.'

'From the little I've seen of Gus, he cares about things. All that stuff about saving the world. Even the quiz. He's interested in people.'

'Mainly in their defects. People ruining the world.'

'Well, they are, aren't they? Ruining the world.'

'Not everyone. You can't tell me that all those nice people that Colin has gathered are world-wreckers? Maybe we should go back and ask them?'

'Is that your way of saying you'd like to rejoin the party?'

'They'll think we're up to something if we don't.'

'Or you could go home and talk to Gus? I've been drinking or I'd drive you. I can nip back round, drop Neville off, and let Linda know to collect you from here when she's ready.'

'I'd rather we went back to the party,' Dima said. 'Colin had more brokering to do.'

'Brokering?'

'Absolutely. He wanted to fix you up with that curator friend of his.'

'Mission accomplished on that score. Are you telling me he's got a raft of other distractions lined up, just for me? Only he needs me in full lady-of-leisure mode to be able to look after Neville.'

'He and Linda have you as their new year's resolution. I shouldn't tell you. Get you out of the house. I'm in on it too, once I think of something.'

'I find that rather insulting.' Or touching. She wasn't quite sure.

'Be insulted if you want. Colin knows so many people. You don't know any. Make the most of it.'

'Back into the fray then.'

'Lead on. Although you'll need to wrestle with the ramp again first.'

The ramp was a nifty gadget. No good for the steep stairs at Colin's but perfect to get Dima's wheels up the shallow front step to Nina's house. It was a concertinaed thing that clicked into place in a way that Nina found oddly satisfying. She was pleased that Dima trusted her to assemble it, not that he had any choice. Flattered too that he'd asked her about Gus. They made their way back to the party in silence, Neville proudly carrying one of Nina's gloves, which she'd dropped while locking the door.

Chapter twenty-seven

The days after the party ran into weeks and suddenly Colin was off on his travels. He brought Neville over one afternoon a few days before he left to run through arrangements yet again.

'It's not as if he hasn't stayed with me before.' Nina tried to sound reassuring and not irritated. A fleeting visitor – the gasman, say, or the Tesco delivery person – would think Nina had a resident dog. Neville had a basket permanently in the corner of the kitchen. There were tell-tale claw marks on the back door.

'He might be discombobulated after the kennels.'

'Don't they vaccinate against that?'

'It's a frame of mind. Not a virus.' Nina had forgotten how literal Colin was when it came to the dog.

'I'm teasing,' she said. 'Honestly, Colin, you don't need to worry. Neville will be fine at the kennel and he'll be fine with me. I'm looking forward to having a furry lodger.'

'You're not to spoil him. He's learning boundaries. We mustn't undo all the excellent work.'

Nina was surprised by the news that Neville had learned boundaries. Perhaps not helping yourself to your host's shoes in the hallway wasn't on the beginners' course. 'I was thinking I could teach him some more tricks.' He'd got good at shaking paws.

'You mustn't hothouse him. I don't want to come home and find he's signed up for a talent show.'

'I was thinking Crufts,' she said. 'They do that agility stuff. Crowd-pleasing. You don't need to worry, Colin. He'll be well looked after. We'll look after each other. You know I'd take him for the whole time if you're concerned about the kennel.'

'I know. I'd already paid for the kennel before I thought of you.' At least he was honest. 'This way, Neville gets the best of both worlds. Some intensive pampering – I've booked him in for grooming and teeth cleaning – and then a few days *en famille*.'

'Does one person count as *en famille*? Although Kate says she will be over all the time if Neville is here.'

'He'll like that.'

'He's going to like all of it. We'll have to set up some Zoom calls so you can see how much fun he's having. I'll send pictures too. We could set him up with an Instagram account.'

*

Colin's visit had been unnecessary, but welcome. Until he turned up, it had been days since Nina had spoken to someone in real life. The person who helped her move an unexplained item from the bagging area and the optician who'd suggested stronger reading glasses didn't count. Jonah had rung one day wanting to borrow her car.

Otherwise it was the curator woman from the party and that had been almost a week ago.

Nina had forgotten all about it when she had a call from an unknown number. Lina. When she'd got over being annoyed at another reference to the rhyming names ('It's clearly meant to be!') and Colin handing out her number, Nina found herself agreeing to go and have a chat about the project. That had happened on Wednesday. The upshot was that Nina had signed up for a couple of induction sessions in February, and Lina would also arrange for her to go and talk to the person who was sourcing the new china. It would be a long time before Nina found out that the phone call was Dima's doing. He'd told Linda to tell Colin to tell the person who might get Nina to do something to get in touch while the iron was, if not hot, at least vaguely warm.

*

The tail end of January always brought new hope. Longer afternoons, early snowdrops, Valentine's cards in the shops if you liked that sort of thing (which Nina didn't). This year, Nina thought there might be more substance to it than the changing of the seasons. Jonah and Kate had gone. In a way, it meant they saw more of each other. Proper socialising without the distractions of haggling over household chores.

Her life was a bit fuller. People she hadn't known a year ago who counted her as a friend. Her turn on the quiz master rota, keeping the tradition alive while Gus fought elitism from beneath the dreaming spires. A project in the offing. Neville's ecstatic greetings every time she took him off Colin's hands. This was the year when things would tip to Martin having been dead for longer than she'd known him. As good a year as any for a turning point.

Not that Nina had any truck with that sort of nonsense.

Part two

Chapter twenty-eight

'Charming old-fashioned B&B, chatty helpful staff Sue and Wendy, comfy beds.' Trip Advisor review.

It wasn't like Jonah to use such short sentences. Even if she hadn't been hanging on every word, Nina would have known something was wrong. 'You're not to worry, Mum.' Never a good start. 'Granny's broken her arm. She says it's complicated. She means compound. They're doing assessments.' He didn't say what they were assessing. 'She says not to visit. I know you'll want to. I looked at the train times. That would be quicker than driving. There's one at lunchtime. I've found you a B&B.'

'How did she sound?' Nina asked when she could get a word in.

'Cross, mainly,' said Jonah.

'That's a good sign, I suppose.' Nina had a million questions. 'And she rang you just now?'

'Last night. She made me promise not to call until this morning. She didn't want you driving through the night.' Now he'd got the main news out of the way, he was talking more normally.

'And she fell yesterday?'

'A couple of days ago,' Jonah said.

'And she's broken her arm?'

'Yes, I already told you.'

'And you don't know how she is, apart from that?'

'Only what I've told you,' Jonah said.

'And she didn't think to call me herself?'

'I'm just the messenger,' Jonah said. 'You can ask her yourself when you see her.'

'And you think I should go?'

'Don't you want to go? I've sorted everything out for you.' He sounded a little aggrieved.

'It's all a bit of a shock,' said Nina. 'I'm sorry to fire so many questions at you.'

'I'm used to it.'

'You said Granny didn't want me to visit?'

'There you go again, Mum. Her exact words were to tell you not to panic and not to get any ridiculous ideas in your head about jumping into your car. She didn't mean it.'

'Are you sure about that?' Nina asked.

'I know her pretty well,' Jonah said. 'You'll need to get a move on if you want to catch the five to one. It'll be OK, Mum. It's only a broken arm.'

*

The train took forever. It hugged the coast on the spectacular stretch below Exeter. From the window, Nina watched people bundled in anoraks walking bouncy dogs on the beach as the daylight faded. She tried her mother's number a few times. It went straight to voicemail. Jonah's words went round and round in her head. Only a broken arm. But complicated. Or compound. Or more likely both.

*

The B&B was called the Wendy House. Left to her own devices, Nina would have chosen somewhere with fewer gnomes. It was clean and the 'self-service check-in' (keys in an envelope under the doormat) meant she hadn't needed to talk to anyone until now. She'd arrived too late to get anything to eat, she told the woman who fussed over her at breakfast, but hadn't starved. She'd had to change trains and there'd been time before the not-very-connecting service to pick up a pasty from a bakery near the station.

That set the woman off on an involved anecdote about pasties and tomato ketchup. 'I wasn't allowed the sauce before I was nine in case I broke the bottle. It was glass in those days. Are you OK for toast? Lovely.' Nina thought that was the end of the story, but no. 'Everyone else, they'd all go in for their tea at the table. I liked to eat mine on the doorstep.' It was hard to picture her as a young girl in such a whimsical scene. 'Let me find you some jam.' The woman moved away from the table, still talking. 'That was a long time ago. I'm sixty-six next month. Are you sure you don't want a cooked breakfast? Sue does a lovely scrambled egg.'

Nina supposed this exhausting prattle was part of the warm and friendly welcome mentioned in almost all the Trip Advisor reviews. 'No, thank you,' she said.

'Just the toast then. Weather's clearing up. Doing a bit of touring, are you? Although I didn't see a car? There's a good bus service – you'd be surprised, goes all the way down to Penzance – and the train of course, you know all about that. Strawberry jam OK? Or would you rather blackcurrant?'

'Visiting family,' said Nina. 'My mother. I don't need any jam, thank you. If I could have some more marmalade, that would be lovely. Thank you.' She pointed at the lonely sachet of feeble orange jelly.

'Aren't we the lucky ones! Still got our lovely mums. And at our age!' The woman had fifteen years on Nina. 'Excuse me a minute and I'll fetch the marmalade from out back. We don't want your toast getting cold.'

The breakfast room fell into grateful near silence. The couple at the other occupied table studied their phones. He spooned sugar into his tea, tapping the spoon against the side of the cup as he stirred.

Chapter twenty-nine

Officially visiting times weren't until the afternoon. Nina had phoned the ward and the nurse had said she could pop in anyway. 'She'll be pleased to see you,' she said. Nina hoped that was true. 'No one's been in yet so you could maybe pick up some bits on your way? The hospital friends have sorted out the basics.'

The hospital was a train and a bus away. The journey was straightforward enough. When Nina arrived, she was directed to a side ward at the end of a long corridor. Her shoes squeaked on the shiny floor. She peered into bays of identical tiny women perched on beds or in chairs, packaged in groups of six, their human sounds no match for the beeping machines. Someone had written names on wipe-clean boards in green marker pen. Mary something starting with an S had been half erased, a forlorn stripped bed in the place nearest the door.

She found her mother in a sea of pillows. 'Hello, Mum,' she said, pecking her on the cheek. 'This isn't so bad. It's good that they could give you your own room.' It was little more than an alcove. The walls were freshly painted a jaundiced yellow. 'I brought you these.' She produced mints, sparkling water and fat green apples from her bag.

'That was nice of you,' Annette said. She wasn't hooked to any machines but had a canula sticking out of her left hand. Her right arm was in a navy plaster cast.

'How are you feeling?' Nina asked. 'I've been so worried.'

'I'll live,' Annette said. 'I told Jonah you didn't need to come.'

'He chose not to believe you,' Nina said. 'Anyway, I wanted to come.'

'It's a long way to travel,' said Annette. 'That train's terrible. As you'd know if you used it more often.'

'It was very scenic,' Nina said. 'Lots of countryside to look at.' She'd found staring out of the window stopped her thinking. 'We went past a field of the most ridiculously small ponies. You'd have thought they'd freeze.'

'Very sweet, I'm sure,' her mother said dismissively. 'Where are you staying?'

'Jonah got me a B&B. Terrible coffee, but it's cosy.'

'I don't know why you wasted money on a B&B. You could have stayed in the house.'

'Jonah thought it would be easier,' Nina said. Her mother was less likely to push the point if she thought it was Jonah's idea. 'Let's see how it goes, shall we? The main thing is to get you sorted out. Tell me what you've been doing to yourself.'

'It was a stupid accident,' said Annette. 'They all are, I suppose. I sat on my arm.'

'Do you know why you fell?'

'The pavements get icy, and all those hills, and my arm was in the wrong place. They've put lots of pins in it.'

'Does it hurt?' Nina asked.

'They've got me on some sort of miracle drugs,' Annette said. 'I can't feel anything. Probably addictive of course.'

'You should have let me know.'

'I knew you'd only fuss. Anyway, I told Jonah. He's promised to visit. I always like seeing him.'

Nina thought she should say something about Jonah always liking seeing his granny. The moment passed. 'The nurses seem nice,' she said. She'd met one for all of a minute. He had a nice smile and the person she'd spoken to earlier had been friendly.

'They're not bad,' said Annette. 'They will insist on calling me "we". How are we feeling? How's our arm doing? Have we moved our bowels? The doctor is twelve, naturally. She chews the end of her biro.'

Nina was reassured by the grumbles. 'Have they said how long they'll keep you in for?' she asked.

'They don't tell me anything,' Annette said. 'Nothing that makes sense anyway.'

Nina stayed for what felt like a long hour before being shooed out so the doctors could do their rounds. It was enough time to make a list of things to collect from the house. She thought Annette must be at least a little bit pleased to see her. It was hard to tell.

*

When she left, Nina took Annette's key. It was a crisp day. She walked the half mile from the station to her mother's house along the steep streets above the bay. She passed

181

a sign promising a 'Beach: 700 metre's', the apostrophe grating. The houses were terraced, with short flights of tall front steps and big picture windows. Some people had filled their windowsills with marine knick-knacks – china fish, twists of old rope, driftwood expensively painted blue and white and overlaid with italic clichés about clear skies and calm seas.

Her mother's house was at the top of the hill. It looked cared for. Cyclamen and winter pansies bloomed bravely. Inside made Nina think of those crime reconstructions you sometimes see where the police know the person is missing because they'd gone out without finishing the washing-up. (People must do that all the time.) A cereal bowl, small plate, knife and spoon had drained on the rack. Most of a mug of milky tea was still in the sink. The rest of the milk was in the fridge with predominantly dairy food, yoghurts and cheese. A bowl of what looked like home-made custard had started to separate. It was funny how it did that, eggs and milk bonding and then unbonding again when things started to go bad. The freezer was full of sensible fish and vegetables.

There was a calendar on the fridge door, held fast with four magnets, which Nina recognised from the same Tate Modern set Jonah had given her for Christmas one year. Neat block capital letters spelled out a busy, organised life of art circles and worthy lectures, interspersed with names Nina didn't know (Sarah, coffee; Chris, harbour walk) and regular Zoom calls with Jonah. The last day of each month had a list of things to fit in the following month – dental check-up, renew insurance.

Upstairs, the wardrobe was half empty. All the drawers were labelled as if someone might need forewarning that opening the one on the top left would reveal pretty underwear that put Nina's own too-many-times-through-the-washing-machine knickers to shame. She didn't recognise the handwriting.

*

'I took a photo of February, on your calendar,' Nina told Annette when she returned to the hospital. 'Quite the social life you've got going. Much better than mine!'

'That's hardly an achievement, darling,' her mother said.

Nina had packed a bag with clean underwear, a couple of nighties (from the drawer labelled PJs) and a change of clothes. 'I've brought your phone charger too.' She waited for a few seconds in case her mother wanted to say thank you and then pressed on. 'The house is very spick and span, not like our family at all!' Growing up, Nina had been embarrassed to bring her more fastidious friends round for tea. Everything was always in such a mess. 'Have you been having a clear-out?'

'You should try it,' said Annette. 'You know what they say. Get rid of what you don't need, use or love. Kept the charity shops stocked up for weeks.'

'It must be easier to look after the house,' Nina said. 'With less clutter.'

'I'm good at looking after myself,' Annette said. 'Or I was, although now I'm not sure, with this wretched arm.'

'Have they told you when it will get better?' Nina asked.

'No, but they've named it for me,' Annette said. 'The main injury is a distal radial fracture. It sounds like the kind of band Jonah would listen to. You know he tries to keep me up to date with the latest music.' *Distal*, Nina thought, *doesn't that mean far away?* 'Another one of them came to see me after you'd gone. All clipboard and bustle, muttering about wanting to do tests to see if I'm bonkers.'

'I'm sure they didn't say that.'

'She didn't call it that. You could tell from the idiotic questions it was what she was driving at. Do I know where I am? Do I know the name of the Prime Minister?'

Cognitive questions. 'That's just what they have to do, Mum,' Nina said.

'I named the last six of our glorious leaders and gave my views on all of them. That soon sent her away.'

*

A skinny nurse stopped Nina on the way out. She had a different uniform to the others that showed she was more important, or maybe less important, than anyone else on the ward. She wanted to know how long Nina would be staying for. She wanted social services to have a chat with Nina about a care package, seeing as how her mother lived on her own and was an older lady. There'd be someone in the office tomorrow afternoon if Nina wouldn't mind popping in.

'Shouldn't you be talking to my mother?' Nina was confused.

'Of course. We'd like you to be involved too. We like to include the loved ones. Your mother is not giving much away. We want to run some memory tests.'

'Mum mentioned tests,' Nina said. 'Is there anything to worry about?'

'That's what we need to find out,' the nurse said. 'She is short-tempered and she had half a tin of cat food in her pocket. An open tin. With a spoon. Something not quite right there.'

'I don't understand,' said Nina. 'What have cats got to do with anything?'

'She fell because she was feeding a cat,' the nurse said. It wasn't clear if she thought Annette or the mystery cat was responsible.

'You mean while she was feeding a cat,' said Nina. 'Not because she was feeding it. Sorry, I know that's pedantic. She told me she slipped on ice.'

'Yes,' the nurse said, 'because she was out in her slippers.'

'She probably only nipped out for a second,' Nina said. The nurse's tone made her want to defend her mother. 'I don't believe she's got a cat, so maybe she was doing a favour for a neighbour. Shouldn't people be concentrating on her arm?'

'The arm will mend. Her bones are in good shape, considering her age. As I say, we want to check a few things. She won't tell us anything and she wouldn't let us ring anyone. She didn't have her next of kin on her notes at the GP. That must be you, mustn't it?'

'Yes,' Nina said. She couldn't think who else it would be. Probably it was an oversight that her mother hadn't added her name to her records. 'She wasn't sure when you'll be discharging her.'

'Too early to say,' said the nurse. 'It's a bad break

and if she's here we can keep an eye on her, check there's no infection. We'll also arrange for someone to do an assessment of her home, to see if it's suitable for her to go back to.'

'Is that all strictly necessary?' Nina said.

'We think it is, yes. So if you don't have to rush back to – is it London you live? – that makes it much more straightforward for us. You say you've been to her house. Did it look OK, like she's managing?'

'It looks very organised,' said Nina. 'More than I remember.'

'And you haven't noticed any changes in your mother's behaviour?'

'No. I don't see her that often. We stay in touch of course. London's a long way.'

The nurse had a judging kind of face. Pursed lips. The thinness that comes from always refusing pudding. Nina felt she was failing the acceptable daughter test. Infrequent visits. Unsure of the status of any pets. Not trusted enough to be listed as next of kin.

Chapter thirty

'I am going to stay a few days, make a trip of it,' she told her mother the next day.

'What's brought this on?' Annette asked. 'Normally you couldn't wait to head back to London. Before you stopped coming at all, that is.'

'Then there's a lot for me to catch up with,' Nina said. 'The B&B is a bit odd but they're nice, and it's handy for your house. I don't think they get many visitors this time of year.'

'I still don't understand why you won't stay at mine,' Annette said.

'We'll see, shall we?' Nina said. 'The B&B's paid up for now. The nurse said you've got yourself a cat. I didn't see any sign of one at the house.'

'Did I forget to tell you?' Annette said. 'We are so out of touch these days.'

'We're in touch all the time,' Nina said. 'All those emails and you haven't mentioned anything about cats.'

'I might have a dozen, for all you know,' said Annette. 'Or one lucky black one, with green eyes, that rides on the back of my broomstick.'

'Well, if you have, you'd better tell me so I can feed it while you're stuck in here,' Nina said.

'I quite fancy being one of those mad cat women.' Annette laughed. 'Do you remember when Debbie had kittens and I ended up keeping three of them? Your father pretended to be furious.'

Nina remembered Debbie. She'd been a scratching, biting animal. It was a miracle any brave tomcat had got close enough to get her pregnant. 'You still haven't answered my question,' she said.

'There was a spare one, a stray, wandering round a couple of times. I felt sorry for it. It's so yowly. I bring food in case I meet it, every time I go out.'

'It seems like a lot of bother,' Nina said. 'Wouldn't it be easier to put a bowl out by the back door?'

'Then I'd have ended up owning the cat,' Annette said. 'It's not fair to take on a pet at my age.'

'You're not that old, Mum.'

'Old enough to know what's best,' Annette said. 'This way, I still have something to look after. Like you've adopted that dog. Jonah sent me pictures. Stupid name, Kevin or some such. Gingery.'

'Neville, and I haven't adopted him. He belongs to a friend. He stays with me sometimes. I enjoy having him in the house.'

'Something to look after,' Annette said. 'Proving my point. Jonah says you are getting very attached to him.'

Jonah had noticed? 'He's a very likeable animal,' Nina said. 'I'm supposed to be fostering him for a few days soon. If I'm still down here, I'll see if Jonah can help, or get Colin – that's his owner – to sort out something else.'

'Bring him here,' Annette said. 'He can stay with me. It would be fun, more fun than if it's just the two of us. I'll need you to move in too, of course. I won't manage on my own, not with a dog as well.'

It hadn't occurred to Nina that supervising Annette's recovery might be fun. 'Let me talk to them, the hospital I mean, and see what they say. I'm meeting the social worker later.' She had imagined camping out at the B&B until Annette was back on her feet. Dropping in every day. Not living under the same roof. Sharing a bathroom. Surely the hospital would say no to that, let alone the idea of Neville.

*

The social worker was relieved, to be honest, she said when Nina went to find her in her office. It would give some breathing space. Take the pressure off to know that family would be there if Mum took another little tumble. Nina could move into the house before Mum was discharged. They could do most of the assessments while Mum was still in hospital and then see how things went once she got home. It was easier now Nina would be there.

'I don't know exactly how long I can stay for,' Nina said. She wished the woman wouldn't keep saying Mum. It made it harder to stand her ground. 'It was more that I could be on hand to, sort of, liaise and coordinate. I'm not qualified to be a carer.'

'No one expects you to be a proper carer.' She hadn't introduced herself. Her name badge said she was a triple M. Mrs Maureen Morley. Nina wondered if she had children lined up to look after her when the time came. Melanie and Michael. 'Everyone understands that it's a short-term thing,' Mrs MM continued. 'Mum's lucky to have a daughter like you. You'd be amazed how many don't bother.'

'It's still not a hundred per cent confirmed,' Nina said, 'that I can stay, I mean. I'm supposed to be looking after someone's dog, so I need to make arrangements for him first. Unless I bring him with me.' She waited for the other woman to ask questions, or object to such a feeble excuse.

'That would be lovely for Mum,' said Mrs MM, beaming widely. 'A nice dog will be good company while she starts to feel better. They've proved it now, you know. Animals boost recovery.'

Nina got the feeling she could have suggested bringing a sabre-toothed tiger and this would still have been welcomed with open arms.

Chapter thirty-one

The chatty B&B woman ('call me Wendy') had suggested the pub as the best place to get decent food in the evenings ('no pasties, though'). Out of season, a lot of places were closed. Nina looked around at the sprinkling of other customers. Mostly little knots of men, in twos or threes, nursing pints and talking quietly. She wondered who they would go home to. They looked like they belonged in families. The food was burgers and 'classic traditional favourites'. She picked at her fish pie. The Mamas and the Papas sang upbeat songs on a tinny loop, old sounds from sunnier shores.

There was no phone signal, so she pretended to be interested in the leaflets about memory loss that the nurse had given her. The tasks looked like they were intended for primary school children. Clock faces to tell the time. Listing words beginning with 'A' ('or we might choose another letter!'). The nurse had asked her to have a little think about her mother. Had she been acting differently? Had Nina noticed anything at all?

Two women came into the pub, bringing damp dogs and umbrellas and laughter. The younger one pulled a scrappy towel from her backpack and dabbed at the dogs. The table was too far away for Nina to listen in. She watched the easy way the women talked to each other, how they made the same gestures. She supposed they were mother and daughter. They looked happy. One of them went to the bar and Nina saw the tip of a brown tail thump gently from under the table when she came back bearing large glasses of red wine.

The place was half empty and nice in a way that Nina found dispiriting. Insipid watercolours by local artists covered the walls. Upended cutlery in aluminium jars on the tables, next to tiny purple winter cacti. She had only a hazy idea about what a Cornish pub would be like. She'd anticipated something saltier than this bland, pleasant, easy atmosphere. Still, it was unthreatening and better than returning to her flowery room at the B&B with a stale sandwich. When the girl came to take her plate away – 'yes, it was very nice, thank you' – she ordered another gin.

She wondered if her mother ever came here. They could come together as part of her convalescence. It was years since Nina had been in a pub with Annette. When she was still living at home, it had been their Wednesday night game – slightly unusual back then, two women drinking together outside London. They would make up stories about the other customers, speculating on their marriages, awarding them political affiliation and hobbies. After a couple of glasses, her mother would sometimes try and test her theories, striking up conversations on flimsy pretexts, with mixed success. They'd hit the bullseye with a starchy couple (Tory, badminton, super way of keeping trim at our age) saying goodbye to a bored son (taciturn, impenetrable), who was leaving the next day to go to university to study, of all things, art history, in, of all places, Scotland. Such a long way away and so terribly Celtic. It had become a family saying, anytime anyone was doing anything out of the ordinary. 'Oh, Nina, do be careful, it's so terribly Celtic.' Then Nina had married Martin (not remotely Celtic) and the easy, laughing evenings had come to an abrupt end.

Chapter thirty-two

Wendy was there at breakfast the next morning, armed with nostalgia. Between sorting out toast and fresh (instant) coffee, she told Nina a long and complicated story about a particular time with a specific pasty. She hoped Nina had liked the pub. She knew she'd been because her niece and great-niece had been in last night dodging the rain. Perhaps Nina had noticed them, with their dogs?

'Honestly, Jonah,' Nina said when she rang him, 'we fret about CCTV and AI and invasions of privacy, but they've got nothing on small-town gossip.'

'It's good,' said Jonah. 'It means someone is looking out for you. The B&B owner sounds like she's got the quaint Cornish schtick down to a tee. She probably hates it as much as you do.'

'Not everyone is as cynical as you, darling. I think she's just one of those people who talks too much.' There were a lot of those.

'What are the hospital saying about Granny?' Jonah asked. 'She rang me last night but didn't know anything. She said you'd brought her apples and that was an odd choice, but I wasn't to tell you.'

'And so, of course you told me.' He was good at passing on information, unless it was important. 'She seems OK. Grumpy about her arm. The hospital have her on some sort of treadmill of assessments. They must have boxes to tick. Age-related. I'm to talk to a dementia specialist this afternoon.'

'We'd know if anything was wrong in that department, wouldn't we?' Jonah said. 'She sounded lucid when I spoke to her.'

'Same here,' Nina said. 'The hospital seem to think there might be something in it. I suppose they've got their reasons. They asked if I've noticed anything different about her. Can you think of anything? I can hardly say I don't know. They'll think I'm a terrible person.'

'They won't. It must happen all the time.' Jonah sounded very grown-up and reassuring. 'She seems the same to me when we Zoom. You should maybe try and talk to her friends. They're the ones who see her regularly.'

'That's a good idea,' Nina said. 'She claims to have texted various people. I'll see if I can get her to introduce me to them.'

'What about her arm? Is she going to be able to manage?'

'We'll find out,' said Nina. 'When can you come down? Granny's been asking. I thought I could nip home, not that a six-hour train ride is nipping anywhere, but go home for a night or two and sort stuff out for if I need to be here for the duration.'

'I'll talk to my boss,' Jonah said.

'I'll need to do something about Neville as well,' said

Nina. 'If I send you the details, would you be able to ring the kennels, see if they can suggest anything? Granny says to bring him here. I'm not sure I can see that working.'

Chapter thirty-three

On her way into the hospital, Nina picked up a newspaper and some oranges.

'Thank you, darling. You know I prefer *The Times*,' said Annette.

That wasn't true. Her mother used to introduce herself to strangers as a *Guardian* reader. It weeds out the headbangers but not the woke, she'd say, and on the whole the latter were more palatable. 'You hate *The Times*,' Nina said.

'When have I ever said that? This one is so preachy.' There was a more complaining tone today. 'And why did you buy new oranges? There are some in a bowl in the kitchen. Unless you've eaten them all.'

'Do you ever think to say thank you?' Nina asked.

'It's important, to be honest,' Annette said. 'If I thank you for *The Guardian*, you might bring it again tomorrow. And I'm sure I brought you up to finish up the old fruit before buying more.'

'I can't get anything right, can I?' Nina said.

'Nonsense, darling.' Annette's smile was quite patronising.

'You told Jonah you didn't want the apples so I got these instead. They're easy peelers so you'll be able to manage them.' It was such a pitiful little kindness. To her horror, Nina felt herself welling up.

'There's no need to get upset, Nina,' Annette said. 'I merely said I don't like that particular newspaper. It's too worthy. And Granny Smiths aren't the best apples, although they look nice and shiny in that special NHS fruit bowl.' Someone had plopped the apples into a grey cardboard bedpan. 'You mustn't get worked up about a paper and some fruit.'

'It's not about the newspaper,' Nina said. 'Or the apples. Which aren't Granny Smiths, by the way.'

'What is it then, Nina? You're all het up and I'm the one who's hurt their arm. You don't see me making a silly fuss.' Annette used the same pull-yourself-together tone Nina had resented all her life.

'All this. Your arm. You. I've come all this way and you don't even seem happy to see me.'

'No one asked you to come, Nina,' Annette said. 'In fact, I think I suggested you stay at home.'

'Of course I came. You're my mother.'

'I am quite aware of that.'

Nina thought of the women in the pub last night. How much they seemed to be enjoying each other's company. She wished Annette would say something about families, how pleased she was to have a daughter, how nice it was that she'd come. 'I'm going to be looking after you, Mum,' she said.

'Yes, and you are doing splendidly, darling.' Annette smiled brightly. 'Here you are, bringing me things, like a newspaper and all this healthy fruit, and keeping me company. The nurses are such busy bees. They don't have time for much in the way of conversation.'

'When you get home. I'm going to be looking after you when you get home. The social worker, Maureen, was going to talk to you about it.'

'And so she has,' said Annette. 'I can't see it working, can you?'

It was the same thing Nina had said to Jonah about the dog. 'What makes you say that?' she said. 'I want to look after you.'

'Do you really? That's sweet of you, darling. Thank you.' Annette patted Nina's hand. 'And, why, exactly?'

'You're my mother.'

'Oh dear. We seem to be going round in circles. I may be going doolally, but I'm fairly certain we both know that I am your mother. It's the looking after me bit I am struggling with.'

'It's not difficult,' Nina said. 'When you leave here and go home, I am moving in so you won't be on your own. We need to talk about how we are going to manage things.'

'I'm not sure that's such a good idea,' Annette said.

'You suggested it,' Nina said. 'You said Neville could come and stay and I'd need to move in too. I can look after both of you.'

'I don't think I said that.' Annette looked puzzled. 'And even if I did, now I am unsuggesting it. I don't understand why you are getting all het up.'

'You know why I'm getting het up, as you call it.'

'I honestly don't,' said Annette. 'Let's talk about it later when you've calmed down. Honestly, darling, you're behaving like a teenager. Now, as you have gone to the trouble of bringing this awful newspaper, let's have a look, shall we? Although I'm just going to ring for someone. I need the loo.'

Annette pressed the buzzer. 'I'm sorry to trouble you,' she said to the nurse. 'I need to go to the toilet and I wondered if maybe my daughter could take me. It would be good practice for her. For both of us. I thought I should ask first. This is Nina. I think you've already met.'

'Yes, hello again.' The nurse barely glanced at Nina. 'The toilet's at the other end of the corridor, on the left. We're a bit unsteady. That arm has affected our balance. We'll take it nice and slowly and we'll be fine, won't we, Annette?'

'We'll be splendid,' said Annette. 'Thank you. Come on, Nina, you can help me on with my slippers.'

They dawdled past the bays of snoozing old ladies and bored visitors, her mother counting steps out loud, Nina two paces behind, chewing her lip. 'Here we are!' Annette announced in a too-cheery voice. A strong smell of bleach poured out from behind a heavy orange door.

'I'll wait outside,' said Nina. Her mother could easily have managed the walk on her own.

'Oh no, darling, I need you to come in with me. I can't do the loo roll with one working arm.'

Nina looked. 'It's not on a roll,' she said. 'You pull it out of that square boxy thing on the wall. You don't need two hands.'

'It's on the wrong side,' her mother said. 'And if I grab the loo roll before I start, then I won't be able to balance to sit down. I need my free hand. Luckily that rail is very useful. It's a pity I don't have one at home. Still, I expect I'll manage.' The stoical tone was unbearable.

'What do you want me to do?' Nina asked.

'The nurse usually comes in when I'm ready for paper and that seems to work. Why don't you wait outside and I'll give you a little shout, shall I?'

Annette hustled her into the corridor. She stood guard outside. *Please, please don't be doing a poo*, Nina thought.

'Ready,' trilled Annette after what seemed like too long a time. Nina opened the door cautiously. Her mother was perched directly on the porcelain, the seat up behind her. She looked so tiny. Her pretty knickers caressed her ankles, a frail silky contrast to the rough dark blue surgical stockings.

'Oh, Mum,' said Nina.

'Don't be silly, darling,' said her mother. 'There's nothing to cry about. If you can scrunch me up some paper, I can manage. Although I might need a bit of help arranging my clothes as well. And with washing my hands too. I can't get the soap around properly and these places are full of germs. I'll give you another shout, shall I?'

Nina retreated to the antiseptic corridor. She knew her mother was making a point. She just needed to work out what it was and what to do about it for the best.

*

'How it feels to...' said Annette. They were back on the ward. 'How it feels to be a middle-class *Guardian* reader with a first-world problem that I overcome marvellously by doing yoga and counting my blessings.'

201

'It doesn't say that,' said Nina.

'It might as well. We could write one together. How it feels for mother and daughter, a little estranged, to bond over trips to the toilet.'

'We managed,' said Nina. It hadn't been as bad as she'd expected. Physically at least. She'd not had to wipe anything.

'We managed,' her mother said. 'But you didn't like it, and neither did I. We don't have to pretend you can look after me, even if it is easier for the hospital.'

'I'm happy to look after you,' said Nina.

'You're not. You think it's your duty. Or that you owe me because I once looked after you. It's not what either of us wants, so let's not pretend otherwise. Why are you looking at me like that? I'm only saying what we are both thinking.'

'I need to go to the loo myself now,' said Nina. Her mother probably didn't mean to be so aggravating. Or so honest. She had to get away before she said anything that would make things worse. 'I'll get us some tea as well, so I might be a while.'

She made her way to the hospital café and parked herself in the little outside area where there were no other people, her umbrella up against the drizzle. A soggy seagull hovered. She dialled Jonah's number. It went straight to voicemail.

When Martin died, she'd waited outside a different hospital, standing in the warm summer rain. A man attached to a drip had offered her a cigarette and she'd accepted, even though she didn't smoke. The doctors were doing all they could, they'd told her. Her husband had hit his head badly and they wouldn't know more until he woke up. If he woke up. They were sorry. They thought Nina should prepare herself.

Annette had picked up the pieces. Nina hadn't had to explain anything to anyone, not even Jonah. Especially not Jonah. 'Granny told me, Mummy. He bumped his head and he's dead, but he still loves me very much. He's with baby Jesus and I can't see him, but he can see me, and I can talk to him and he'll hear me.' They'd agreed never to fob Jonah off with religion, but Nina had been grateful. It saved a lot of questions.

This time around no one was going to die and no one was going to pretend to believe in God. *Five weeks*, Nina thought, *and we can go back to normal*. Or six. Broken bones took six weeks. It was stupid to get upset. They'd get used to each other. They could come up with a system for the practical things. If they unrolled and tore the loo roll, they could pile sections on top of the radiator. Her mother would be able to reach it from there. They'd buy convenient clothes. Drawstring trousers if she could get her to agree. Six weeks would fly by.

*

'There was a queue at the café,' Nina said when she got back to the ward. 'I gave up on the tea. I bumped into Maureen again. She's very well organised. Rallying all sorts of people. Someone called Agnieszka is sending someone to the house tomorrow. I can ask about arranging the bathroom differently. So you can reach everything.'

'And what else are you going to ask about?'

'What do you mean?'

'What about the things they can't fix? It's a couple of months, Nina. They'll have to sort me out with proper carers. For the bath. Cooking, although I daresay I can ping a microwave. Doing up my bra. You need two hands for that.'

'I can do all of that. Maybe not the bath. You're really saying that you don't want me to help.' She waited for her mother to contradict her.

'Not with this, no I don't.'

Nina was shocked by how certain she sounded. 'I want to look after you,' she said.

'You don't.'

'I do.'

'Come on, Nina, this isn't a pantomime. Oh yes you do, oh no you don't. If you can arrange to be here away from your London life, whatever that is, then it would be lovely to have company. You can even make the odd bit of cheese on toast. I'm not having you doing all the dressing and bathing and loo stuff. You're not that kind of daughter.'

Nina wondered what kind she was. They'd been such friends. Nina had never understood all the other girls' complaints about how interfering and embarrassing mothers were as a breed. Annette was level-headed and fun and had known when to make herself scarce. It was a pity she and Martin had taken against each other. There had never been time to make that right.

Chapter thirty-four

As promised, the experts Mrs MM had mobilised came to find Nina on the ward. The dementia specialist was first. She didn't have a name badge, which seemed very unfair. It instantly put anyone talking to her at a disadvantage. She took Nina off to the side and explained that Annette had refused to take the numerical reasoning test, protesting that she still remembered her times tables, and shops and banks and utility companies did the rest. Often someone wouldn't do the tests because they were afraid they'd fail, especially in the initial stages. Annette hadn't known the date when she came into the hospital. In some people, the number skills were the first to go.

'Your mother is very articulate,' the specialist said. 'Excellent with words.' It seemed this was not seen as entirely positive. They'd asked Annette to list words beginning with 'p' and she had chosen things like 'psychology' and 'philanderer' then given them a lecture about distinguishing between the actual letter and the phonetic pronunciation when they set their pitiful patronising tests.

'Yes, she's always been waspish, I'm afraid.' Nina felt

rather proud of her mother. 'I'm guessing that's a good sign though, that she challenged you.'

'Not necessarily. Did you have a little think like the nurse asked? Have you noticed anything out of the ordinary in the way she's behaving? Any moods?'

'I've racked my brains and so has my son, and basically no,' Nina said. 'The only thing that did surprise me – it's a good thing, I think – is that she's gone tidy. Organised, you know, at home. She's thrown away most of her house plants. Labelled drawers.'

'And that's a big change?'

'Oh yes. She had a back-to-nature, free spirit thing going on for years. She used to go on marches. Greenham Common.' The woman looked blank. 'You're too young to remember that,' Nina said. 'That's another thing, she'd never have read *The Times*. She didn't approve of the owner.' Again, the woman looked blank.

'So what you are describing could be said to be a personality change?'

'I really don't know. I don't think so,' said Nina. 'I don't understand what's going on here. My mother's only broken her arm. I don't understand why she's having all this rigmarole.' She supposed that there were protocols or dementia targets or both when someone old came into hospital. No wonder her mother was being difficult. She forced what she hoped was an understanding smile. 'I'm arranging to stay around for a couple of weeks, as you know, so I can help my mother settle back in at home. She's right-handed so that arm is going to be a real pain for cooking and getting downstairs because the banister's on the wrong side, but I daresay we can work something out.'

'Agnieszka will see to all of that. My tests are different.'

'You won't find anything.' She felt quite certain. They'd been circling each other for years. Even so Nina would still have noticed if her mother was losing her mind.

*

Nina had only been back on the ward a few minutes when another new person arrived. She had a yellow name badge. Agnieszka. Her surname was so long it had been printed in a different font. She was the discharge coordinator. She was very pretty. She explained that discharge on different system to dementia assessment and no one have full picture until someone visit house to decide support needed.

'Surely some things are obvious,' said Nina. 'Her arm, for example. How is she supposed to get dressed on her own? Or have a bath? Will you be able to sort out some help with that?'

'The information I am having is that you living at house,' said Agnieszka.

'Maybe,' said Nina, 'but there are things I can't do.'

'Lots of things,' her mother said. 'It would be quicker to list the things that Nina can do.'

Agnieszka ignored her. 'First we visit house. Then we decide,' she said.

'I decide,' said Annette.

'Maybe,' Agnieszka said.

They are like buses all these health people, her mother had said as Agnieszka clacked out of the ward on her impractical heels. It was funny how they were only turning up now because Nina was here. As if Nina knew anything.

Chapter thirty-five

After the discussion about the oranges, Nina had broached the subject of the other food in the house. She didn't think her mother would mind her raiding the freezer, but it was polite to ask. 'I can't keep going to the pub,' she said. 'Do you mind if I cook at your house? I can restock when we know when you're coming home.'

'There's fish. Lots of it. You could leave some in the lane. For the cat that's not mine. A couple of forkfuls would be plenty. Thaw it first, please.'

'Won't the gulls take it?'

'They might. Or, let's try being optimistic for once, they mightn't. For me, Nina. Please.' Like a child, one more spoonful, just for Mummy, and then maybe we can read a story together.

*

Most of the fish was in hard blocks, in freezer bags with few identifying clues. Nina recognised sardines, fused together in a shiny silver ball, and mackerel. Something white that probably wasn't cod because there's a shortage.

Pollock, maybe, or haddock? Nina only ever shopped in the supermarket where everything came with instructions. Could you cook real fish from frozen?

On the bottom shelf, she found a packet of Tesco Finest fish fingers. She tipped two onto a baking tray that had seen better days. She was struggling to understand Annette's oven when there was a knock at the door, then a rattling of the letterbox. 'Annette,' called the voice. Female. 'Are you there?'

Nina opened the door. 'I'm Annette's daughter,' she said. 'Nina. Can I help you?'

The woman on the doorstep was young. She had a badly crocheted long yellow scarf, with orange pompoms on the end. Purple curls flowed from under an orange knitted hat. 'I'm Sarah,' she said. 'I live sort of opposite. The one with the green door, only it's dark so you can't see it.'

'Sarah?' said Nina. 'There's a Sarah on my mother's calendar.'

'4.30 today,' said Sarah. 'That's me. Only she didn't answer so I thought maybe she forgot again. I saw the light was on in the kitchen, so I knocked.'

'So you did,' said Nina. Again. The girl said her mother had forgotten again.

'Has something happened?' Sarah asked. 'We haven't seen her for a few days. Mum said she'd probably gone away.'

'Look,' said Nina, 'I'm in the middle of getting my supper, but if you want to come in for a minute, that would be better than freezing out here.' Sarah followed her into the kitchen while Nina explained about the fall. 'She's going to be fine,' she finished.

'That's a relief,' Sarah said. 'We all love Annette. You must be Kate's mum. I met her in the summer, with her husband, Jonah.'

'I'm Jonah's mum. Not Kate's. They're not married. Unless there's something they're not telling me.' Jonah might do that. He'd think it was modern. He wouldn't think she'd mind. 'He mentioned something about a neighbour who's a dance student when he was last here. Is that you?'

'Performing arts,' said Sarah. 'Annette introduced us. Kate knows all about lighting. Annette's helping me with a living history project. We're creating a performance piece about campaigning women.'

'She'll enjoy that,' said Nina. 'Right up her street.' The oven pinged to tell her it was hot enough. 'I was about to cook these,' she said, pointing to the fish fingers. 'There are plenty more if you'd like to join me?'

'I'm a vegan,' the girl said. Of course she was. That purple hair. 'But anyway, Mum's expecting me home. I only stopped by because I saw the lights.'

'Is there any chance you could come back tomorrow if you've got time? I'd like to chat with someone who's spent time with my mother recently. It will help the hospital sort her out.'

'She's definitely going to be OK?' Sarah asked.

'Absolutely.'

'I can bring Petroc too, if you like,' Sarah said. 'Tomorrow. He's my uncle. He knows Annette the best.' She didn't explain.

'That would be helpful. Thank you,' Nina said.

'I'm sure she said Kate was her granddaughter,' Sarah said. 'Maybe she got mixed up again.'

*

Later, Nina rang Jonah. She was back at the B&B. 'According to this Sarah person, Granny's adopted Kate. Told Sarah she was her granddaughter, no less.'

'Kate will be flattered,' Jonah said.

'She also told Sarah that you and Kate are married,' Nina said. 'You don't have something to tell me, do you? Only, I would be sad to have missed the chance to wear an embarrassing hat.'

'We're not married,' Jonah said. 'Although now you've reminded me about the hat I'll have to see if Kate would be up for it. I remember Sarah. Granny press-ganged Kate into taking her for coffee and telling her about stage lighting, as a plan B in case she doesn't make it as a performer. Like, they are totally different things. You know Granny when she gets one of her ideas.'

'I do indeed. And I'm glad you are not married. Although you should be by now. Don't keep a girl like Kate waiting too long.' She was digressing. 'Sarah tells me she's putting on a play about female campaigners and somehow got wind of Granny's stint at Greenham Common.'

'Granny's very proud of that,' Jonah said. 'She's always saying what a shame it is that none of the rest of us take on the establishment.'

'I suspect she's overegged the crusading heroine bit,' said Nina. 'The point is, this Sarah girl sees a lot of Granny so is a good person to talk to.'

Nina had wondered about the calendar, the jolly-sounding appointments. In her mind, Sarah had been silver-haired and mischievous, leading her mother into slightly bad habits, a gin and tonic in the late afternoon. Not an earnest teenager, the daughter of the family across the road, willing to be impressed by exaggerated tales of polite and intermittent activism.

Chapter thirty-six

Agnieszka was sending someone to the house at 10am, or so Nina had understood. In the event, she turned up herself. She looked younger in her ordinary clothes. 'Normally is coming OT. Today has flu, so here is me. Hello, Meena.'

'Nina,' said Nina.

Agnieszka explained that the visit was somewhere between a formality and very crucial and took photos of the stairs and the bath. 'House is nice,' she said. 'Stairs not so good. Maybe we put bed downstairs for now. Downstairs toilet excellent.'

Nina didn't follow. 'So you are saying that my mother can come home if we bring her bed down here and presumably she doesn't have a bath until she can manage the stairs?'

'Maybe, yes, is solution. And you staying so all OK for cooking and shopping. Is for not many weeks.'

'What about her supposed dementia?'

'Outpatients assessment. Nothing confirmed yet. And must talk over also with Annette, of course.'

'Of course,' said Nina. 'I'm sorry to ask questions, it just doesn't seem very satisfactory.'

'Everyone does best, but no money,' said Agnieszka.

'There would be place in home also, care home, but private, expensive.'

'I'll talk to my mother later.' From Nina's googling, she couldn't imagine her mother tolerating any of the beige places on offer. The people in the brochures smiled too much.

'I drive to hospital now,' Agnieszka said. 'I give you lift?'

On the way, Nina asked whereabouts in Poland she was from. She hoped it was Poland. Agnieszka was a Polish name. Nina and Martin had been to Krakow so they could talk about that.

'Sopot. By the sea,' Agnieszka said.

'Like Cornwall then,' said Nina.

'Not so much,' Agnieszka said.

'Have you ever been to Krakow?'

She hadn't, and conversation about Poland ran dry.

*

'It's the other end of the country,' her mother said when Nina told her. 'Near Gdansk. You remember: Solidarity, the beginning of the end of Soviet domination.'

'Vaguely,' Nina said. She'd never understood her mother's fascination with politics.

'So what did she have to say for herself? Agnieszka.'

'She came to assess the house,' Nina started.

'I know,' said Annette. 'Most intrusive. And you asked her where she was from, which is also intrusive and judgmental, if you don't mind me saying. You wouldn't have asked her if she'd been British.'

That was true, Nina thought. Somehow it was

acceptable to be nosy if someone spoke with a foreign accent. 'I was making conversation,' she said. 'It was better than her going on about rearranging your house, before we had a chance to talk to you.'

'Very thoughtful of you. Are you going to tell me what she's got in mind?'

'She didn't like the stairs.'

'That's hardly her business.'

'It's completely her business. It's her job to say if it's safe for you to go home.'

'Safe for who?'

'For you. For all of us.'

'Safe?'

'Yes.'

'Not convenient or welcoming or happy or warm or any of those things that homes are meant to be?'

'Those too,' Nina said, fighting to stay patient. 'It's hard to judge if you were OK before you fell if you never tell me anything about your life.'

'If you talked to me more before I fell, you wouldn't have to judge.' Her mother sighed. 'Email's hopeless.'

'Are you coping? I met Sarah last night. She said you keep forgetting when you've arranged to meet her.'

'Sarah's a teenager, darling. You know what they're like. Unreliable.'

'She also thought Kate was your granddaughter.'

'Well, she sort of is, isn't she,' her mother said. 'Such a lovely girl. So right for Jonah. Now, darling, perhaps you could go away until visiting time. It was kind of Agnieszka to give you a lift. It means you are very early. The doctors will be here soon and you'll be in the way.'

Rain was bombarding the hospital windows. Nina walked along the corridors, past brisk young doctors. Too much purpose. She passed the multi-faith prayer room, its sign blu-tacked to a green door. It would be somewhere quiet to wait. The door groaned as she pushed it open.

The room was empty. Someone had left a cheese and onion crisp packet and last Friday's *Daily Express* on one of the seats. No window and harsh lighting. She picked up a shiny booklet from the scuffed table at the door. 'Prayer Room – Instructions,' she read. It seemed an odd choice of word. The badly printed pages explained that the room was for everyone no matter what their faith to pray and reflect. All kinds of harassment would not be tolerated.

The rest of the booklet contained short poems and proverbs, in English, Arabic, Chinese and languages she didn't recognise. The ones in English were largely geared towards the gloomy end of things. The Lord keeping you company in the valley of death. Most people in hospital got better or were being born. There was little mention of that, at least in the carefully inoffensive Christian section of the leaflet.

Her mother had always wheeled out the baby Jesus at the first sign of difficulty. Nina didn't think she was a true believer. She raged against the terrible things the Church had done – 'all churches, Nina, not just our lot; the Muslims and Hindus and the rest are as bad'. Some of the Ten Commandments were useful, and miracles were always cheering. You could never have too many loaves and fishes, and none of the rest was the baby Jesus's fault.

Eleven-year-old Jonah had liked the idea of his dead daddy helping Mary and the angels bring up the baby whose real dad was busy fixing the world.

The door creaked, serenading a couple with a swaddled infant. 'Sorry,' the woman said.

'No, no, it's fine, I was just leaving,' said Nina. From the beaming smiles, she guessed that they'd come to say thank you for their baby, with its shock of black hair.

*

When she got back to the ward, she found her mother in proper clothes, sitting in the chair. Nina's heart sank. 'Are they discharging you?'

'Don't look so horrified, darling. Aggie suggested that you take me for a walk around the car park to see how I get on outside. For the assessment.'

'Aggie?'

'Agnieszka. From Sopot. She's a very interesting woman. Do you know her uncle worked at the very shipyard where all that Solidarity stuff started? Did you get lunch?'

'You're going outside?' said Nina. 'It's bucketing down.'

'It'll stop,' said Annette. 'We've got all afternoon.'

Nina's heart sank a little further. 'I got a sandwich in the café. Tuna. I stumbled across the prayer room earlier. There was a lovely young couple in there, with a baby. Looking for blessing, I suppose.'

'I don't really hold with all this religious stuff,' said her mother. 'All those gods and what have you, and the money they spend!'

'You seem to be quite a fan of the baby Jesus, though. You go on about him quite a lot,' said Nina.

'Do I? How funny. I used to always wonder what would have happened to him if he'd been born now, in this country or the US or somewhere. Wouldn't he have been taken into care?'

'Do you believe in any of it? I've never asked before.'

'There's lots of things you've never asked. Too wrapped up in yourself, that's always been your problem, Nina.' She said it so kindly that Nina wasn't sure if she was being horrible.

She was saved from replying by the arrival of a nurse. 'Now, Annette, do you want to change back out of those clothes? At least the top half? You look a bit constricted.'

'We're going out,' said Annette. 'Aggie arranged it.'

'I think you're getting a bit muddled, dear,' said the nurse kindly. 'We only wanted to have a little try, see how your clothes work.'

'They work very nicely as a straitjacket,' Annette said. Someone had wedged her into her sweater with some force. The left cuff had caught on her canula. Her broken right arm and its plaster were jammed against her body, the cashmere so stretched Nina doubted it would ever regain its shape. The sleeve hung limply empty.

'You managed very well with most of it. You'll need to get your daughter to bring you something looser for your top half. A poncho would be nice if you have one.'

'Can a poncho be nice?' Annette asked. 'Outside of Peru, I mean.'

'We need to think about what's practical,' said the

nurse. 'You'll need your shoes too. I don't think anyone's brought those in for you yet.' She looked at Nina, who registered it as another failure on her part.

Chapter thirty-seven

There was a small van parked outside when Nina returned to her mother's house after visiting was over. Sarah was sitting on the front seat talking to a man about Nina's age. 'I told him not to go in the house, in case you got back and he scared you,' she said. 'I've got to go but waited to introduce you. This is Petroc.'

'Pleased to meet you,' said Nina. 'That's a fine Cornish name.'

'Isn't it?' Petroc said. With his oval face and shiny head, he looked like an egg. 'My parents were blow-ins. From Leicester originally. They wanted us to fit in so went for the most Cornish names they could think of. They might have overcompensated.'

'Sarah said you know my mum really well,' Nina said. Well enough to have a key to the house, it seemed. 'Thanks for introducing us, Sarah.'

'You're welcome. Bye then,' said Sarah. 'I've got a rehearsal. Say hello to Annette. Tell her the show's going great.'

Nina turned to Petroc. 'Won't you come in?' she said. 'I'll put the kettle on.'

'Thank you,' Petroc said, wiping his feet on the mat. He explained how he fitted in. He was a handyman, although with a limited range, the kind of things that anyone half-decent at DIY could manage. He'd do bits of cleaning that needed equipment or a lot of elbow grease. Ovens. Patios. His real job was as the joint owner-manager of a small hotel, the Harbour Walk. In the off-season, Petroc and his husband had come up with a scheme to offer low-key social activities – Scrabble and Mahjong were popular – and practical help to anyone who would pay. Mainly retired people or people on their own. 'It's a kind of private members' club,' he said. 'There's a fee to join and strangely people like that – they think it means exclusivity. It's good business for us as they come and have cream teas, and in the summer we'll invite them to have dinner in the restaurant for a tenner, on the nights it's not full.'

'Harbour Walk,' said Nina. 'It's on the calendar. It says Chris, not Petroc. I'd assumed it was some kind of outing.'

'Chris is my husband,' Petroc said. 'He was hoping to rope Annette in to giving a talk to a local history group. We're experimenting with hosting events. Anything to diversify.'

They talked for a bit about his business and the tourist business in general. Petroc knew Wendy and Sue's place, where Nina was staying (although she's not even called Wendy, he told her. The guest house had been called the Wendy House once upon a time, and the name stuck.)

'So what's Annette done to herself then?' he asked. 'Sarah said it was her arm.'

'It could have been a lot worse,' Nina said. 'They're trying to work out if she can come home, but not sure the house is suitable.'

'We could fix up another rail, on the opposite wall,' Petroc said. 'I've been telling her to do that. Those stairs are quite steep.'

'That would be helpful,' Nina said. 'I think it's all a bit more complicated, though.' She explained about the cat and about the cognitive testing. 'You see her quite regularly,' she said. 'Does she seem to be struggling?'

Annette was sharp and argumentative, Petroc said. She did sometimes lose words, or make them up (he had thought for a while she was trying it on in their Scrabble games). He'd helped her label all the drawers and cupboards and they'd made a sort of reference guide for the days she felt muddled. The cat was the local tart, he said; it lived with several families. He didn't know it had tricked Annette into contributing to its upkeep.

'What about Sarah?' asked Nina. 'I can understand a girl her age being interested in all that Greenham Common stuff. How did she even find out that Mum was there?'

There'd been something on social media. Annette had got into an argument with a couple of polite young men on the edges of an environmental rally. Something about men causing most of the problems, so they couldn't also wave banners about – it was hypocritical. Greenham Common, that was a proper protest. She'd been arrested, briefly. Disturbing the peace.

'Arrested?' Nina was horrified.

'She was unarrested again pretty quickly,' Petroc said. Someone had filmed it and one of Sarah's brothers had recognised one of the old ladies he ferried to and from Uncle Petroc's place.

'I hope she hasn't been overstating her Greenham days,' said Nina. 'She only went a couple of times as I remember it. She used to make my father drive her most of the way, then drop her off. She couldn't be doing with the camping out and the chanting. But she's always loved a cause.'

'She's great. A real live wire,' Petroc said. 'The supper club I mentioned. It's like an old-school political salon. We get someone to talk about an issue of the day. Annette's one of the stars, especially since she was arrested. She has lots of opinions. It was what gave Chris the idea about hosting the history group.'

Nina could imagine her mother holding court. 'She never said,' she told Petroc. 'Not that she was arrested. I daresay they got more than they bargained for there.'

'It gave her something to dine out on,' said Petroc. 'She probably thought you'd worry if she told you.'

'I don't think that's it,' Nina said. 'She's a bit vague about her life down here. I get all the generalities. She talks to Jonah, my son, more than she does to me.'

'She talks about you all the time,' Petroc said.

'Really?'

'Really. She's very proud of you.'

Nina doubted that. It was what mothers did. When she talked about Jonah, it was always how settled he was with his job and Kate. Never that streak of selfishness that sometimes kept her awake at night. It was such a balancing act. Your world revolved around your squeaky new baby. You still had to bring it up to understand that it wasn't the centre of anyone's universe. Not yours. Not even its own. 'I dread to think what she's been saying about me,' she said. 'Or what she'd say if anyone asked her today. We're both finding the hospital a bit of a strain.'

'Have they said when she can come home?'

'No. The visit today, the home assessment, was all part of that. The girl was talking about bringing a bed downstairs. She didn't look very convinced.'

'Let me know if you need things shifting. Although you'd struggle to fit a bed in the lounge. Is she up for visitors?'

'She's grouchy,' Nina said. 'That might just be with me. If you want to risk it, she'd probably be pleased to see a different face.'

'I'll message her and ask her. Do you have plans this evening?'

'Phone calls.'

'If you want, you can come to ours. Any friend of Annette's and all that. Chris is making a lasagne and there'll be loads. I do have an agenda, too. If you come, then I'll tell you about it.'

'I need to make my calls,' Nina said. The invitation had taken her by surprise. She didn't know if she was in the mood to eat pasta with strange men. Her mother's fan club.

'Tell you what,' said Petroc, 'I'm going to call in on my sister, Sarah's mum, for an hour or so. I'll pop back and if you're still here, I can collect you. Worst case, I can drive you back to the Wendy House. You don't want to be walking in this.' Rain was hammering the windows, given new confidence by the wind coming off the sea.

Chapter thirty-eight

When Petroc had gone, Nina rang Linda.

'Nina! This is a nice surprise. Are we seeing you on Friday?'

Quiz night. She'd forgotten. 'I can't. I'm in Cornwall. It's been a blur. I've not had time to tell anyone.' For the second time that afternoon, she ran through the events of the last three days. 'It's ridiculous,' she said. 'It's only a broken arm, not something catastrophic like happened to Dima. If she was twenty-five or forty-five, they'd let her home with none of this fuss.'

'But she's not,' Linda said. 'And if they did tip her out of an ambulance onto her doorstep, what would you do?'

'Survive,' said Nina. She'd always find a way to cope. 'Anyway. I didn't ring to moan.' Not totally true. 'I was wondering if you'd heard from Colin? Jonah tried calling him and I messaged. He's not got back to either of us.'

'Nothing for a few days,' Linda said. 'Neville business, I assume.'

'I'm supposed to be taking him next week. You remember the kennels were full?'

'Colin said. I told him to find somewhere else. He insisted you were happy to babysit.'

'And I would have been,' Nina said. 'I've been looking forward to it. But I'm needed down here and it would mean both of us staying at my mother's.' Something occurred to her. 'I don't suppose you and Dima could take him? Muddy would be in his seventh heaven to have Neville to play with.'

'Yes. And Dima would be in his seventh hell. If they have seven hells. I think it's nine, isn't it? Nine circles of hell.'

Nina pulled her back to reality. 'Dima's much fonder of the dogs than you give him credit for,' she said. 'And this is Neville the lapdog.' It had been the pub quiz, the first time Nina had set the questions. Neville had sat stock-still for maybe ten minutes, watching Dima eat a burger, very slowly, with his hands. Then he'd jumped into Dima's lap. 'Hey, bud,' Dima had said, 'd'you wanna share?' It had been so gentle and so surprising Nina hadn't known where to look. Colin had done the talking. 'No, Neville. Down. You know you're not allowed to do that.' Nina hadn't thought anyone believed him.

'That was one time,' Linda said, 'and Neville in the pub and Neville in your home are totally different propositions. As you should know. Dima's not really the issue. He's my fall guy. I'm the one being difficult. I'm not taking on Colin's dog. Not even for a couple of days. He's the most badly brought up animal.'

'He's always an angel for me,' Nina said. She wasn't sure why she was lying.

'You have lower expectations,' said Linda. 'Colin can

sort something out. He left me his sister's number, for emergencies, so if you don't hear back from him, let me know and I can give her a call.'

'Thank you.'

'Never mind the dog. Tell me again what the hospital was saying about your mother's house?'

'There's nothing more to say. It's apparently not suitable if she's on her own and magically suitable if I'm there.'

'And how do you feel about that?'

'You sound like my therapist. How I feel is completely immaterial,' said Nina. 'Mum can't stay in the hospital forever.'

'And that's your problem how, exactly?'

Linda, of all people, must understand that. 'I'm her family,' she said. 'It's my job to look after her. Like you and Dima.'

'I married Dima,' Linda said. 'It seemed like a good idea at the time. We chose to be together. Better. Worse. Sickness. Health. No one expects the worse and sickness bits when they trot out all that. Cutting loose would be a huge palaver with lots of lawyers and haggling. There's nothing written down anywhere that chains you to your mother. From everything you've ever said about her, you're not even close.'

'It's not that easy,' said Nina.

'You need to make it easy. If you're worried about it even a tiny bit, then don't do it, Nina. Don't be nice.'

'She did so much for me when Martin died,' Nina said.

'Yes. And that's lovely. It's also irrelevant.'

'What would you do if it was your parent?'

'Also irrelevant. Doubly so as they are both long gone.' Linda was matter of fact. 'It's up to you, Nina, but take it from me. You don't want to be a live-in carer.'

'I don't suppose anyone does,' Nina said.

'Unlike most people, you have a choice, Nina. You need to dump all the emotional crap on this one.'

It sounded straightforward when Linda put it like that.

Chapter thirty-nine

Nina was sorting out emails when the doorbell rang. She opened the front door just enough to see Petroc wrestling with a too-big umbrella. 'Your carriage awaits,' he said. He'd driven his van up as close as it could get to the house. 'Where to? The Wendy House, for another evening of 24-inch screen telly and individually wrapped biscuits? Or your mother's favourite *salon privé* for home-made lasagne and a chance to pry into the finer details of her life?'

'Well, since you put it like that,' Nina said. 'Let me shut down the computer.' She'd sent a long email to Colin asking if he could make other plans for Neville. She'd enclosed links to seven other boarding kennels. Jonah had promised to check too.

'It's the weirdest thing,' Nina said as she fumbled for her seat belt. 'I've never been inside a van before.'

'Why would you have?' said Petroc. 'They're for practical people.'

'I might be very practical for all you know,' Nina said.

'I'm hoping not. I don't want you stealing all my customers.'

'You're safe from me,' Nina said. 'I can barely hang a picture. Is there a lot of demand for the handyman services? I have this idea in my head that people in Cornwall are going to be a lot more practical, as you call it. Able to fix things.'

'There wouldn't be enough to do it full time,' Petroc said. 'And I wouldn't want to. It's a bolt-on for the people who use Harbour Walk. There's always someone who needs a shelf putting up or taking down.'

'You're not a professional carpenter? I always thought that would be a nice thing to be. There aren't many jobs that are creative and useful.'

'Before I met Chris and we got into the hotel game, I taught. Politics. Possibly useful. Definitely creative, treading on eggshells to get kids to see different points of view.'

'No wonder my mother likes you. She's always been very interested in politics,' Nina said. 'It's quite the career leap, though.'

'I'd like to say I've never looked back,' Petroc said. 'Still, it's always good to try new things.'

'So people tell me.' Nina couldn't remember when she'd last tried something dramatically new.

The van turned right at a roundabout and headed down a steep hill. 'Here it is, in all its glory,' Petroc said. 'If you imagine there was no driving rain, then straight ahead of you is the stunning picture-postcard view of the harbour with its twinkling lights.'

'I know the very postcard you mean,' Nina said. 'Jonah's sent me that one at least twice.'

Petroc pulled into a small car park. From what she could see through the rain, the building wasn't at all what

230

Nina expected. The name, Harbour Walk, and the idea of genteel social gatherings (she didn't know where she'd got genteel from, it was hardly her mother's style) had made her think of something imposing or charming or possibly both. This was a low, wide, modern building that looked more like the headquarters of an insurance company than a holiday retreat. Perhaps it would look better on the inside, or in better weather.

'*On est arrivé*,' said Petroc. 'You'd better take this.' He handed her the giant umbrella. 'And look down when you walk. In this wind, all sorts of debris blows up onto our driveway. I'll run ahead and get the door.'

She made it to the entrance without incident. 'I thought I might do a Mary Poppins any minute,' she said. 'That wind! Although this has kept most of me dry, apart from my feet.' She propped the green and yellow umbrella in the corner.

Indoors, the building wasn't like an office at all. The walls were painted the creamy blue that Nina associated with Provence (although she'd only been there once). On one wall, there was a map showing the locations of various shipwrecks. She'd read somewhere that over the years, there had been a staggering number – four or five thousand. Cornwall was a magnet for unexpected death.

'You can hang your coat up on those hooks and leave your shoes in the hallway too, if you prefer,' Petroc said. 'There's a loo there if you want to freshen up. We'll be just through that second door. Can I offer you a drink?'

'Water, thank you,' Nina said. 'Fizzy, if you've got it.' She wanted a clear head. 'I'll join you in a minute.' The beautiful tiles on the hall floor continued into a plain white cloakroom. She approved of the high-quality natural seaweed handwash, individual sage green hand towels and quilted white paper. The basin taps were so shiny she was almost embarrassed to use them.

*

A polished, dark wood bench ran the length of the hallway as far as a simple central staircase. The space was lit by plain glass lamps. The overall effect was soothing, a calm contrast to the storm raging outside.

Opening the second door, Nina found herself in a dining room, extending into a sunroom. The shaker-style furniture was perfect for the space. The room had none of the trappings from the Wendy House that shouted B&B – the breakfast buffet table pre-loaded with cheap muesli and single-serving boxes of Rice Krispies. No pile of tiny paper napkins. You still wouldn't mistake it for a private house. There were too many tables and chairs and the small wingchairs in the bay window had the look of a waiting room.

Petroc appeared from the door at the opposite end of the room. He handed her a glass of sparkling water. He was followed a moment later by a man with an impressive beard. 'Hi,' the man said. 'I'm Chris.' They were like Jack Sprat and his wife, Chris with so much hair and Petroc with almost none. 'Your mum's told me lots about you!'

That seemed unlikely to Nina. There was nothing about her life that her mother would think interesting enough to share with her friends (if that's what Chris and Petroc were). 'It's lovely to meet you,' she said. 'I'm afraid my mother has played her cards rather close to her chest when it comes to telling me about her social life. You are on the calendar – Chris, Harbour Walk. Until Petroc explained, I was envisaging sou'westers and Cap'n Birdseye.'

'The Harbour Walkers,' Chris said, 'which is a criminally misleading name as we don't arrange any walking. No sou'westers needed. Annette's one of the mainstays.'

'Petroc said she was giving talks,' Nina said. 'On politics.'

'She's very passionate,' Chris said. 'We're basically a social club, without the alcohol licence. Even when the B&B is full, this room is free in the daytime and most evenings, so we host a handful of activities.'

'Petroc said about the Scrabble. And the supper club.'

'The supper club is extra,' said Chris. 'People can subscribe to be a Harbour Walker. They get access to this room and the gardens, which I can't show you in this weather. And anyone can suggest and run an activity.'

'It sounds like an excellent idea,' Nina said. She'd have to tell Jonah about it later. It all seemed a lot of work to her, but it must make sense for the space to be used. She wondered how much it cost to sign up to play Scrabble or sit in someone else's garden.

'We weren't sure when we started,' Chris said. 'Luckily, it's taken off quite nicely. We've got to know a lot of local people too, which is a change from the B&B where it's all strangers passing through.'

'It's very kind of you and Petroc to invite this passing stranger,' Nina said.

'You're Annette's,' Chris said. 'So you can't be a stranger. How is she getting on? I can't believe she didn't let us know.'

'She didn't let anyone know. Not until they'd operated.'

'The surgery all went well?'

'She should be fine,' Nina said. 'We're in the hospital discharge process. And as I was telling Petroc, they're asking questions about her mental state. I think that's an age thing, something they have to do.' She waited for Chris to agree with her.

'I'm not sure if that's standard or not,' Chris said. 'Come and sit at the table. Petroc's sorting out the food. We can give you our non-expert opinion over dinner.'

*

Nina normally had a low opinion of lasagne. Rubbery pasta and stodgy fillings. This one was light and herby. 'I can see why the supper club's a success,' she said. She noticed that neither of the men was drinking. 'This is the kind of food I'd want to cook for myself. It tastes like a lot of effort.'

'It's pretty easy,' Chris said. 'The trick's to not go overboard with the cheese. Now, what can we tell you about Annette?'

'The hospital are asking if she seems different. They're a bit vague about what they are driving at. The only thing I've noticed is she's tidied up the house, which I see as a good thing.'

They didn't know any more than Petroc had already told her. Annette was with them two or three times a week.

234

She turned up or didn't, and they hadn't worried when she didn't appear at the weekend. Mentally, she seemed as switched on as anyone. There were occasional lapses. They were very fleeting. The labelling that Nina had seen in the house had been Annette's idea. Future-proofing, Annette had said. If Petroc was making labels anyway (for the fuse box, which didn't reassure Nina) he might as well make a few extras.

'Sarah said something about forgetting appointments,' Nina said.

'That was just the once,' Petroc said. 'She's very aware.' He didn't say of what. 'Keeping active. Eating fish. I get her a bit extra when I'm at the market.' Nina thought of her mother's freezer. 'All that sort of thing. She knows how to look after herself.'

'She's always been very independent,' Nina said. 'We both are. But her arm's affected her balance. It's quite tricky to see how she's going to manage.'

'That's why I've lured you here,' Petroc said. 'I've got an idea. Let's finish eating and I'll show you.'

*

While Chris was clearing the table, Petroc led Nina back into the hallway. He opened a wide door at the far end, past the stairs. A small living area led through to a bedroom and walk-in shower room. Off the other side of the bedroom, there was another door, leading to a separate bedroom and another bathroom.

'This is our disabled suite,' Petroc said. 'We realised that people like to come to Cornwall with an elderly parent. You'd be surprised how few places are well geared up for that, outside the big hotels. It's usually the first to get booked up.'

'It's nice and self-contained,' Nina said. She wasn't sure about the interconnected bedrooms.

'Do you think Annette would like it?' Petroc asked.

Nina was alarmed. 'You're not suggesting that me and Mum could move in here?' Sleeping in the next room. Nina didn't think she'd cope with that. The walls in a modern building like this would probably be rather thin.

'I was thinking Annette,' Petroc said. 'Although you'd be welcome too. If she doesn't need nursing care and it's a matter of being able to flit between bedroom and bathroom, she could stay here.'

'We could ask her, I suppose.' Nina was dubious. 'It's a lot for you to take on.'

'She wouldn't be the first,' Petroc said. 'One of the other Harbour Walkers did a few days here in November. Mates' rates. It's business for us, not charity.'

'I'm trying to picture Mum as a houseguest,' Nina said. 'She always claims to like her own space.'

'My guess is she'd love it,' Petroc said. 'She's always saying that we're a home from home.'

'I don't know,' Nina said. 'She's going to need help with day-to-day things. Getting dressed.' It looked a long way from ideal. Surely if you were in hospital, you'd want to get home to your own stuff?

'They'll be able to find someone to help with that,' Petroc said. 'The offer's there if you want it. You have a chat with Annette and see what you both think.'

'I'll do that,' Nina said. 'Thank you so much for suggesting it. And for rescuing me this evening.'

'Sometimes people want a bit of company while they get back on their feet,' Petroc said.

Nina wasn't sure if he was talking about her or her mother. 'I can see that the walk-in shower would be handy,' she said. 'It's certainly something to think about.'

'Come through and have some coffee before you go?' Petroc said. 'We can probably answer all your questions. As I say, Annette wouldn't be the first.'

'Thank you, but no. It's been a long day. I should be on my way now.' She didn't want to be charmed into agreeing to something before she'd had time to consider. 'I'll talk to Mum when I see her tomorrow.'

They went back into the dining room so she could say goodbye to Chris and did that little dance people do when one person wants to get a taxi and someone thinks they should offer a lift, even though it's pouring with rain and they don't fancy the roads. Life would be a lot easier if everyone said what they really thought. Always assuming they knew what that was.

Chapter forty

The Wendy House looked drab after the sleekness of Harbour Walk. It smelled of air freshener. Nina took off her coat and shoes, still squelchy from earlier, and settled onto the faded floral duvet with her phone. Six missed calls from Jonah.

'Where've you been?' he said when she rang him back.

She explained about her evening. 'Granny talks about those two,' Jonah said. 'She was suspicious at first, thought they were on a racket trying to get old ladies to change their wills. I offered to check them out for her, but she laughed at me. Said she'd met enough charlatans in her time to be able to sniff them out for herself.'

'She never mentioned them to me.'

'Well, she doesn't, does she? Mention anything to you about what she's up to, except the broad-brush stuff. You're as bad as each other.' Jonah sounded unfazed by this filial failing. 'That could be a plan,' he said when she told him about the offer of the disabled suite. 'Good business for them too,' he said. 'Mates' rates has got to be better than having it empty.'

Jonah and his eye for business. 'Their finances aren't our concern,' she said. 'I'm trying to think what will be best for Granny.'

'From what you've said, she can't go home. I can have a look when I'm down there if you like. Give you my expert opinion.'

Expert in what, exactly? 'That would be helpful, darling, thank you,' she said.

'Actually, I mostly rang about Neville,' Jonah said.

'I take it there is no room at the inn?'

'None of the inns. Kate rang round about a dozen of them.'

Kate. 'I thought you were going to do that?' Nina said.

'Yeah, but Kate wasn't working today and she likes Neville nearly as much as you do. Anyway, no one can take him. Apparently you have to book miles in advance.'

Nina wondered how hard they'd tried. 'When's he due out?' she asked. As if Neville were in prison. Or hospital. 'It's Friday, isn't it? Remind me how Colin's dog has become our problem.'

'Your problem,' said Jonah. 'You were the one who offered.'

'Granny's still saying he could come to Cornwall,' Nina said. 'I can't work out if she's being serious.'

'I could leave him at Paddington, with a label. Like the bear,' said Jonah.

'Don't joke. It might come to that.'

'We've got a couple of days,' Jonah said. 'We'll figure something out. I've already let Granny know this bit, but I've taken a few days off from Thursday. So I'm going to come and visit and cheer her up.'

'That's lovely, darling. She'll be thrilled to see you.'

'I know,' said Jonah with that certainty that she'd find presumptuous in anyone else. 'She said she's looking forward to having someone different to talk to.'

Sarah. Petroc. Chris. Jonah. Even Agnieszka. It seemed to Nina that her mother was happier talking to anyone other than her daughter.

Chapter forty-one

The rain had cleared overnight, leaving a shell-pink sky and slightly warmer air behind it. Nina stuck her head round the breakfast room door to tell Wendy that she wasn't hungry this morning and was going for a walk. The couple at the other table looked crestfallen at the thought of having Wendy all to themselves, or maybe she was imagining that.

She'd been here four days and still hadn't seen the sea properly. A huddle of dog walkers had gathered a third of the way along the beach, watching as their dogs played in the waves. 'Morning!' one of them shouted to her. 'Morning!' she shouted back.

There'd been a bossy sign on the path down. Dogs only allowed November to March. Nina wondered where they all went in the summer. Maybe there was a meadow somewhere where they lolloped and trampled buttercups. She thought of the shipwreck map on Chris and Petroc's wall. This morning the sea was almost flat, too benign to topple even the flimsiest of boats.

Two collies bounded out of the water, running towards her and shaking themselves dry. 'Pugwash! Barnabas! Oh, I'm so sorry, did they soak you?' a woman said.

'Only a bit,' Nina said. 'Those are excellent names.'

'Pirate names,' said the woman. 'My kids' idea.'

'They suit them.' The pirate dogs had rushed back to play in the ripples, splashy leaps giving way to strong swimming in futile circles. 'They obviously love the water.'

'I think all dogs like the sea,' the woman said.

'Is that true?' Nina said. 'Can I ask your advice? I might be borrowing my friend's dog for a few days. He lives in London. I'm wondering how he'd get on if I brought him here.'

'You never know until you try. What breed is he?'

'We're not altogether certain.' She thought of Neville's orange curls. 'Part poodle and then it's anyone's guess.'

'Poodles are good swimmers,' the woman said. 'There's always a gang of us on the beach about this time, in the winter, if you wanted safety in numbers first time you bring him.'

'Thank you,' said Nina. By now, a dozen or so dogs were careering around people who chatted in twos or threes or shouted above the wind into their mobile phones. It looked friendly and chaotic. A bit like the park at home, only wetter. A lot wetter. They must get through a lot of towels.

'I'd better go and see to my two.' The woman pointed to where the pirates were wrestling at the water's edge with a long-haired dog that would take someone forever to get clean.

'Thank you for your help.' Nina sniffed. The chilly air was making her nose run. 'Is there a café somewhere? I can see some people have got cups.'

'Right at the end,' the woman said. 'Don't be tempted to go any further. It's all riptides round the other side of the headland, and it only takes one wave.'

'Thank you,' Nina said again. She carried on across the wet sand towards the café. It couldn't do much business at this time of year. Feeling guilty about Wendy, she ordered a coffee and a bacon roll. The coffee was excellent. She'd have to come here again.

*

'How are you today? I've got lots to report,' Nina said as she arrived on the ward. Her mother was sitting in the chair beside the bed. Nina looked at the flaking skin that had worked its way through the navy-blue elastic stockings and added E45 to the list of things to bring in next time.

'Petroc and Sarah were here this morning,' Annette said. 'They probably told me all your news. You can tell me again. I'd like to hear your version. See if it matches.'

'There's not supposed to be any visiting in the mornings,' Nina said. She was a little put out that Petroc had got in first.

'There are always exceptions to be made. Especially for someone as winning as Petroc. He said you all had a lovely time last night and that you were very nice. You must have been on your best behaviour.'

'They were very hospitable,' Nina said. 'It's quite the set-up they've got going. I'm surprised you never mentioned it.'

'You never ask, Nina,' Annette said. 'Everything's always news of Jonah and Kate or things you've heard on

243

the radio. If I say that I've been to a drama group or an art talk, you never comment.'

It was true, Nina thought. Over the years, since Martin, they'd become expert at not knowing much about each other's lives. 'I'm asking now,' she said. 'Would moving in with Petroc and Chris for a bit be better than any of the other options on the table?'

'Options on the table,' Annette said. 'Let me see. That implies choices. Negotiation.'

'No one is negotiating, Mum,' Nina said. 'It's up to you.'

'How considerate,' Annette said. 'As I understand it, I can't go home unless someone puts a bed downstairs and someone manhandles me upstairs twice a week for a bath. That someone might have to be you and we know how well that would go.'

'They can sort out carers to help with that,' Nina said.

'Yes, because carers grow on trees,' said Annette. 'I can't stay here. I could probably go to an old folks' home. I can't come to London to stay with you because you haven't invited me.'

'I haven't invited you because it's inconvenient. Too far away,' Nina said.

'We both know that's not true, darling. You don't want me cluttering up your house and I don't want to be the unwanted elderly parent.'

'You'll never be unwanted,' Nina said.

'Inconvenient then,' said Annette. 'You said so yourself. Don't let's pretend, Nina. Harbour Walk will be splendid. I told Petroc yes and he's going to square it all off with the social worker.'

'Shouldn't we discuss it?' Nina said. She felt bounced. 'It seems very sudden.'

'There's nothing to discuss. It will be a holiday for me. A home from home.'

Nina thought she should push the issue, but what if her mother changed her mind? They'd have to go round the whole thing again. 'If you're quite certain, we could give it a try, I suppose,' she said.

'That's all settled then,' her mother said. Her expression made it clear that the subject was closed. 'It means you can go back to London whenever you want.'

'I was going to go for a day or two when Jonah gets here,' Nina said. 'We'll do a switch around. Like those weather houses, where one person is in and one out depending on if it's rain or sun.' They'd had one on the mantelpiece when Nina was small, a beautifully carved souvenir from a Swiss holiday. It had been that or a cuckoo clock, her mother had told everyone, and who could be doing with all that wooden chirruping day and night?

'You are planning to come back?' Her mother sounded like she cared.

'Yes. I'll bring the car. Then we can drive to appointments, and you can get a lift between your house and Harbour Walk any time.'

'That sounds splendid,' Annette said. 'And you can bring him with you.'

'Now you've lost me. Bring who?'

'Kevin.'

'Kevin?'

'Colin's dog. Jonah said it was being evicted from the kennels. We can't have another animal roaming the streets. Look at the trouble that cat I tripped over has caused.'

'You mean Neville,' Nina said. 'I'm worried that will make everything much more difficult. He's very lively.'

'Nonsense,' Annette said. 'It will give us a focus. Something to talk about while we wait out my recovery. We can take him for walks. They've told me how important it is to keep mobile.'

'Let's see how it all plays out,' said Nina. 'Hopefully Colin will have sorted something out by the end of the week.'

'It would be fun to have a dog,' Annette said. 'Although he'll have to stay in the house, with you. No pets allowed at Harbour Walk. Too destructive.'

Nina pictured Neville chewing his way through Annette's buttercup-yellow cushions and scraping his claws down the picture window. Then she pictured her and her mother arm in arm walking carefully along the beach to the café, Neville barking at the waves and chasing his new pirate friends. *It could work*, she thought. She half hoped they'd get the chance to find out.

Chapter forty-two

As Nina checked out of the B&B, Wendy pressed a warm pasty into her hand. 'It's a tradition,' she said. 'A last taste of Cornwall. Come back soon!'

I'll have to, Nina thought. She didn't say anything.

*

She'd only been away a week, but her house felt musty and unloved. Cold. The weeping fig in the corner of the living room had shed some leaves. Neville's spare basket was in the kitchen, next to two empty bowls. A lead and a roll of poo bags were still on the table where Colin had left them when he'd come to say his goodbyes. Somehow, the doglessness of it all made Nina feel sad.

She put the new seaweed handwash, a gift from Chris and Petroc, into the downstairs shower room. The room still had that freshly grouted smell, all these months after Jerzy had added the finishing touches. An ensuite would have been lovely, but there'd been a limit to how much they could mess with the pipework, and this was a good compromise. No one had stayed over yet and no one except Neville had needed to take a shower. Colin, Dima and the man who'd come to fix her broadband had all used the toilet. They'd left the seat up, except Dima.

She hadn't expected to be home this early. In a triumph of experience over hope, the trains had run to time. She and Jonah had managed to coordinate their changes at Reading to overlap by forty-five minutes, long enough for a cup of coffee. Nina had insisted on this. *A proper handover*, she thought, although handing over what wasn't clear. Jonah had been dismissive. 'Nothing to sort,' he'd said. 'I'll talk to everyone.' He turned out already to have keys to Annette's house. When had that happened?

She rang Linda and then Kate. Both phones were switched off. They must be working. There was still no word from Colin.

Nina looked around for something to do. It was too dark to go for a walk and a quick inspection of the cupboards confirmed there was enough in the house to make something pasta-ish for supper.

Colin had left a detailed ring binder file that he'd labelled 'Neville: Operating Manual' and the pick-up instructions from the kennels. She flicked through pages of disclaimers. 'Theft Prevention Measures' meant she needed to bring proof of identity and the signed authorisation form Colin had completed, discharging Neville to her custody (the kennels needed to work on their use of English). Check-out was midday tomorrow. Neville was ahead of Annette, who would have to wait until Monday, and only then if a new X-ray showed them that everything was knitting together as it should.

*

Linda and Kate returned her calls early on Friday.

'Jonah says he tried to ring you last night,' Kate said. Nina's phone begged to differ. 'He arrived in time for the end of visiting,' continued Kate, 'so he's already seen Annette. He's dealing with everything and says you are not to worry and to focus on Neville.'

'I was rather hoping you might be off today, Kate,' Nina said. 'We could brave the kennels together and then get lunch somewhere.'

'Sorry. I'm working. I'd have gone with Jonah otherwise.'

'I hope it's an interesting project,' Nina said. Kate had had a run of dreary assignments.

'I have the thrilling prospect of tweaking the lighting for a new installation at one of those ludicrous galleries in Mayfair,' Kate said.

'Does whoever buys the art also buy the lighting, I wonder?' said Nina. 'It seems a bit pointless otherwise.'

'It's Mayfair,' Kate said. 'People with money to waste. The paintings are all under wraps. They look terrible from the catalogue. They're called things like *Horizons of Angst*.'

'Hardly up your street.' Nina stored up the title of the painting to tell Dima. His art had pragmatic names like *4pm Sky* and *10am Shore*. The kind of thing Nina would happily hang on her walls if she lived in a bigger house.

'God, no,' Kate said. 'It's so pretentious. Apparently the angst melts away under a certain slant of light. Which is where I come in with my superpowers.'

'I recognise that phrase from somewhere,' Nina said.

'Emily Dickinson. The artist's muse, although she'd turn in her grave.'

'Handy to know that you can magic away angst with a couple of strategically placed lightbulbs,' Nina said. 'I'll bear it in mind when Neville or Mum get too much.'

'I'll be happy to help with either or both of them,' Kate said. 'Unfortunately just not this weekend.'

'It's probably for the best,' Nina said. 'Neville would get far too excited if both his favourite women turned up.'

'I'm sorry I won't see you,' said Kate. 'I'm free on Monday. I guess you'll be away by then? Unless you've decided to stay? Jonah's quite happy holding the Cornish fort. He's having a great time making himself indispensable.'

'I'm not sure what to do for the best,' Nina said. 'If the kennels can keep Neville, that'll make life easier. No one's been able to contact them. Mum's suggested taking him to Cornwall. Does that seem mad to you?'

'Annette's such an animal lover,' Kate said. 'I can see her and Neville getting on very well together.'

'Sometimes I think you know her better than I do,' said Nina.

'I never met my grandparents,' Kate said. 'I wanted to get to know Jonah's.'

'You're doing a good job of that,' Nina said. 'I'm starting to realise how little I know about my mother. It's hard to know what she wants.'

'I can ask Jonah to ask her if you like,' Kate said. 'Just about Neville. You're on your own with the existential stuff.'

'Would you?' Nina said. 'She's more likely to tell him the truth.'

'For what it's worth, I'd take Neville to Annette's unless she tells Jonah otherwise. You were looking forward to having him to stay.'

'That was before all of this happened,' Nina said.

'Life can't stop because your mum fell over,' Kate said.

'I'm worried about her, Kate. Not just the fall. She went out in her slippers. In the freezing cold.'

'That mightn't mean anything. She probably couldn't be bothered to put her shoes on,' Kate said. 'Faffing around with laces.'

'I hope you're right.'

'Not much point in fretting,' Kate said. 'From what Jonah has told me, it sounds like the hospital are doing all the right tests. Give her my love when you are back down there.'

'Thank you, darling. Have fun with the arty-farties.'

'Sadly, I think not.'

'Any luck with the job-hunting?' Nina said.

'I've got an iron in the fire,' Kate said. 'I'm not saying any more in case I jinx it.'

'Promise I'll be the first to know?'

'Jonah might have something to say about that,' Kate said. 'Take care, Nina. I'm sorry I can't join you for the great Neville reunion. Tell him to send me a postcard from his seaside adventure.'

Nina felt better for talking to Kate, but it wasn't the same as spending time together. The conversation was too brief to help her make sense of the last few days.

Linda's call was more satisfactory. She was full of approval for the Harbour Walk scheme. She couldn't join Nina this morning, something about a PhD student with a referencing crisis. She absolutely insisted that Nina come to the quiz that evening, to celebrate.

'What are we celebrating exactly?'

'Glass half full, please,' Linda said. 'It sounds like things are going from worse to not so bad for your mum. It'll be easier to figure out what to do next if she's safely tucked up with her gentlemen admirers.'

Linda had news of Colin too. 'I spoke to one of the girls, the nieces. The oldies have gone off-grid on some manufactured outback adventure. They are back on Saturday.'

'I'll set up a Zoom, if I can work out the time zones,' Nina said.

'Be clear with him,' Linda said. 'I am forever reminding Colin that Neville is his responsibility. He'll realise that one day.'

'He takes his responsibility very seriously. He's left me reams of instructions for how to handle Neville until he gets back.'

'I bet he has,' Linda said. 'Good luck at the kennels, and we will see you later?'

'You will,' Nina said. 'With or without Colin's furry friend.'

Chapter forty-three

In the early days of their friendship, Colin, never short of clichés, told Nina that Neville had rocked his world. All thanks to the Hound-dog Hotel. Nina had admired the website with its springtime colours and unlikely backstories of the current crop of rescues. It was heart-warming, the number of abandoned pooches finding loving forever homes through the power of photos and imaginative prose (or in Neville's case, poetry).

Driving through the duller parts of Surrey on Friday morning, Nina imagined a country house retreat, with amiable dogs free to frolic in grassy fields before sleeping on blankets not unlike the stripy one she'd stretched across the back seat of her car. Colin drove a hatchback. Much easier. She hoped it was OK to put a dog in the back seat without any kind of restraint. She didn't want to put him in the boot like a hostage. *Careful, Nina,* she thought. *Plan A is to persuade them to look after Neville until Colin is home.*

The entrance to the kennels was marked by a large sign. Welcome to the Hound-dog, with a black and white photo of the King of Rock singing to his droopy basset hound. She remembered the dog was called Sherlock. Someone had made it wear a top hat, which was probably why it looked so depressed.

Elvis and his dog were the extent of the place's charm. Turning off the busy road, Nina found herself surrounded by concrete, gravel and breeze blocks. She followed the arrows to reception, which was in the one red-brick building in the complex.

'Yes?' The young man at the front desk looked like he would be more at home in a mobile phone shop. He had that hunched air of knowing more than was healthy about algorithms.

'I'm here to collect my friend's dog,' Nina said. 'Although I was hoping also to speak to someone about booking him in for longer.'

'Name?'

'Nina Gilmour. The booking is under Colin Colindale.' Colin's parents had liked the name, he'd told her, and they'd done him a favour. It had made it easier when he was first learning to write, what with the repetition.

'No. Name of dog.' This boy could only operate in monosyllables.

'Neville,' she said. 'I don't know his surname. He's adopted.'

'Wait there.' The boy pressed buttons on a shiny gadget. A few minutes later, a woman appeared. She wore a long sweater with a Scottie dog pattern. Stud earrings shaped like very small Alsatians. She looked altogether more suited to canine care than the pale youth. Her lipstick was a little too pink, as if she'd found a shade she liked when she was twenty-four and never upgraded.

'Thank you, Toby,' said the woman. She turned to Nina, smiling pinkly. 'How can I help you?'

'As I just explained, I am here to collect a dog.'

'Yes. Neville Colindale,' said the woman. 'Nina, isn't it? Colin said that you'd be collecting him first thing. Still, better late than never. I'll need to see your ID of course, as a precaution.'

Nina handed over her driver's licence. 'Do you also have some ID?' she asked.

'Oh, silly me. I forgot to introduce myself. I'm Amanda, the director of Hound-dog. Leader of the Pack, you might say.' She gave what Nina assumed was intended to be a winning little laugh.

'Pleased to meet you,' Nina said. In the song, the Leader of the Pack came to a noisy end. She decided not to mention this. 'I believe my son emailed you, about whether we can extend Neville's stay?'

'I am sure I replied,' Amanda said. Nina was sure she hadn't. Jonah would have said. 'If you'd like to come through to my office, I'll fill you in on what's been going on with Neville. He's a lovely dog, of course.' The 'of course' didn't bode well.

Amanda led her through a room that needed hoovering into an overheated office. A pinboard on the back wall was covered in polaroid photos of smiling people with their dogs. 'Very old-school,' Amanda said, 'but people like it. It's also handy if the adoption breaks down – which it does sometimes, sadly – to have a picture so we can remember who's coming back.'

Nina thought it was odd that all the dogs were so attractive. They wouldn't be out of place advertising toilet

255

paper or insurance. She'd read somewhere that most of the dogs that ended up in rescue centres were Staffies or enormous or ugly. Such a concentration of cuteness didn't ring true. 'As I was saying,' she started, 'I was rather hoping you might find a way of hanging on to Neville for a few days longer or be able to recommend someone else.' She explained about her mother and her need to return to Cornwall.

'That must all be very difficult for you,' Amanda said. Nina recognised the meaningless, professional, empathetic tone. 'I'd love to be able to help.'

'But you can't,' said Nina.

'We're closed next week. I know, silly Amanda, half term and so much demand.' She fluttered a hand. 'We've fostered out the rescues and the paying guests are going home.'

'There's nothing you can suggest?'

'I didn't say that. We need to think about what's best for Neville too. The poor chap has exhibited abandonment issues. He misses his family.'

Abandonment. Niall had tried that one on her in one of their therapy sessions. He was wondering, he'd said, and tell me if I am off the mark, did Martin's dying like that make you feel abandoned? She'd given him short shrift. The suggestion stayed with her, nagging at her every time she thought about how long to stay in Cornwall.

'I have a family,' Nina told Amanda. 'It's small, so not difficult to keep track. I would remember if it included my neighbour's dog.' This woman was highly annoying with her whimsical dog-motif clothes and her lilting voice. Still, there was no need to be so rude. 'Neville's not my dog,' she continued in a more conciliatory tone, 'and I'm worried about how he and my mother will mix. If he's missing Colin, then I am not much of a substitute. I can't give him my full attention. Not with all this going on with my mum.'

'My main concern is for Neville. I should warn you that he's chewing his paw. It's quite sore and raw.' Neville's poor sore raw paw. A tear-jerking ditty if ever Nina heard one. 'We've had the vet look at him several times,' Amanda continued. 'It will add a fair chunk to Colin's bill, unfortunately, but it's welfare first round here.' She went on to theorise that perhaps Neville remembered his longer sojourn (what normal person uses that word?) and was confused about why he was back. 'Why don't I go and fetch him, and you can see for yourself?' She left the room, her boots creaking, before Nina had a chance to answer.

The young man from the front desk appeared at the office door. 'Mum says to wait in meet and greet.'

'Meet and greet?'

'Yeah. Through here.' He led her back to the big room with the hairy sofas. 'It's where people meet and greet the dogs.'

'Thank you,' Nina said.

'S'alright.'

'How long have you worked here?' she asked. The boy had stayed in the room with her, which made conversation seem necessary.

'I don't,' he said. 'Work experience.'

'Are you hoping to work with animals one day?'

'No.'

They lapsed back into awkward silence, broken a few minutes later by the cajoling and carrying voice of Amanda. 'Come along. It's cold out here. There's someone here to see you.' A moment's quiet and the voice started up again. 'Come on, boy. Don't let's be silly.'

'Maybe if I went out there?' Nina said to the youth, who was blocking the door.

'Dunno if that's allowed,' he said.

He was a useless sort of a boy. No gumption. 'Well, it can't do any harm,' Nina said. 'If you could let me through, please.' She stood in front of him, holding steady eye contact until he moved to the side.

'Door's there,' he said, unnecessarily. The front door was propped open with an umbrella stand, cold air pouring in from outside.

'I thought it would save time,' Nina started, stepping into the driveway where Amanda was half coaxing and half dragging Neville. The rest of her sentence was drowned out by furious barking. Neville pulled at the lead, his tail beating against Amanda's legs in a way that Nina hoped was a little painful.

'Why don't I take him?' she said to Amanda, prising the lead away from the other woman. 'Hello, you. No, no jumping. You know that rule. And you're supposed to have a bad foot. We'll go inside and have a look, shall we?' She led him back into the hairy-sofa room and sat down. The hopeless boy had vanished. Neville jumped onto her lap and started licking her chin. 'Stop that, please,' she said. 'Show me your paw.' It looked fine to her, a little bald in patches. Nothing to suggest horizons of angst.

'You have a lovely way with him,' Amanda said. 'I can always tell a dog-lover.'

Nina was suspicious of the flattering tone. In her line of business, Amanda must meet nothing but dog-lovers. 'We are good friends, Neville and I,' she said.

'He does look pleased to see you.' The saccharine tone was back.

Neville had sunk onto the sofa beside Nina. She rubbed his ears gently between her fingers. 'I'm pleased to see him,' she said. She couldn't leave him again. It would break his heart.

'Neville will be happy to be going home with Auntie Nina, won't you, boy?' Amanda reached out a hand to stroke the dog, who growled. Nina wanted to believe it was in disgust at the cloying tone.

'As I explained before,' she said, 'Neville and I are friends. He is not my nephew. I am doubly sure of that because I don't have brothers or sisters, and because Neville is only a dog.'

'Oh, but they are so much more than just dogs, aren't they?' Amanda simpered.

'So it says in your brochure,' Nina said. It was true, of course. Neville was gazing at her with so much love she wanted to cry.

Toby was fetched from his phone calls to collect Neville's belongings. There was a flutter of paperwork. A polaroid snap (two, so Nina could keep a copy) and they were on their way.

Chapter forty-four

The pub had a pleasantly fuggy feeling. Most of the quiz regulars were there. Several stopped Nina on the way in to ask after her mother. She was touched by how news of the accident had spread.

She joined Dima and Linda at their table and described her trip to the kennel.

'You didn't like her, then?' said Dima. 'I wonder how long it took her to notice?'

'She was unbelievably irritating. All fake smiles. Neville didn't like her either.'

'The ever-empathic Neville,' Dima said.

'I don't know much about boarding kennels,' Nina said. 'I thought the people would be more genuine. Caring.'

'It's a business. Just like any other.'

'They've certainly made a tidy profit out of Neville.' Nina had ended up paying the vet's bill.

'But Neville's fine?' said Linda.

'As you can see.' Neville was under the table, patrolling for dropped bits of crisp. 'They made some song and dance about him having chewed his paw. Trying to justify the massive additional costs.'

'And you've decided to take him to Cornwall?' Linda said.

'I don't see there is any other choice,' Nina said. 'He's been moping, apparently. I can't bear the thought of sending him somewhere else strange.'

'I'm so sorry we can't take him,' said Linda quickly.

'Heartbroken,' added Dima.

'I'm not sure which of you sounds less sincere,' Nina said. 'I'll manage. He was so pleased to see me it was quite flattering.'

'Neville's not the only one,' Dima said. 'We've missed you.'

'I've only been away a few days,' said Nina.

'Just the days I needed your collaboration on the quiz,' Dima said. 'It's the intellectual equivalent of cupboard love. But I understand that Cornwall beckoned.'

'Tell us the latest about Cornwall,' Linda said. 'How your mother's doing, all of it.'

'Note that we have our priorities,' Dima said. 'Dog first, mother second.'

'Nina third,' said Nina.

'Are we having a pity party?' Dima asked. 'I missed the memo.'

'I'm stating facts,' Nina said. 'There's so much to think about with Mum and with Neville I've hardly had time for myself. I don't know if I'm coming or going.'

'Does it feel like that?' Linda asked. 'You must be exhausted.'

Too exhausted to go over it all again. She gave the edited highlights, brushing over the things she'd found difficult and talking up the bouncy dogs on the beach and the ingenuity of Harbour Walk. 'The hospital are a bit vague. Hopefully things will get clearer when she's out.'

'And you'll definitely go back on Monday? With Neville?'

Nina wished Linda wouldn't keep asking. 'That's the plan,' she said. 'It was Mum's idea to bring him and astonishingly the hospital are in favour. I'm off to the pet superstore tomorrow to get him a proper car seat.'

'An exciting weekend, then?' Dima's expression was hard to read. 'Preparing for a big adventure.'

'I'm hoping it won't be too much of an adventure,' Nina said.

'Let's hope it's not for too long,' Dima said. 'Your pub quiz needs you.'

Nina looked around. People she hadn't known a few months ago who greeted her as a friend. Dogs she knew by name. Familiar faces smiling at her.

*

Dima had compiled the quiz questions. Nina reckoned he'd done so with her in mind, although it was a bit hit and miss. Real names of pop stars was an old standard, but Noddy Holder (Neville) wasn't normally starry enough to feature alongside Elton (Reg) and Gaga (Stefani) and Freddie (Farrokh). A round on Unhealthy People included someone who'd discovered the Colles fracture, which was one way of breaking a wrist. Nina wondered if this Dr Colles had been proud of such a paltry legacy compared to Hodgkin and Alzheimer with their more devastating ailments.

Even with the additional help, she and Linda trailed in fourth out of the five teams. They lingered for over an hour after the quiz was over. Dima looked at Neville's paw and said that Colin should demand a refund on the vet's bill. Nina told him about the paintings Kate was lighting. He knew of the artist, he said, and no disrespect to Kate but it sounded like she was missing the point. Something about the interplay of words and images firing the deeper emotions. He was explaining it to her in a way that was quite fascinating until Linda interrupted to show her a photo of Colin petting a koala that had popped up on Facebook.

She'd left the car at home, wanting what now felt like an ill-advised drink. Walking through the cold streets took longer with Neville, who stopped to sniff and mark his territory at every gate. Their route took them past Colin's house, lit up by the random programme-timer switches he'd shown her at some length. Neville stopped only briefly before pulling Nina forward to her own dark home.

Chapter forty-five

Neville was an early riser. Nina was woken before seven by a paw prodding at her face. His fur was frayed. There was nothing wrong with his claws. 'I suppose this means you want out?' she said. She pulled on her dressing gown and followed him downstairs.

The first time Neville had stayed overnight, he'd trashed the kitchen. She'd learned to move anything edible or chewable out of range. His metal food dish, licked clean, was at the bottom of the stairs. There were faint scratch marks on the wooden floorboards where he'd nosed it through from the kitchen. She put it back in its place and dropped in a handful of dry food. Medium-breed turkey and chicken. It smelled horrible. 'Don't tell anyone,' she said as Neville scurried in damply from the garden. Colin's instructions had been to feed him once a day. 'My house, my rules. *Comprende?* *I must be going mad*, she thought. *I'm talking to him in Spanish*. She fetched the towel from the downstairs bathroom and rubbed at his coat. 'There. Does that feel better?' she said. Less than twenty-four hours since the dog had moved in and already she was seeking his approval.

Checking her phone, she found an email from Colin. At last. It was very unColin-like. The last written communication she'd seen from him was the convoluted stuff he'd given her about Neville, which basically said walk him, feed him, be nice to him, remember who's top dog (that last one was already proving a bit ambivalent). This message was brief and comprehensible. It was mostly about being sorry – about Annette, about being out of contact, about the hassle. He was setting up a Zoom from his sister's account. They could sort everything out then.

She took a picture of Neville, now curled up angelically on the rug. 'Someone's been missing you,' she wrote. 'Give us a bit of notice of the call so we can make sure we're home.'

*

Nina took Neville for a quick run in the muddy park before heading off to Pet Pet Pet ('Love is all around') without him. He'd been a disconcerting passenger yesterday, barking and prone to poking his head through the gap between the front seats. 'I'll be back in a couple of hours,' she told him. 'Please try not to destroy anything.' He looked at her as if he understood, then slumped into his basket with a sigh.

As a child, Nina had liked pet shops. There was one at the end of the high street that sold small things that lived in bowls or cages. Occasionally there would be a kitten or puppy ('the last one, no one wants the poor mite'). It was a scruffy little shop staffed by a husband and wife who wore dove-grey overalls. They'd only ever had one of each type of animal inside, with the rest kept in the shed behind. Nina's parents used the shop as a bribe. If Nina was patient while they got school shoes or ear drops or light bulbs, they could go and ask if the nice man at the pet shop would let her stroke the spare hamsters.

Pet Pet Pet was nothing like the shop Nina remembered so fondly. The world had moved on. It was illegal to sell dogs and cats in shops now, of course. Evidently, there was more than enough money to be made from the dazzling array of unnecessary and expensive objects that filled the 'Furriest Friends' aisles.

The shop was enormous. It had a pleasingly anarchic feel. Most people had brought their dogs and their small children. Some of the toys in the Fun aisle (Nina thought that sounded like something in a sex shop, not that she'd ever been to one) looked suitable for both groups. She was tempted by a tall, plush structure that looked vaguely like a tree trunk, filled with squeaky squirrel toys for your dog to find and, she gathered from the label – 'Price includes four spare squirrels' – destroy.

She found her way to the Adventures aisle where a helpful member of staff quickly pointed her to a padded box. He explained that this was a luxury tethered booster seat with detachable harness that was practical and stylish. He also told her that she'd been breaking the Highway Code by having Neville loose in her car the day before. Nina thought that Amanda from the kennels should have mentioned that.

'It's going to be a long drive for him,' Nina told the man. 'All the way to Cornwall. Is there anything you recommend to make it easier?'

There were so many options. Where to start? There was a website dedicated to people who drive with dogs. If Nina looked at that, there'd be a list of motorway service stations that were dog-friendly. For the car, he recommended the calming toys, the relaxation sprays, the soothing treats, the special heavy-duty poo bags, the dog travel sickness tablets. He was a brilliant salesman. It doesn't end with the journey, he said. For the destination, there was the dog wetsuit, since the sea was colder than the Thames, and the special skincare for dogs that have been on the beach.

People had put a lot of time and effort into creating the perfect product for any canine eventuality. When she'd finished choosing (everything from the top of the range), the salesman helped her load her trolley into her car. He tried to sell her a roof rack, but she resisted.

*

'You could spend a fortune,' Nina told Jonah later. 'As indeed I did.'

'We've had this discussion before, Mum,' Jonah said. 'Someone, more than one someone, has been very ingenious monetising people's obsession with their dogs. Neville would probably be OK with something to chew and you stopping from time to time to make a fuss of him.'

'He likes his new padded cell,' Nina said. She'd taken Neville for an experimental drive. The trip had been a huge success with none of the agitated barking from the day before. It had taken some coaxing and a bribe to get him to jump out of the car back into the house. 'They only had the harness in purple,' she added. 'He looks quite ecclesiastical.'

'You've got too much imagination,' Jonah said. 'Did you ask about keeping him under control in the house, like I said?' Nina had told him about being woken up and been rewarded with a long lecture about not letting Neville have the run of the place.

'They suggested a crate. Colin won't wear that. He's got strong views on keeping animals in cages.'

'Colin's not here,' Jonah said. 'I'll talk to Granny about it. It's her house.'

'Thank you. That would be helpful.' She wasn't sure how, exactly. There wouldn't be room in the car for a crate unless they got something collapsible.

'Granny's looking forward to Neville coming. She thinks it will be fun.' The same thing she'd said to Nina. 'I've taken a few extra days off, though, just in case. That way you can always take him home again if it doesn't work out.'

'And your job's OK with that?' Nina asked. Jonah wasn't always able to take leave when she needed him to do something.

'They are. I told them they can use me as a case study for how their flexible leave for caring for dependants policy can apply to literally anyone. They loved my logic.'

Nina thought it more likely that they'd agreed quickly to stop him going into too much detail. 'That's very clever of you, darling,' she said. 'Granny emailed to say how pleased she is that you are staying on.' Her mother's email had been kindly meant (probably). Jonah was much more use than Nina around the hospital. The nurses liked him

268

and he didn't flap. He could talk to everyone on Monday after the X-rays and get things moving. 'How was Granny today?' she asked.

'Granny's Granny,' Jonah said. 'Being Queen Bee. Sarah came to see her. She wanted to discuss her script. Petroc was there too. He brought Scrabble for if they ran out of things to talk about, which they didn't because you know how Granny likes talking.' She wasn't the only one. 'They got onto the Suffragettes and Sarah asked if Granny had been one.'

'I can imagine how that went down.'

'It was funny. Granny said something on the lines of "yes dear, I am in good nick for someone who is at least 150 years old", and it took ages for Sarah to twig. It wasn't like being in hospital at all, apart from someone kept coming by to take blood pressure.'

'I'm glad you enjoyed yourselves. You obviously cheered her up.'

'Not just me,' Jonah said generously. 'She gets on brilliantly with Petroc. He told her they're rolling out the red carpet for her residency. You know, like an artist in residence. She already runs their art club.'

'I had no idea,' Nina said.

'Well, it's hard to keep up with Granny,' Jonah said. 'I'm going over to Petroc's in the morning with some of her stuff. Then, if the hospital let her out, it will all be ready for her.'

'That's very thoughtful of you. Thank you. Speak tomorrow.'

It sounded to Nina as if everyone was getting on fine without her. 'At least you still need me,' she said to

Neville, who had pulled his lead down from the hook in the hallway and was looking at her pleadingly. A gentle stroll around the familiar streets before bedtime would help them both sleep.

Chapter forty-six

It didn't help that Nina was already in a bad mood before the Zoom call with Colin started. She looked up the time zones when the invitation arrived to find he'd set it up for 7am, which was either incompetent or inconsiderate. He'd used his sister Judy's account and his slightly fuzzy picture was captioned 'HeyOzJude!' Nina had never understood why people needed to create clever usernames. Couldn't they see how tiresome they were?

It didn't help either that she set up the laptop on the kitchen table, as usual, in full earshot of Neville. She hadn't thought it through. She didn't entirely believe that dogs recognised voices or faces. All that nonsense about Facetiming your dog. Weren't animals all about smell? Colin would want to see Neville. Sure enough, after a casual 'Hey, Nina', Colin started calling, in the same voice he used in the park. 'Neville! Neville! Say hello, Neville!' Neville had a limited vocabulary, but he knew his name. By the time Nina managed to quell the barking, her patience had gone.

'I've shut him in the living room,' she said. 'He's not happy about it so we need to make this quick.' She could hear Neville clawing at the door.

'How is he?' Colin said. 'Australia's amazing. He'll have to come with me next time. You both will. You'll never guess what I've been up to.'

'Colin,' said Nina, interrupting a boastful account of his new bush-tracking skills (which she thought would be unnecessary in suburban Perth, let alone south-west London). 'I am pleased that you are having a lovely time. I now need you to concentrate on Neville.'

'Amanda said he was happy to see you,' Colin said. 'She emailed me to say that the transfer had gone well.'

'I'm glad she thought so,' Nina said. 'Did she also tell you that I'm going down to Mum's? So I need to be sure that you are OK with that.'

'Neville will love it,' Colin said. 'He's never been on holiday.'

Did he have to be so relentlessly positive? 'There's a lot that can go wrong,' Nina said. 'Boisterous animal meets old lady with broken arm. She has pottery on display in the house and outside the coast is full of riptides.'

'He's got more sense than to get into a rip,' Colin said. 'You can always keep him on a lead if you're worried. And he doesn't often break stuff. Not anymore.'

'Did Amanda also tell you that the kennels claim to have been forced to treat what appears to be an imaginary injury without your consent because you had gone off stalking koalas or whatever it was you were doing?' She paused. The scratching at the living room door had stopped and Neville was now whining. 'I paid his vet's bill, in case you were wondering.'

'That vet was brilliant. Amanda says Neville's fine now,' Colin said. 'Are you OK, Nina? You sound stressed.'

'The beer hasn't totally numbed your perceptions then.' In the background behind him, Nina could see a stereotypically Australian deck, with attractive people clustered round a barbeque enjoying themselves. She half expected Kylie Minogue to spring perkily into view.

'Why wouldn't I be OK?' she said. 'My mum's in hospital. Your dog is howling my house down.'

'What do you want me to do, Nina?' Colin said. 'I'm sorry about your mum. I truly am. I'm not sure what I can do to help, not from this distance?'

It was a good question. 'Nothing,' she conceded.

'Send me your bank details and I'll pay the vet's bill straightaway.'

'It's not about the money,' Nina said.

'Neville will be fine,' Colin said. 'You know how soppy he is for you. He'd follow you anywhere.' He looked so happy and relaxed, it was unbearable. 'Aren't you going to ask me if I'm having a good time? You wouldn't believe the things we've seen.'

'Are you having a good time? There. I've asked. You need to excuse me, Colin. I need to organise your dog.' She pressed 'leave meeting'.

Very constructive, Nina, she thought. Probably better than dissolving into the grumpy self-pity she could feel rising in the back of her throat. A missed opportunity even so. She'd made a list of questions to ask him. When exactly was he coming back? That was one. But mainly things about Neville.

273

Chapter forty-seven

A tentative February sun was teetering into a baby-blue sky. 'We'll go for a pre-breakfast walk,' she said to Neville. 'Not before your breakfast, obviously.' She waited the fifteen seconds it took him to eat and they headed out into the fresh morning, towards the river.

Life always seemed better beside the water. It was one of the things that had brought her and Martin to this overpriced corner of London with its wild tides, grand buildings and meadows. This early in the day and the year, only a couple of boats forged against the flow, long-sleeved rowers cajoled by sleepy coxes.

They crossed the bridge and pottered past the fancy restaurants and the canoe club, up to the Terrace Gardens and into the steep fields beyond. She let Neville off the lead. He lay down at her feet. 'This is the part where you're supposed to run around,' she said. He sat up when she threw the frisbee. 'Fetch!' she said in her most encouraging voice.

Neville showed no sign of moving, not even when she walked away from him. She picked up the frisbee, then continued the climb up to the famous Turner viewpoint, turning back every minute to see if he was following. *Really*, she thought, *it's Jonah all over again.* I don't want to go, Mummy. I want to stay here. Usually when they were at the swings but sometimes (and she'd been proud of this) at the library. The tedious game of Grandmother's Footsteps that would end happily with Jonah running into her arms – Wait for me, Mummy, wait for me, don't leave me, not never. 'You don't leave your family, silly,' she'd said each time, never thinking what a cruel lie that would turn out to be.

Nina stopped at the top to catch her breath and the surge of joy that always swept up from the sight of the river, far below. A certain slant of light. Generations of people had looked on the world from this very spot. It was still the only view in England protected by law. All those artists and poets had done their best to capture the magic. It wasn't enough. You needed to be here to feel your heart trapped between the sky and the land, London to your right and in the other direction the boundless reaches of the west.

Neville watched silently as she retraced her steps back down the hill to join him. She clipped him back on his lead and they wandered towards the gardens to see if the café was open yet.

*

They'd been home for about half an hour when her phone rang. Linda. 'Is everything alright, Nina? Colin messaged me. He said you were in a state.'

'I'm not in a state,' Nina said.

'He said you were in a bad mood. He'd never seen you like that before. He thought you were having second thoughts about Neville. And that you were pissed off about the vet's bill.'

'I didn't say that. We spoke stupidly early this morning. I wasn't at my best and he worked Neville up into such a frenzy I could barely hear myself think.'

'I talked to Dima,' Linda said.

'Things must be serious.'

'I'll ignore that,' Linda said. 'If you're worried about taking Neville to your mum's, and I can see why you might be, we can look after him. Gus is home for reading week so he can help.'

'And Dima is OK with this idea, is he?'

'OK is putting it a bit strongly. As you know, the main objector was me, and Colin told me I was being selfish.'

'Pots and kettles,' said Nina. She was still annoyed that Colin had been so blasé about Neville. And that he was so obviously enjoying himself on the other side of the world.

'Although there is another option,' Linda was saying.

'There is?'

'Always,' Linda said. 'Colin's back in ten days or so. From what you were saying the other night, your mum has plenty of other people to run around after her. You could simply stay home. Neville can have his playdates with Muddy in the park. If you need to go out, you can lock him back into his own house. You know Colin left me the keys.'

Nina didn't know that. She'd have thought that she was a more obvious choice, living round the corner and having custody of the dog. 'I couldn't do that,' she said.

'Why not?'

It was a good question. 'My mother. She told me she needs me. She's never said that before. She must have meant it. And what if I lose her?'

'She's got a broken arm,' Linda said. 'It's not going to kill her.'

'You don't know that.' Nina was thinking more about the memory assessments. 'In any case, I want to go. Mum did so much for me when Martin died. And she's got this whole life going on, with all these people I don't know anything about. We can get to know each other again.'

'You're sure?' said Linda.

'I'm never sure of anything,' Nina said.

'Is anyone?' Linda said. 'It's up to you, Nina. So long as you know that the offer's there. Drop Neville off with us in the morning if you change your mind.'

'I probably won't,' Nina said, 'but thank you. What about Colin? I was snappy with him. He was obviously dying to tell me about his adventures.'

'Don't worry about Colin, Nina. From what he told me, he was his usual clumsy self. Worry about you. You've got a lot on your plate.'

Nina was touched. She'd forgotten what it was like to have a friend who'd check up on her. Two friends. Even blunderbuss Colin had interrupted his sunshiny fun to call in the cavalry.

*

Neville came to sit beside her. 'You'd like to go to the seaside, wouldn't you?' she asked him. He wagged his tail.

'You'd like to stay in London, wouldn't you?' He wagged his tail. He was a lot more easily pleased than most people.

There wasn't any reason not to go. There was a limit to how much could go wrong. If she stayed here, she'd worry. She'd pack the car tonight. They could set off early and take a meandering route through charming small towns that would provide suitable pit-stops. It was a long old journey, but it didn't have to be stressful. Neville would be happy in his booster seat ('The stylish design will please your dog and be the envy of all his canine friends'). Nina would trade down from the real life of Radio 4 and sing along to cheesy music.

If she timed it right, they'd arrive before dark.

Part three

Chapter forty-eight

Four weeks later.

'We're going to miss you.' Petroc looked genuinely sad. He handed Annette a bunch of daffodils, cut from the garden. He'd wrapped a ribbon around them and tied one of those slippery bows that proper florists can do. It was the same colour as the flowers.

'Is that everything?' Nina asked Annette. 'You've certainly been accumulating stuff.' The clutch of bin bags reminded her of when Jonah had moved out.

'That's the thing about getting out of hospital. People think they need to visit, and because they are visiting they think they need to bring presents. Most of it will have to go to charity shops. You can take it to London, Nina. Less chance of anyone recognising their gift and getting offended.' Annette was sitting on the bed. Neville, who'd awarded himself exemption from the 'no pets at Harbour View' rule, was sitting beside her, watching carefully as Nina packed.

'You have been godsends,' Nina said to Petroc. 'I don't know how we'd have managed without you.'

'Don't be silly, Nina.' Her mother was sounding more

like herself every day. 'You'd have installed me somewhere with a Care Quality Commission rating and a television room and I'd have taken up Beetle. You remember. That game where you throw dice to earn limbs or antlers for an insect.'

'Antennae. Not antlers,' Petroc said. 'Don't knock care homes, Annette. It's brilliant that you can choose to live somewhere where they'll look after you properly if you can't cope on your own.'

'Choose is an interesting way of putting it.'

'There's always a choice, Annette. Like you could choose to stay on here for a few more days if you want to.'

'That's very kind. I'm ready to go home. See how I get on. A month is already quite a long time. I'm in danger of getting too comfortable.'

'We'll hardly be strangers,' Nina said. 'I've already signed us up for the supper club on Wednesday.' Had it only been a month? It felt longer.

Petroc helped shove everything into the car. It was no different to any other day, Nina told herself. Collect her mother and take her back to her house from where they could plan their day. Only this time, Nina would leave Annette there for the night, rather than taking her back to Harbour Walk and escaping to what Nina was starting to think of as her and Neville's own home from home.

*

The holiday rental had been Kate's idea. So many of the most sensible suggestions came from Kate. 'It's better than I'd expected. Very claustrophobic,' Nina had told her when Kate asked how it was all going now Annette had been out of hospital for a few days. The Harbour Walk end was working brilliantly. Annette had somewhere safe and manageable for sleep and ablutions. Petroc and Chris seemed to adore her. She could do most things for herself. Agnieszka had sorted her out with morning carers who came at unpredictable hours to help her get dressed. Annette cancelled them after a week. If she was roping in her hosts to help instead, no one was saying.

The time away from Harbour Walk was trickier. Nina would pick her mother up most mornings after breakfast. It made for long days. There was something unnatural about being together in Annette's house for hours on end. Nina was relieved each evening when her mother said brightly that she was ready to turn in and asked Nina to run her back to Petroc and Chris. It wasn't lost on anyone that this happened so early. Some days, it wasn't even dark yet.

'You don't need to sit with her all day,' Kate had said when Nina rang her to fret.

'I don't have anywhere else to go. It's a small town. I don't know anyone. There's only so many times I can take Neville for a walk, and I can't leave him alone with her unsupervised for long.' Neville had mistaken Annette for someone who appreciated gifts. He busied himself collecting anything he could fit in his mouth and dropping it at her feet. It had been entertaining, briefly. 'This arrangement's not great for Mum either,' Nina continued. 'The idea is that she can slowly settle back into her own routine. She can't do that with me clucking around.'

'I'd enjoy watching you cluck around. Nina the

283

mother hen. Presumably Annette could spend the days at the Harbour Walk place. It's not like they turf her out at 10am.'

'She doesn't want to do that. If she'd normally be there anyway, that's one thing, but she's adamant that she wants to be home. I can't blame her and it's useful seeing how she manages.'

'It must be lovely to be able to spend time together.' Kate was from a happy family.

'Come on, Kate. You know that's true only in very small moderation.'

'Get your own place. If you're sure you're not coming back to London any time soon, rent an Airbnb. There must be loads in that part of the world. I'll get Jonah to do some googling. He'll enjoy that.'

Nina was dubious. 'It will need to be nearby and accept dogs,' she said. 'Colin doesn't seem to be in any hurry to come and fetch Neville.'

Colin had been back in England for a fortnight. Nina had given it a day before ringing him. He'd had a brilliant time. Now work was catching up with him, a new commission. If Nina didn't mind, could Neville stay with her a few more days? It was going to be tricky to find time to get to Cornwall. Nina would be coming home soon, he presumed. (Colin was good at presuming.) It would be OK with Colin, and he was sure with Neville, if the dog extended his seaside holiday.

'To be fair to Colin,' Kate said, 'you do appear to enjoy having Neville. Jonah says he's all you can talk about.'

'Does he, indeed?'

'He feels vindicated. He's always known you needed

a dog. It makes sense, though. Getting a rental place. If you're sure you're staying down there for the duration.'

And so it was that Nina and Neville moved into a large one-storey annex to one of the grand houses on the main road up from the town. It had been built as a granny flat by the well-spoken couple who checked her in. The granny, who was really a great aunt, was in long-term care. The annex had been renamed the Holiday Box, with planning permission to rent it out. There was a big garden and hospitable dogs that were delighted to welcome Neville into their pack. It was less than ten minutes' walk from her mother's house. There was a minimum stay of one month. As Jonah said when he told her about it, that was better than having to worry about being bundled out too soon.

*

Once Nina and Neville had their own space, the new routine kicked in. Nina left Annette at home on her own for longer periods each day. They worked out what she could do with one fully functioning arm (make a cup of tea) and what was still off limits (go upstairs – although the physio, who it turned out Annette had known for years, said it would only be a few days now that the cast was coming off and now that Petroc had fitted a rail on the other wall from the banister). She couldn't walk confidently to the shops yet, not on her own, but she could unpack groceries delivered by men who reversed beeping vans up the narrow street.

'You can go home, Nina,' her mother said frequently. 'As you can see, I can manage perfectly well.' Nina chose to interpret 'home' as the holiday rental and not back to London.

Neville would come with Nina to collect Annette in the mornings. He'd stay at the house until he became too much of a nuisance. Then Nina would walk him and take him back to the Holiday Box to hose off seawater. After that, it was up to Annette whether Nina returned to her house, and whether Neville came too. The first couple of times she left him behind, Nina was worried he'd wreak havoc. She came back to find everything in order. He was calmer here than in London. She wondered if it was the sea air.

Chapter forty-nine

'I'm going to start as I mean to go on,' her mother announced when the last of her bags were in the house. 'First I'm going to unpack.' She insisted on carrying things to her bedroom by herself. Nina forced herself to stay in the kitchen and not watch. Neville had hopped into his car seat as normal that morning and it only occurred to Nina now that it would have been better not to bring him, not today. She held onto his collar. He sat rigid, listening as anxiously as she was, ready to jump into action at the first sound of a crash. He liked to make himself useful.

'Honestly, darling, I could tell you were both holding your breath,' her mother said when she was safely downstairs.

'You can't really blame us. You don't have to be carrying stuff.'

'Of course I do. Laundry. A cup of tea. Do you know Petroc or Chris brought me a cup of tea every morning? A girl could get used to that level of service.'

Girl. It put Nina's teeth on edge. 'I can come and do that in the morning if you like. Or stay over, given that it's your first night at home.'

'What would be the point of that?'

'To be sure you're OK.'

'We've practised enough, Nina.' That was true. They'd rehearsed everything. Annette climbing in and out of the bath (fully clothed, they didn't need to be too realistic), holding on to the grab handles that Petroc had installed. Annette opening the front and back doors. Loading the washing machine. Assembling a meal that didn't need a lot of chopping. Turning the oven on and off. 'There's going to be a first night on my own at home. It might as well be today.'

'I could leave you Neville.'

'Thank you, darling. I didn't know he had assistance dog superpowers.'

'He's company. And he'd bark if anything went wrong. Probably.'

'He's a happy creature,' Annette said. 'That social worker was right about that. He's been rather good for you.'

'Her theory was that he'd be good for you. You're the patient.'

'Not for much longer! I do like him, and he has Petroc wrapped around his paw. The only animal allowed in the building unless they're dead and being cooked. How much longer have you got him?'

'Monday. Colin messaged this morning. He's asked me to ask Petroc if he can stay there. Hopefully you'll get to see Neville's beach boy act before he goes home.'

'One thing at a time. I'm going to get used to the house first and save outdoors until the spring's more established.'

'I wonder what you'll make of Colin,' Nina said. 'He's quite unusual.'

'Jonah's told me a lot about him. He's fascinated by his job. He did try to tell me what it is. I didn't really understand.'

'He works for himself. Computer animations. He's given up explaining it to me too. He and Jonah can natter for hours about customer bases and whatnot. Colin and I talk about more normal things. Dogs. Houses. Our friends.'

'It was about time you started to make friends.'

'So you've been telling me all these years.'

'Activities. That's the secret.'

'And yet I met Colin by stopping what I was doing to help him out.'

'You've always been a kind person. You take after your father.'

'You have your moments too.'

'Thank you. I think that was a compliment.'

'It was.'

'Splendid.'

This could be a moment, Nina thought. They could have a proper conversation about their lives. Hopes, dreams. The loss of their husbands. Instead, she said she'd take Neville for his walk while it wasn't raining and pick up something for lunch on the way back.

Chapter fifty

When Neville was tired of the beach, Nina left him in the Holiday Box and went back to Harbour Walk. Chris let her in. People were playing backgammon on beautiful wooden boards. Petroc was out on a job somewhere. 'I know you're not open officially until Easter,' Nina said. 'I wondered if you could make an exception for a friend. Neville's owner. It would only be one night, next Monday.'

'Get him to call us. Or I can message him. I'll do that now if you've got the number? *Mi casa* and all that. You got time for a brew?'

She said hello to the backgammon players and followed Chris into the kitchen.

'Thank you again for putting my mother up,' she said. 'And indeed my friend.'

'Builder's? Or herbal? I've got lemon and ginger or chamomile or mint.'

'Lemon and ginger, please. Mum was very impressed with the cup of tea in the morning routine.'

'All part of the service. Also checking up on her. Don't tell her.'

'Wouldn't dream of it. I've been trying to persuade her to let me stay over, just for her first night home. She won't hear of it.' Nina knew she hadn't tried very hard.

'That would only postpone things.'

'That's what I told myself. Although I'm not quite sure what we're postponing.'

'Annette's lived on her own for how long?'

'Forever. Since my father died. She claims to like it.'

'A lot of people do. It wouldn't suit me.'

'I'm not sure yet how much it suits me,' Nina said. 'It's funny with Mum. She's so into organising people and talking, always on her own terms. She doesn't want anyone to stay with her. Except Jonah and that's only for holidays.'

'She's used to her own space.'

'She didn't even want me staying in the house. She'd suggested it, but once it happened, she got very twitchy.'

'You got round that with the holiday let.'

'That was Kate's idea. My not-quite daughter-in-law. Mum was very happy when I told her.'

'It seems to me that what you are postponing is seeing if Annette can manage on her own.'

'Yes. She managed here, didn't she?'

'Yes.'

'And she doesn't seem to be struggling, memory and so on? Petroc started talking about care homes, giving them a plug. I did wonder if he was hinting?'

'You saw as much of her as we did,' Chris said. 'She's not noticeably muddled. She didn't leave the shower running or anything like that. Physically she's frailer than a few months ago. More than the broken arm. She's a bit wobbly on her feet.'

'It's a pity her house isn't more suitable.'

'Suitable for what?'

'I don't know. For being old in, I suppose.'

'You're looking for things to worry about,' said Chris. 'Unless you would actually move in with her, which from what you have both said is not going to happen, then the only thing to do is see how she gets on at home and if it doesn't work out, cross that bridge.'

'Cross that bridge to where, though?'

'There'll be somewhere. At a price. If you can afford it, there are some good places round here. All those baby boomers who retired here and forgot to die before they got old. You could go and visit a few of the homes. See how the land lies.'

'That's not a bad idea.'

'Happy to be of service. Maybe not mention that to Annette either, though.'

A casual drive round local care homes couldn't do any harm. *You must reach an age*, Nina thought, *when people start going behind your back. If you are lucky enough to have anyone who cares enough to engage in small subterfuge. You must reach an age where a morning cup of tea is less about kindness and more to make sure you haven't fallen out of bed in the night, or that, if you have it, might not be too late to call for help.*

*

She left Chris and returned to her mother's house in time for a soup and sourdough late lunch, both from an overpriced bakery in the main street.

'I would have scrambled some eggs,' her mother said. 'I am perfectly capable.'

'They'll do another day. I had to pop into town and this sounded interesting.' Leek and celery wouldn't have been her first choice. 'Healthy, too.'

'Thank you. I gather Colin is taking my room at Harbour Walk.'

'How on earth do you know that?'

'Jonah told me.'

For a minute, Nina thought her mother was getting Jonah and Chris confused. It turned out there was a rational, if convoluted, explanation. Jonah had indeed been first with the news. He and Kate had stayed in Nina's house overnight ('he didn't tell you in case you made a fuss and he said that also he knew you'd be pleased he was keeping an eye on it for you'). They bumped into Colin in the street, or rather Colin made a beeline for them and spelled out the arrangements in rather a lot of detail.

'Jonah felt a bit overexplained to, so he rang me to see if I could shed any light,' Annette continued. 'We had a very nice chat. He told me not to let you go all Florence Nightingale. He put on that serious voice he uses when he's being a proper grown-up. That wouldn't go well, Granny. He understands us much better than we do.'

'I hope you put him straight,' Nina said. 'Did he say why he was staying at mine?'

'Something about the carbon monoxide alarm going off. You should talk to him about it.'

'I would have, if he'd asked me.' Carbon monoxide. Life was so full of hazards.

'He shouldn't have to ask to stay at your house. It's no different to you moving in here while I was in hospital.'

'As I recall it, that was your suggestion. No squandering money on a B&B.'

'Well, maybe Jonah doesn't want to squander any more money on rent. I rather got the impression he's hoping to move back home for longer.'

'Of course they can stay as long as they want. Carbon monoxide? It doesn't bear thinking about.'

'Don't fuss, Nina. The alarm did its job. It works out well all round. Since you're not showing any signs of going home. They can look after the house for you.'

'I'll call Jonah in a bit.'

'Unless you do want to go home, of course? You can't hide down here forever. I am perfectly fine now. As you can see.'

She didn't look perfectly fine. Or did she? It was hard to tell. She'd dripped a little bit of soup down her front, leaving a green splodge on her cardigan. Dinner medals. That was what Martin had told Jonah, a messy and enthusiastic eater whose school shirts were permanently stained by tomato ketchup. 'We don't need to decide anything yet,' Nina said.

'We don't have to decide anything. It's up to you, Nina. Don't let's have sourdough again. The crusts are too difficult.'

Chapter fifty-one

After lunch, Nina tried again to suggest that they went out. Annette said she wanted to rest. Instead, Nina took Neville back to the beach. The rain had held off. It was a blowy, grey, nothingy sort of day. She found herself wondering what would have happened if the men hadn't died.

Nina and Martin had been together a few months when his father killed himself. A showy sort of suicide (*Selfish too*, Nina thought. *That poor train driver, how would you ever get over something like that?*). Martin was furious. He blamed his mother. She'd interfered, like she always did, trying to push doctors and therapists and various crackpot hokum theories his way. Religion too. According to Martin, his father was never going to swallow all that spiritual hogwash. That hadn't stopped his mum going on and on about the blessing of being alive. The beauty of the earth. She hadn't been able to accept that his father was ill.

Somehow, Nina had got so swept up in trying (failing) to stop Martin hating his mother, she barely had time to think about anyone else. Her own father had died undramatically in his sleep the previous year. Heart failure, which outraged Nina because he had such an enormous heart. They mourned for ages, proper stop-all-the-clocks grief, but you have to get over things eventually. Nina fell in love (a great distraction). Annette sold the family home and was finalising a move to Cornwall, where she had friends from her art school days. She was coping well. Nina was glad she didn't have to worry about her mum while she helped Martin deal with the shock and the copious administrative fallout from a death that involved police, coroners, and health and safety inspectors. She neglected Annette for weeks. Months. It made it much worse a few years later when Martin died his technicolour death, flashing blue lights and blood, and Annette rode magnificently to the rescue. 'Look at me!' Annette seemed to be saying. 'This is the correct way to support someone who is grieving.'

Martin and Annette had disliked each other even before they'd been introduced. They were both prone to prejudice anyway, and Martin's animosity towards his own mother made things worse. Annette wasn't happy either. Nina couldn't have found anyone less to her mother's taste if she'd tried. 'I know these public-school types,' Annette had said, sniffing as Nina rattled off a potted biography. When Nina asked her who she'd met who'd been to public school, she muttered about all the worst politicians and changed the subject.

'Greenham Common?' Martin had laughed. He wouldn't have pegged Nina for a flower-power child. She seemed too sensible for that. Nina never minded being called sensible. It was an underrated quality.

Martin and Annette met a few times before the marriage. The first was in a curry place. You could tell a lot about someone from the way they approached curry, according to Annette. Evidently, there was a wrong way and a right way. Enthusiastically ordering something from the less familiar reaches of the long menu and inviting everyone to dip naan bread into the sauce was the wrong way.

When it was clear there were going to be wedding bells, Martin had taken Nina's mother out for afternoon tea. Annette hated the idea. Doilies and a pianist. White aprons. Martin wanted to reassure her that their different backgrounds were nothing to worry about. Annette had been furious. He thinks he's better than you, Nina. He wants to move you to a better part of London. A Leafy Suburb. (Nina loved that leafy suburb.)

The problem was all in Annette's head. She wanted a bohemian daughter. A classless society was all well and good but only within boundaries. Poverty would be worse, of course, but marrying money would only spell trouble.

Then there was his personality. He was forever trying new things. You only live once, he'd say. You have to pack in as much as you can. Nina had often thought that it was Martin's unselective enthusiasm that her mother struggled with most. Of course it's your choice, darling, Annette would say. You're a quiet person. I worry for you that all that rushing at life will get tiresome.

Rushing at life. The phrase came back to Nina as she watched Neville skitter across the beach, stopping as he always did where the first ripples hit the sand before leaping into the cold sea. So much energy. It was strange to think that his life was already half over. Hers too, of course, more than halfway through. She was sorry that the happiest part was already behind her.

Chapter fifty-two

Back at the Holiday Box, the owner's dogs were playing in the garden. They came to help while she rinsed seawater and sand off Neville with the garden tap, then herded him into their game. This involved a lot of ear-biting and barging and mercifully little barking. It would give her half an hour's peace. She went inside and fired up her laptop.

There were three emails she had been saving for when she had time to think. The first was called 'Volunteering?' from Lina. Colin's party was a lifetime ago. Now winter was over, things were revving up again. If Nina wanted to get stuck in, she'd be very welcome. Only would she please make contact so that they knew if she was still interested?

The second was from Dima. It was a lot of quiz questions from the sessions she'd missed ('You can see we lack your flair!') and a brief message. He'd possibly be in Cornwall the week after Easter visiting a client. If she was still there, he could swing by.

The third was from Niall. He hoped she had found working with him helpful. If she wanted to renew her membership, please would she let him know. She'd forgotten he called his clients 'members' of his therapy practice. Some claptrap to do with fostering a sense of belonging in one's life. The email was only lightly personalised. Niall felt there was still more to explore. He name-checked Martin, Annette, Jonah, Kate and Neville. However, if she wanted to discontinue, please would she also consider completing a short survey or posting a Google review.

Dima was the easiest. He would see some of Cornwall at last. He could stay an extra day or two after dealing with his client. Do some painting. Sky and light. Bluebells on clifftops. 'I'm not sure yet if I'll still be here. I'll let you know,' she wrote. 'Your clients are probably putting you up. If not, check out this place, friends of mine, and they are wheelchair accessible.' She ignored the voice at the back of her mind that told her that no one in this day and age travels to see a client in person. His ulterior motives were up to him.

She sent a much longer reply to Lina, the volunteer-hunter. Reading it back, she thought the sentiments might have been more appropriate for Niall. 'I am absolutely torn,' she wrote. 'If only Cornwall wasn't so far away. I know I can't put my life on hold forever. But I can't abandon my mother. I will quite understand if you find someone else. If it's possible to keep things open a little longer, I would like to know more. It would be nice to have something to look forward to back in London,' she wrote, before crossing that sentence out.

She sent the shortest message to Niall. Can we book a phone or online session? I am not ready to fill in your client satisfaction survey quite yet. He could knock himself out reading between the lines.

Neville was still playing in the garden. They'd progressed to a form of leapfrog, each of the dogs taking it in turns to jump over the others. Leapdog. She saved the feeble pun to tell her mother. She put his water bowl outside in case he got thirsty and left the door ajar so he could come back in when he was ready without barking the street down. She was going to miss him when Colin spirited him back to London.

*

Chris had given her the names of care homes that housed, or had housed, regulars at Harbour Walk. It couldn't do any harm to look and maybe make some speculative enquiries. They looked less depressing than when she had first googled a few weeks ago, although at least one of them was something she'd looked at before. She made some phone calls. Without exception, the people who answered were lovely. They'd be more than happy to welcome her and show her around – her mother too, of course – with no obligation. We do have a waiting list, one of them said, but it's never very long.

It was something to think about next week, when Neville had gone home, and when they would have a better idea of how Annette was managing away from the safe haven of Harbour Walk.

Chapter fifty-three

The new week brought surprises. On Monday, Annette decided that this was the day she wanted to join Nina and Neville on their beachy walk. By now, they had made a few gentle forays to dull indoor destinations. The pharmacy. The newsagents. The bakery where Nina had bought the soup and bread that her mother hadn't liked. It sold nice food too, Annette said, including a vegan ginger cake that Sarah would eat, if she dropped in unexpectedly, which she apparently often used to do before Nina was at the house all the time. People were funny about intruding on family, apparently.

Getting ready was slow. Her mother needed better shoes than the slip-on loafers she'd been wearing in the street. Her fingers still weren't working properly. She couldn't tie her shoelaces. The slip-ons had been a hasty online purchase. Proper old-lady shoes, Annette said. She wore them rather than asking for help. No good for the beach, however. They argued for a bit about whether unwillingness to let Nina tie the laces on her walking shoes trumped desire to get some proper sea air.

Neville's joy at having two companions to shake

seawater over was uncontainable. The fine weather had brought several dog walkers out. Two or three greeted Neville and Nina by name. 'You've been making friends, I see,' her mother said. She didn't sound altogether happy.

Nina wondered if she was jealous, or perhaps just surprised. 'A dog will do that for you,' she said. 'People always say that. I didn't realise how true it was until this one came along.' She patted Neville who had wandered over to find out why they were walking so slowly.

'It's a pity you're handing This One back.'

'He's not mine to keep.'

'Try telling him that.' Neville was cavorting several feet in front of them, stopping every few seconds to make sure they were noticing him. If Nina so much as moved a hand or her head, he came running back, tail wagging. 'What are you going to do now, Nina?'

'Shove him into Colin's car and wave them both off with a happy smile. I'm not going to cry.'

'I don't mean about Neville. What are you going to do about everything?'

'Everything?'

'I've been watching you. All this endless fussing over me. Spending weeks down here, which you don't need to do, not on my account. You're missing home.'

'What makes you say that?'

'It's what you talk about. Jonah and Kate. Colin. And this Dima character. He of the pub quiz and the art and the anarchist son and the cleverly designed apartment. He comes up rather a lot, I've noticed.'

'The son is hardly an anarchist.'

'And now Jonah has moved back into your house. You can get your old life back.'

'It's still his home, as you were so keen to remind me. And it's temporary. While they look for somewhere else.'

Nina and Jonah had had a long discussion. Not discussion. Monologue. The landlord's delay in fixing the boiler was a last straw. It wasn't as if it was even going to cost him anything. It was a new boiler so almost certainly under guarantee. If he'd acted when Kate had first rung him, complaining that the heating kept cutting out, then maybe it wouldn't have come to this. There was more. Jonah hadn't wanted to admit it before. Nina had been right about the flat. It was too small and up too many stairs and too noisy. The windows didn't fit properly. Also, the downstairs neighbours had a baby. The hallway was always cluttered up with prams and Huggies, and they put notices on the door saying, 'please be quiet on the stairs', 'please don't wake Baby'. ('They named her Baby, Mum. What kind of people call their baby Baby?')

There was a break clause in the rental agreement. If Nina didn't mind, Jonah and Kate could stay at hers while they plotted their next move. Also, Jonah said, that was better for Nina than leaving the house empty while she looked after Granny.

'I don't understand why you're delaying going home,' Annette said.

'I'm not going back to London until I am sure you can manage.'

'You being here is stopping me from managing. Always there to give me a lift or go with me to the shops or to take me for a walk. Tie my shoes. You're going to be even worse when the dog's gone. At least he's a distraction.'

They'd reached the far end of the beach. Nina was sorry that her mother hadn't enjoyed it more. She didn't seem to take much pleasure in the sea or the gulls or the fuzzy white flowers that were beginning to show on the low cliffs. She didn't want to stop at the café. They could get a perfectly good cup of tea back home, and in any case there was rain in the air. On the way back, she didn't want to talk either. At the house, she made herself a Marmite sandwich (Nina had to open the jar) and went unsteadily upstairs to lie down. Nina thought she was sulking. She couldn't work out why.

Chapter fifty-four

The day's next surprise came in the early afternoon. Nina's phone rang. 'We're at Harbour Walk! Come and find us!' Colin. He must have set off early, she said, and sure enough they'd been up before the lark to beat the traffic, and the roads – he gave a lot of detail about the route – had been clear and here they were.

'Who's we?'

'Linda. Didn't she tell you she was coming?'

'I've not spoken to her for a few days. Do you want to come over? I'm still at Mum's but I can meet you at my place. It's only about twenty minutes' walk from you, or there's parking. Neville's not altogether welcome at the B&B.'

'Chris has sorted us out afternoon tea. He thought you and your mum might want to join us. I can catch up with Neville later.'

'Mum's asleep, I think. I'll check.'

Nina rang off and went quietly up the stairs. Her mother was awake, lying fully dressed on top of a bright yellow bedspread, Radio 4 chuntering gently in the background.

'Don't you think it's odd that he doesn't want to see the dog straightaway?' Annette said as Nina explained the afternoon's plan. 'Fishy.'

'Another hour won't make any difference,' Nina said. 'Not after all this time.'

'I feel sorry for Neville,' Annette said. 'The wretched animal must already be confused by his recent lifestyle changes.'

'Neville will be fine,' Nina said. She felt sorrier for herself. 'Do you want to join us for afternoon tea? Chris asked for you specially.'

'I'm tired, darling. That walk this morning has taken it out of me. You go and enjoy yourself. We can regroup later.'

Neville was asleep in the corner of Annette's kitchen. Nina stirred him and walked him round the corner to the Holiday Box. There was no sign of the resident pack. 'Sorry about this,' she said. 'You're going to be home alone for a bit. If you're good, there'll be a nice surprise for you later.' He sat in his basket without protest, watching as she hung up his lead.

She found Colin in the lounge at Harbour Walk. He was deep in conversation with two of the regular visitors. Linda was nowhere in sight. 'Don't say you're going to steal him away,' one of the women said to Nina. 'It's not often we get a new person to talk to.'

Colin got up and hugged her. 'Nina!'

'Don't sound so surprised. Hello, Colin. I see you've made yourself at home.'

'How can you not? This place is amazing.'

Nina remembered how impressed she'd been that

first evening when Petroc had taken pity on her. And the myriad kindnesses over the long weeks when Annette was camped out in the disabled suite. 'It's a lovely spot,' she said. 'It's good to see you, Colin. There's a lot to catch up on.' She turned to the two Harbour Walkers. 'There's no hurry, so please don't feel you need to leave on our account.'

Chris appeared from the kitchen with half a ginger cake. It looked familiar. He confirmed that it was indeed the same cake Annette had bought the other day. Petroc had popped in over the weekend to see how Annette was getting on, while Nina was out somewhere. It was funny her mother hadn't mentioned it.

The five of them sat on two sofas around a low coffee table and talked about Australia. Or rather Colin talked about Australia with one of the women, who turned out to be Australian. Nina hadn't noticed the slight accent until now. Colin found out more about the two women than Nina had in over a month of wandering in and out of Harbour Walk.

At last the women left, helping Chris carry teacups into the kitchen on their way out. 'You made it then,' Nina said. He looked well, she thought. A bit thinner. 'The jet lag's worn off by now?'

'Right as rain. How's your mum doing?'

'Better than we thought a few weeks ago.'

'So you'll be coming home soon?'

'Still playing it by ear.'

'And Neville's been no trouble? I do really appreciate you looking after him.'

'He's been no trouble. He took a few days to settle. He

likes it now. We both do. He'll be pleased to see you. We can go and surprise him.'

'Can we wait for Linda?'

'Linda. Of course. How come she's with you?'

'To share the driving, mainly. And she fancied a break. You can ask her yourself. She's only popped out to stretch her legs. We've had a long trip down.'

With his audience of strangers gone, Colin seemed subdued, at least by Colin standards. Nina didn't understand why he wasn't rushing to see Neville or coming up with grandiose plans to explore Cornwall in the twenty hours before he headed back to London. She'd braced herself to be shown lots of photos of his Australia trip. So far, his phone remained undisturbed.

He brightened up when Linda arrived, bearing plastic souvenirs. 'For Gus,' she said. 'A plastic Cornish pisky. Environmentally dodgy and culturally exploitative. So much to complain about.'

'Hello, Linda. Your hair is amazing.' The limp grey plait had gone, leaving a complicated swingy bob, shot through with unnatural colours. Nina had never known Linda take any interest in her appearance.

'It was a whim. An expensive whim. I was suddenly sick of looking at the same thing every day. I'm not sure it suits me. It's been good for the bathroom drains. No more long hair clogging the plughole.'

'That's a motivation they don't include in those "new hair, new you" articles.'

'New hair, same me.'

'I'm glad to hear it. You didn't tell me you were coming with Colin.'

'Long story. Call it another whim. I hope you don't mind?'

'It's a lovely surprise. Can we all go out to dinner? There's a good pub. Neville can come too. I'll need to check with Mum, of course.'

'Sounds like a plan. Where is Neville?'

'At my place. Colin and I were waiting for you before heading round there.'

The three of them set off along the harbour and up the slope towards the newer part of town. Colin talked, picking out features and asking questions that Nina couldn't answer. The street names all start 'Tre'. Does that mean something in Cornish? When was St Piran's day; it must be around now or were there always lots of flags? Why is Cornishware blue and white? Didn't Nina think it was interesting that she'd been in Cornwall all this time and knew so little about it? It was as if she'd only scratched the surface.

They debated the best way to break the news to Neville that Colin had come to find him. When they got to Nina's street, she left the others in the little park on the corner. 'My holiday flat is quite a small space,' she said. 'Better to bring him here where there's less to break if he gets overexcited.' She wanted one last outing with Neville. One last chance to pretend they belonged to each other.

Neville, already overjoyed to see her, broke into an ecstatic little dance as she took the lead off its hook. She dawdled attaching it to his collar and walked as slowly as he would let her. Her eyes were running in the wind. *He's not your dog,* she reminded herself. *It's your own fault that you've got so fond of him.*

Linda met them at the park gate. 'Colin thought we shouldn't spring two people on him at once. He's over there.' She pointed at a bench in the far corner of the park. Neville sniffed at Linda's shoes, wagging his tail. 'Not spectacularly excited, are you?' she said. 'I always suspected you loved Muddy more than you love me. Let's roll out the big guns.'

She took Neville's lead from Nina and headed towards Colin. After a few paces, Neville dropped to the ground in a reasonable imitation of a sheepdog plotting its next move. His body tensed. 'Who's that?' Linda asked. Neville moved forward a few feet, then dropped down again.

'This might take a while,' Nina said. An image of Neville straining to reach her when she rescued him from the kennels popped into her mind. She knew it wasn't fair to make comparisons. 'Maybe if you let him off the lead, Linda. Then he can go at his own pace.'

Colin was practically in touching distance before Neville made up his mind, launching into a clumsy sprint and hurling his front paws into Colin's ample lap. Colin bent forward to kiss the top of his head. Neville ran from Colin to where Nina and Linda were standing and back again, jumping at all three of them, before coming to a stop at Nina's feet. Nobody spoke and nobody barked. As reunions went, it was a strangely muted affair.

Chapter fifty-five

Despite two pieces of ginger cake, Colin was hungry. They arranged that he, Linda and Neville would go straight to the pub while Nina went to check on her mother. She found Annette at her kitchen table. 'You can come with us,' Nina said, confident of a refusal. 'If you're not too tired.'

'I think I should,' Annette said. 'You can drive us. It will be a chance to meet your friends. Only if I am not cramping your style, of course.'

There was no right answer to that.

Nina had grown fond of the pub. The landlord knew her and Neville by name. Neville's favourite table was by the real flame gas fire. He would lie there irrespective of whether Nina was nearby or at another table altogether.

This evening, Colin and Linda had got the fire table. They both stood up as Nina walked in, with Annette behind her. Neville stayed put, guarding his place. He rolled over onto his back, his tail thumping, displaying what was left of his genitals.

'What an absolute pleasure,' Colin said to Annette as Nina introduced them. 'I'm so happy to meet you.' Old-fashioned charm. 'And this is Nina's other friend, Linda.'

'Imagine Nina having two friends,' Annette said. She was a lot perkier than earlier. 'Until recently, she didn't have any.'

'You'll have to forgive my mother. She's very direct.'

'Direct must run in the family. Nina has many friends, Annette – may I call you Annette?'

'You may. Nina and I have led such separate lives. I need you and Linda to tell me all about her.'

'All in good time,' Colin said. 'We want to know about you. I've heard quite a few stories already. Chris was telling me that you're the brains behind Harbour Walk.'

'Hardly the brains.' Annette looked pleased. 'I like to think my ideas helped the social aspects get off the ground.'

Nina watched fascinated as Colin drew information from Annette, flattering her with admiring comments. He had a way of making people talk about themselves.

'That's enough about me,' Annette said as the barman came to clear away their main courses. It had taken a round of drinks and hearty portions of fish and chips to exhaust the topic. 'Can you two help me out? I'm trying to convince Nina to go home. And now I've met her friends, I can see that she'd have more fun than she can stuck here with an old woman like me.'

'Not this again.'

'This again.'

'From the little I've seen, I can quite see the attraction of Cornwall,' Linda said. 'I'd stay longer myself if I could.'

'You need a reason to be in a place,' said Annette. 'There are too many people who wander here because it's

312

pretty. They've watched too many sea shanty movies and then they don't know what to do with themselves.'

'You made the move,' Nina said. 'Never looked back.'

'It made sense. I still had friends from my art college days. I had roots. A reason for being here. And once I was here, I made an effort to get to know people.'

'Nina's here for a reason,' Colin said. 'And who can blame her? Not everyone gets the chance to hang out with their mum. I can't believe Nina's been keeping you to herself for so long.'

'Hang out with?' Annette's lip curled.

'That's what people do. Nina and Jonah. Or Linda here and her son, Gus. Always laughing. Families enjoying each other's company. You can't beat it. I'm only recently back from seeing mine. Australia.'

'That's a long way to go for a visit. Nina normally only makes it as far as Devon.'

'I was only able to go because of Nina. She's the only person Neville will allow to babysit him. He worships her.'

'I've noticed.'

'Back home, he spends as much time at her house as he does at mine.'

'More. At least recently,' Nina said. 'It's going to be weird him not being around.'

'You'll be back soon enough, won't you, Nina?' Linda said. 'I don't agree with you, Annette, that people need a reason to be in a place. If you're a free agent like Nina, why not take a few weeks out? That's what I'd do if I wasn't tied to my job and my everything else. We'll still be there for her when she gets back.'

Linda was looking tired. Her bright hair didn't suit

her. It couldn't compensate for the drawn expression. 'At the moment, my house is full of Jonah,' Nina said. 'My little granny annex is very appealing. Not to mention all that mother-daughter hanging out we are still to enjoy.'

Neville was getting restless. It was their sign that the evening was over. 'We won't all fit in my car,' Nina said. 'His car seat takes the space of two people. I'll take Mum home first and come back for you.'

'We can walk,' Linda said. 'Work off some of that food.'

Outside the pub, they bundled Annette and Neville (after a quick pee against four different parts of the fence) into Nina's car. Neville curled himself into his seat, not watching as Colin and Linda headed down the hill.

Nina expected comment from her mother on the way home, but Annette was quiet until they were almost at the house. 'They're nice,' she said, 'and fond of you.'

'Of course. They're my friends.'

'Fond of each other too.'

'As I said, we're friends. We all get on well.'

'I'm glad,' Annette said. 'Friends are important. More so than family in the long run. Don't neglect them for long, Nina.'

Chapter fifty-six

Nina invited Linda and Colin to breakfast before they started the long drive back to London. She'd collected doggy belongings on the sofa, ready to load into Colin's car. Neville pulled the dog wetsuit onto the floor. He refused to wear it but had adopted it as a favourite chewing toy, leaving trails of rubber crumbs everywhere. When Colin and Linda arrived and squeezed themselves round the tiny table, Neville got up only briefly before resuming his steady destruction of the wetsuit.

After they'd eaten, they carried everything outside, Neville dancing between them. 'That's a lot of luggage for one dog,' Linda said.

'I got a bit carried away. He's not used most of it. I've left the harness and the dog seat in my car, Colin, in case you need me to mind Neville when I'm back in London.'

'You don't know when that will be?'

'I want to make absolutely sure Mum will be OK before I commit to anything.' She'd said this so often, she wasn't even sure it was true anymore.

'Which involves what, exactly?'

'A couple more outpatients appointments. Physio. And a bit of waiting and seeing.'

'You can't wait forever. Your mum's right about not putting things on hold.'

'You were right, too, Linda. What you were saying last night about me being a free agent. I don't have anything tying me to anywhere. For now, I want to be here. I'll come back to London soon. If only to visit my pal here.' Neville had come to stand beside her, pressing against her leg.

'Provided we know where your priorities lie,' Colin said. 'We'd better make tracks. Leave you to get back to your mum. Come on, young man. Time to hit the road.'

Neville pressed himself closer to Nina's side. 'Nev! Silly sausage! Time to go home.' Colin pulled gently on Neville's collar. Neville whined. Colin lifted him up and plonked him down in the back of the car. Neville jumped out again and ran back into Nina's little apartment, wedging himself behind the sofa.

'He's resisting arrest,' Nina said. 'Maybe he thinks you're taking him back to the kennels.'

'Not helpful, Nina.'

'No. But possibly true. He'll be OK when you get him home, I'm sure. If you and I shift the sofa, Linda can grab him.' She bumped one end of the sofa across the floor.

'That went well,' Linda said. Neville had wriggled free and was now careering round the garden, barking. 'Are there any more of those sausages from breakfast? We could bribe him.'

'Let me talk to him.' Nina walked slowly across the garden and sat on a damp chair on the patio. She waved at her landlady through the kitchen window. 'Neville?' He seemed to think about it for a moment, then came and sat in front of her, resting his head on her knee. *The problem with this arrangement is I don't speak dog,* Nina thought. One of the problems. The blind adoration in Neville's eyes was overwhelming.

Linda came over and pulled up another chair. 'Colin's waiting in the car,' she said. 'Says he can't bear to watch.'

'We can try again in a minute. Poor Neville. He must be very confused.'

'He doesn't look confused to me. He wants to stay with you. It's not surprising really, given how much time he spent with you, even before Colin waltzed off to Australia.'

'Colin loves Neville.'

'He's also defeated by him. How time-consuming he is. That was the word he used. Not exactly a declaration of unconditional love. He was fretting on the way down here about how he's going to juggle Neville and his work projects without you on hand to babysit. He feels horribly guilty too.'

'Sounds like you had a proper heart to heart.'

'It's a long drive. You must have noticed how quiet he's been since we got here. Apart from when he was performing for your mother.'

'She was very taken with him. Singing his praises. Mum hasn't always taken to my friends. He did well.'

'He's a lovely man.' Nina noticed the tone. 'Brilliant with people. He's also a selfish man who can't quite be arsed to look after his dog properly. You know that's why he's delayed coming down here?'

'I assumed he was tired after all that travel and had things to catch up on. And it's not like I'm in a rush to let our furry friend go.' She patted Neville's sides.

'You should tell Colin that. Ask if he'd like to leave Neville with you for a bit longer. Until you come home.'

'I can't steal his dog.'

'You'd be fostering him. Like you have for these last few weeks. Neville's already voted with his feet. His paws.'

'Then you'll have driven down for nothing.'

'Not for nothing, Nina. We came to see you too. Let me fetch Colin and we can see what he thinks. Although maybe we can go back inside. You can have too much sea air.'

Nina put the kettle on. Neville hovered in the garden looking wary, but when the heavens opened, he scuttled inside and settled under the table.

Colin and Linda sat back in the same seats they'd been in for breakfast. They talked about Neville and whether Muddy was missing their walks together. Neville joined in with other dogs, Nina said, but he hadn't got a special friend. Now that he was staying a bit longer, they could work on that.

'Speaking of special friends,' Linda said. There was something else Nina probably needed to know. If she hadn't already guessed.

Before they left, Colin sat on the floor (no mean achievement) reaching under the table to pull a squirming Neville into a hug. Then Colin and Linda were gone, promises of see you soon carried away on the wind.

Chapter fifty-seven

'What did I tell you? You're acting as if it was a surprise,' her mother said.

'It is a surprise.'

'Then you haven't been paying attention. It was all he could talk about last night. Linda the feminist lawyer. Linda and her peculiar son.'

'Gus isn't peculiar. He's an activist. You'd get on.'

'Linda's courageous hair. Very arty, I must say. Linda's dog. Linda's dog's friendship with his dog. You're quite the matchmaker, aren't you, Neville?'

'I didn't notice any of that. We spent most of the evening talking about you.'

'As I said. You weren't paying attention. Do you know you got up six times to check on Neville? I counted. Colin didn't go over once. You could see he wasn't interested in taking him back.'

'That's not fair. It was Linda's idea to leave him behind. And Neville's too. You should have seen the fuss he made when they tried to get him into the car.'

'You got what you wanted.'

'I didn't want anything.'

'You never do. Or if you do, you never say so. Not clearly enough, anyway. You wanted to prolong your holiday with Neville and now you're doing exactly that.'

'It's not a holiday.'

'Of course it's a holiday, Nina. A dinky holiday let by the sea. Walks on the beach. Tea and scones overlooking the harbour. No responsibility. You look well on it. But I have a feeling home is going to seem more attractive now.'

'Based on what, exactly?'

'Poor Dima will be on his own once Gus goes back to university.' Annette looked triumphant. 'I thought it was odd that Dima was going to come and see you. You obviously like him. You talk about him such a lot.'

'Now you are being ridiculous.'

'Am I? I wonder.'

Annette was leaping to too many conclusions. She often did. She was right about Neville, of course. Nina had been dreading going back to life without him. This way she'd have him for longer, maybe as long as she'd be in Cornwall. In all likelihood, he'd still spend many nights at her house once she was back at home.

But Annette had read too much into what Colin and Linda had said about everything else. They had made a temporary arrangement. That was all. Dima and Linda hadn't separated. Not exactly. Everyone needed breathing space from time to time. It had been Dima's idea. Linda was staying with a friend. They'd see how they got on before having a proper discussion. Very civilised. Very lawyerly.

What about Gus, Nina had asked, surely you want to be there when he's home? Gus taking study leave was the only reason Linda agreed to take a break. Dima always said he could manage. He'd never had to try for more than a couple of days, and never with Muddy at home. Gus was going back after Easter. They'd cross that bridge later. It had all been quite sudden. They hadn't really thought anything through.

There was nothing going on. They'd only mentioned it to Nina because Jonah was living in her house, round the corner, so might notice that Colin had a woman staying. It wasn't a woman, Colin said. It was only Linda. That's how he thinks of me, Linda had said. Only Linda. There is nothing going on.

Chapter fifty-eight

'Colin's got a different dog. A brown one,' Jonah said. 'He's a fast worker.'

'That will be Muddy. He's Neville's bestie.' Nina didn't explain further. Jonah would work things out soon enough. Although if Muddy had moved in already, things must be more serious than they'd let on.

'He didn't introduce him. Just said that Neville was having such a lovely time with you, he'd decided to let him stay longer and that this other dog had stepped into the breach. Apparently, it's easier to manage than Neville. It's a drab-looking thing.'

'Don't be taken in. When he and Neville get together, it's mayhem. They drive Colin crazy.'

'Colin thought Granny was brilliant. No, magnificent, that was the word he used. I'll tell her he said that. She'll be pleased. He said that she looks very well and is very independent, better than he'd expected from what you'd been saying.' There was a short pause, as if he was working up to something. Sure enough. 'I suppose it means you'll want your house back? Although you're welcome to stay here with us, of course.'

'That's so thoughtful, darling. Very generous. I am welcome in my own home. It will always be your home, too. You don't have to move out again until you're ready, no matter when I come back.'

'Kate said you'd say that.'

'How is Kate?'

'Funny you should say that. She's right here.' Definitely working up to something. 'I'll put her on.'

'Nina! Hi.'

'Hello, darling. Not out tripping the light fantastic somewhere?'

'They're not using me this week. I've got some good news. We wanted you to be the first to know.'

For a minute, Nina thought it was going to be a baby. It was less dramatic than that. Also a tiny bit devastating. A new job. A proper job with a single organisation rather than being co-opted into different crews at short notice each month. Near Leeds.

'Leeds?'

'In Yorkshire.'

'I know where it is.' A long way away. 'I take it this is why you haven't rushed to find another London flat?'

'That and Jonah's sense of obligation to house-sit for his mother in a comfortable suburban house where someone else pays the bills.'

'Ever considerate.'

'That's Jonah to a tee. Tell me you're pleased for me, Nina. It'll be odd not being in London, but we love it up there. Halfway between both sets of parents. And the job's a real chance to get established somewhere I want to be.'

'Of course. I'm thrilled for you. Or I will be. When I get used to the idea. We'll have to have a proper celebration when I'm home. Now give me back to Jonah. I want to know what his grandmother's been telling him.' She needed to change the subject before she said anything important.

'You won't tell Granny, will you, Mum?' Jonah sounded uncharacteristically anxious. 'We want it to be our news.'

They really had told her first. 'My lips are sealed,' Nina said. 'You know she'll have a million questions. And opinions.'

'That's what's so brilliant about Granny.'

'If you say so, darling. When did you last speak to her?'

'This afternoon. She rang to tell me she'd walked to yours on her own. She sounded very pleased with herself.'

'She was. It's a big step. We walked back too, with Neville.'

'It's good news,' Jonah said. 'She's looking forward to everything getting back to normal.'

Whatever happened next, it wouldn't be normal. Jonah and Kate were going to be hours away. Her mother had turned into someone she would always need to worry about. She'd thought seeing Martin's mother again would be a one-off (quite a pleasant one, as it had turned out). With Jonah moving north, she'd be more of a fixture. Nina would need to work out how to make friends. If it wasn't too late.

'Granny didn't tell you what we talked about?' Nina asked.

'She said you were worrying about Neville. If Colin was missing him. As I said, Colin's got a different dog now.'

Annette and Nina had talked about Martin. At last. Annette had started it. It had been lovely to see Nina with real friends. How relaxed she was. And how chatty she was with Petroc and Chris and the nice people who said hello on the beach. 'Like my old Nina,' she said.

'What old Nina?'

'Before you got tangled up with that man. That deadening man.'

'You mean dead.' Her mother could be so insensitive.

'That too. But I mean deadening. He flattened you, Nina.'

'You didn't like him. Right from the off.'

'More to the point, he didn't like me. Right from the off.'

'He didn't not like you. He thought you disapproved of him.'

'He was right about that.'

'Why are you bringing this up now?'

'He stopped you in your tracks.'

'I wasn't in any tracks. I was any other middle-class girl, in a pretend bohemian flatshare in a dingy bit of London, wearing black trousers to my first grown-up job and racking up points for seeing the artiest film or most avant-garde exhibition.' Nina could see her twenty-three-year-old self, all smoky eyeliner and too much mascara. If she'd been young now, she'd have used those awful caterpillar false lashes.

'You were having fun.'

'I expect so. It was a long time ago.'

'You were so interested in things,' Annette said. 'You'd ring and you'd be fizzing with some bit of grim theatre you'd seen about incest or how one of the flatmates was going to Cambodia and how you might go too; you were reading up about it.'

'I was never going to go to Cambodia.'

'Maybe not. You took an interest is my point. Once you met Martin, you weren't interested in any of your own things anymore.'

'That's not true.'

'You stopped noticing anyone else.'

'That's not true either.' Martin attracted people. The house was always full. He'd had a billion friends. His funeral was standing room only.

'And your dreams.' Annette sailed on. 'You were doing that spreadsheety job as a stepping stone to something more creative.'

'Pipe dreams,' Nina said. 'I was going to do ceramics and be like Grayson Perry, although he didn't exist then, as a famous person I mean, and you need actual talent. And you have to be an interesting person.'

'You've always been an interesting person. Martin stopped you from seeing that. He drowned you out.'

'That's not fair.'

'He kept us apart too.' Annette reached her good arm across the table, briefly resting her hand on Nina's wrist. 'Is there any more tea in that pot?'

'I'll make some fresh. How do you figure that out?'

'Any time I suggested coming to stay, there was always an Edward or a Giles or a Bill with an earlier claim on the spare room.'

'A lot of his friends were outside London. He was very hospitable.'

'And all those times I invited all of you down here. A lovely family holiday in Cornwall. As often as not, Jonah came on his own, from when he was very little.'

'Eight,' Nina said. 'He was eight the first time. It was your idea as I remember it. Martin and I spent the whole three days by the phone in case he rang wanting to come home. He had a great time.'

'And so did I,' Annette said. 'The first of many great times with Jonah. It is true, darling. Martin used you to run away from his own life and he kept you away from yours.'

'He was my life. For twelve or thirteen years. He was my life.'

'Longer than that.'

'No. Jonah was born eighteen months after we met.'

'The years since. I'm happy that you had a great, true love. Lots of people don't manage that. And look what he left you. A glorious son. Not to mention all the sordid material things like money and a nice house. But he died, Nina. It's been too many years. Don't waste any more time on things you can't change.'

Her mother had always been good at boxing up the past. Pushing on to the next thing. Nina was different. She liked her memories. No one could ever ruin what she'd had.

Chapter fifty-nine

Leeds would be happening much too soon.

The idea had been planted over Christmas. Maud had told Kate about a new immersive centre (whatever that was) that had been given Lottery funding as part of a regeneration of another of the old mill areas. You wouldn't have thought there'd be any left by now. There was nothing romantic about textiles. Children's lungs had got clogged up with cotton and wool. That problem had been shifted to faraway countries, out of sight and out of mind, leaving big spaces to turn into flats and galleries and a creative vision that needed people who understood the interplay of sound and artificial light. People like Kate, otherwise so normal and delightful, who chose to make her living fiddling about with light bulbs.

Jonah would easily find a brilliant job. He was very confident of that, with his London experience. In the meantime, he mostly worked from home these days. They would stay with Maud for the first few weeks until they found their feet and could then even possibly buy somewhere.

Also, they'd probably get married. Nina might get to wear that embarrassing hat she'd threatened. Soon, if they could fix it.

Also, and at this point Jonah started to leak words in big clots as he did when he was flustered, he knew it was silly but also nice if she thought about it and Maud and she had hit it off and it was all the wrong way round but Maud wanted to ask Nina for her blessing to take Jonah under her roof so that Nina wouldn't worry that Maud was stealing them for Dad's family. 'So I said you'd ring her. She's always in on Tuesdays, around 5pm is a good time.'

Nina rang and they talked for a long time.

*

'I had an interesting conversation with Maud yesterday afternoon.' Nina and Annette had given themselves the evening off from each other. They were doing it more and more.

'That's splendid, darling. So clever of Jonah to bring you together again.'

'I'm not sure about again. I feel guilty looking back. Like I could have tried harder to get Martin to make it up with her.'

'It wouldn't have made any difference.'

'You don't know that.'

'I do. You can never get anywhere with that kind of man. Always so sure they're right. He'd jostled you into marriage before you had a chance to find that out.'

'The wedding was my idea. Even if I hadn't got pregnant, I didn't want to waste a single day of my life not married to Martin.' There'd be time enough for that later. Not that she'd known when she asked him. 'Maud said she spoke to you beforehand. I don't think I ever knew that.'

'We did talk, yes. You and Martin were from such different backgrounds. We were worried about both of you. We also didn't think it was our place to interfere.'

Not interfering would have been a first for her mother. 'That's not how Maud remembers it. From what I can gather, you went on the offensive. On the lines that she should remember that I was your daughter, not hers.'

'Yes. She rather took that the wrong way.'

'How would you expect her to take it?'

'I wanted to make sure you weren't swallowed up. You'd fallen for this overbearing man with silver spoons coming out of his ears. Pedigree dogs and horses. They'd have had you wearing cashmere sweaters and drinking sherry.'

Her mother wore cashmere. You could get quite good quality from Marks and Spencer. 'They wouldn't. And it would hardly have mattered if they had. It was unkind too.'

'It's all in the past now, Nina. I don't know why she's bringing it up now.'

'She's worried that you'll be as upset at the idea of Jonah moving in with her. She wants to avoid any more rifts.'

'Jonah knows what he's doing. You hadn't a clue. Your rich, handsome Prince Charming stampeded in to whisk you into a shiny new life. The rest of us didn't get a look-in.'

'The rest of us being you.'

'Yes. I was on my own, Nina. I agree it was unkind. I wasn't thinking straight. It wasn't that long after your father died. I didn't want you disappearing too.'

'Wouldn't it have been better to talk to me?'

'To be fair to me, darling, you weren't really listening to me around then. You went a little bit teenage for a while.'

Nina remembered slamming some doors. It wasn't surprising. She'd been getting the hang of adult life when Dad had inconsiderately died, vacating the space at the centre of her mother's attention, until Annette upped sticks and moved a long way away. 'Maud's worried now that it's all going to come round again,' she said. 'She doesn't want us to feel threatened by her taking in Jonah.'

'Do you? Feel threatened.'

'Of course not. I'm pleased that Jonah and Kate will have someone to help them out while they find their feet.'

'You should make sure Jonah knows that. He's worried about how you'll react. That you'll find a way of stopping him.'

Nina was outraged. 'I've never got in the way of Jonah doing anything.'

'Are you sure about that? He lived at home for longer than he needed to. You socialise with his girlfriend. He spends part of his holiday visiting me, so you don't have to. It's a lot of pressure on him, propping you up.'

'Jonah's said all that, has he?'

'Yes. Not in so many words, but yes.'

It wasn't the answer Nina was expecting. 'Of course I'll miss Jonah being an hour away, and Kate too, of course. Turning up the whole time wanting something or suggesting something. I'm still happy for them. They're where they want to be.'

'That's splendid, darling. Well done.'

'You don't sound as if you believe me.'

'I believe that you want to believe it. It's not easy, letting go. Jonah's sharpened the shears and shredded the apron strings. It can feel like you're being abandoned, but you'll find it liberating if you let it.'

Liberating. 'Which one were you?' she asked her mother. 'Abandoned or liberated?'

'Goodness, we are getting deep all of a sudden.'

'I want to know.'

'Abandoned. I got over it. It made it easier to put my energy into making things work for me down here.'

'You always seemed busy. And happy, almost like you didn't miss Dad at all.'

'I'd have said the same about you at the time. Trotting around after your dashing new beau and not a backwards glance.'

'I looked back all the time,' Nina said. 'Martin's parents were such a mess – his depression and her religion. I felt so lucky in comparison.'

'You never said.'

'We don't talk about things. Not really. Dad dying when he did was terrible for both of us.'

'And Martin dying was terrible for all of us. Not only you and Jonah. Me as well, and Maud, of course – she lost her son. The thing is, though, Nina, it happened. All of it. You can't change that, and you don't have to stop missing him. But you've got all that time in front of you.

Now Jonah is properly fledged, it's your chance to forge something new. For you. Not for me and not for Jonah.'

*

'He's just like his father,' Annette had said when she met newborn Jonah. Nina had secretly hoped her son would look like her, right up until the moment she met her perfect baby. He stayed perfect as he grew into a good-looking boy. Those beautiful brown eyes. He'd looked so heartbreaking at the funeral.

Now there was something magical about seeing how similar he was to Martin as she'd first known him. She was proud that she'd got him safely into adulthood where he could make his own life, hundreds of miles out of her reach.

Chapter sixty

Easter came and went with hot cross buns and chocolate. The town was less appealing with so many holidaymakers taking up space. There was a grim bonnet parade in the high street. Nina supposed it was difficult to carry off a daffodil-topped hat with aplomb.

Petroc and Chris invited Nina and Annette to what turned out to be a mostly family Easter lunch. Sarah was there, tucking into roast lamb. Evidently no longer a vegan.

Annette was doing well. She showed Nina the letter that she'd had after her most recent hospital appointment, the one she'd refused to let Nina take her to. ('There is a perfectly good bus.') A masterpiece in hedging around. 'While diagnosis is notoriously difficult, on the balance of probabilities, we feel that this lady's presentation does not suggest grounds for serious concern.' They could do more investigations. These were intrusive and unlikely to be warranted at this stage. 'Gobbledigook,' Annette had said. 'It means they've decided I'm not losing my marbles. At least not yet. Or not all of them.'

'That's good, I suppose. Although it doesn't explain why they were worried about you in the first instance.'

'You didn't see me when I fell. I was all over the shop. They were happy to jump to conclusions. I might have helped them do that. It was too tempting to give them problematic answers.'

'And you're sure you're fine?'

'No one's ever fine, Nina. I don't always remember where I've put things. Even obvious things, like the teabags or my toothbrush, that always live in the same place. I'm not going to worry about that until I have to. And you must stop interfering.'

Nina had smiled. Interfering was a family tradition. She'd need a little longer to break the habit.

Chapter sixty-one

Harbour Walk opened for the season the week after Easter. Dima was to be one of the first visitors. Nina still wasn't very clear why he was coming. His client had bases in more convenient places. She supposed there was posturing to be done. Bringing a lawyer down from London. The myth that all the best people congregated in London persisted in spite, Dima said, of copious evidence to the contrary.

'It's a shame about the weather,' Nina said. He'd arrived mid-afternoon, chased by plump clouds. 'I'd imagined you painting the sky.'

'Perched on a clifftop in my chair and a smock. I could see it would be a fetching sight.'

'Artists flock here. The light's completely different from in London.'

'Technically it's all just light, isn't it? I'm not overly familiar with the physics. I didn't come this whole ten miles out of my way to see the light. I came to see you.'

'You're my first actual visitor. Jonah's been, although that was for his grandmother. And Colin, of course, but he came for Neville.'

'He didn't do such a good job of that.' Neville had greeted Dima rapturously.

'No. I felt guilty for a day or two, kidnapping his dog. Now I'm glad.'

'Colin said much the same thing. Says it's reassuring to think that you're not here on your own.'

'I'm not really on my own,' Nina said. 'Obviously Mum's here, and you've met Chris and Petroc, they've adopted me, and I've got quite friendly with the neighbours too, my landlords. They keep an eye on Neville for me sometimes. And lots of dog walkers.'

'It's not home though, is it? How many of these people do you really know? Your absence from London has not gone unnoticed.' He put on the teasing tone that made it hard for her to know how much he was joking. 'Gus was outraged when he came home and found you were still missing in action.'

'Gus was?'

'Gus. You made quite an impression on him. Your pep talk in January. He's only just told me about it.'

She hadn't been going to say anything. Dima had been drunk when he suggested it. Then she'd been lent Neville for an afternoon and was walking him along the river when they saw Gus sitting on his own in the beer garden of the White Swan, drinking an incongruous bitter lemon. An old-lady drink. He had the sad look and runny nose of someone who'd been waiting round for the lack of anything better to do. 'Bit cold out here,' she'd said. 'Neville and I are on our way to the café. You can join us? I could do with picking your brains about the quiz. Me and your dad made an OK job of the questions. We haven't got your pizzazz.' She'd been surprised he'd said yes. It hadn't taken much to get him talking. 'For a moment, there, you reminded me of Jonah. He used to go off in the most enormous mood.'

'Not in a mood,' Gus had said. Oh, but he was.

'I didn't say anything clever or original,' Nina said now to Dima. 'I told him about Jonah. How he blamed himself for being away having a lovely time when his dad's accident happened. Gus and I ended up having quite a complicated philosophical discussion about the concept of blame. If it's ever helpful.'

'Nothing wrong with a bit of healthy blame,' Dima said. 'It keeps my profession afloat.'

'Lovely for you. But it's rubbish for human stuff. When shit just happens. Not karma. Not anyone's fault. Just shit. That's what I told Gus, anyway.'

'Well, luckily for peace and harmony, he bought it. Saying shit twice. That sealed the deal. Linda doesn't let him swear.'

'They've had a lot to contend with. Our boys.'

'We all have. Other people have it worse. Linda and myself, we want to make sure Gus remembers that. He's a clever, rich kid. We don't want him turning into a jerk.'

'I don't think you've got anything to worry about on that score.'

'He's gone back to Oxford now. He says to tell you to get your ass back to London before he's back for the summer.'

'How very flattering. Not even a please?'

'Absolutely not.'

Annette was desperate to meet Dima. 'He sounds exciting,' she told Nina. 'American and an artist and a lawyer and a cuckold.'

'Please don't mention the latter. Even though it's not true. And that's an awful word.'

'What do you take me for? Even you must admit it's intriguing, a man whose wife runs off with Colin. It's only natural to speculate.' She'd always been nosy. Nosy and judgmental. It was where Nina had got it from. The difference was that Nina was trying to overcome it. She'd carefully not jumped to conclusions about any of the people she'd met since coming to Cornwall (apart from the sour-faced thin nurse, or pretty Agnieszka or purple-haired Sarah).

*

The pub was fully booked and there was no conceivable way of getting Dima up Annette's steps, so they ate at Nina's. It was a fish stew that Annette assembled at her house. She was getting quite capable now with her damaged arm. All Nina needed to do was stick it in the oven.

Annette was at her most charming. It was as if she'd remembered her manners and polished them off for the evening. 'Nina tells me you've come here to paint,' she said to Dima. 'I hear you're a wonderful artist.'

'That's very kind,' Dima said. 'Nina says the same about you.'

'We are all artists in this family,' Annette said. 'Apart from Jonah. He's too like his father.'

'Of course. I know Nina's a ceramicist.'

'That's overstating it. I studied ceramics. The history as well as the practice. I haven't done any for ages.'

'She was quite good,' Annette said. 'I've got some of her work in my house. People admire it.'

'Quite good's very damning. Code for not nearly good enough. I'm interested in it, though. Like all that old china Colin has. You'd love Colin's house, Mum. It's full of stuff.'

'It's why he was so keen to get you together with Lina,' Dima said. 'She's a mutual friend, Annette. There's a new conservation project at one of the historic houses near where we live. She wants to enlist Nina's help with the porcelain collection they're building up.'

'That sounds splendid. Right up her street. I've been telling Nina for years to get involved in projects. You never do, do you, darling?'

'Maybe it was never the right project,' Dima said. 'What about you, Annette? Are you also into ceramics?'

'Watercolours. I used to sell a fair bit. I painted angry scenes, protests and the like, using the prettiest techniques that people associate with flowers and rivers and ballerinas. For a while, it caught a wave. Now I run an art club and the odd painting workshop at Harbour Walk.'

'Plants or protest?'

'Plants, largely. They have a very beautiful garden for inspiration. I cover protest in my other club. History, society and debate. It's basically a nice noisy talking shop for people who are tired of ranting at the news.'

'I should bring my son along next time I'm here,' Dima said. 'He loves finding new people to debate with.'

'He'd be very welcome,' Annette said. 'We're all old fogies. It would be a change to hear from anyone young.'

'Gus loves politics,' Dima said. 'Activism. You might get more than you bargained for.'

'Sounds like my kind of person,' Annette said. 'Do you just have the one child?'

'Yes.'

'I never understood how people could bear to have more. That explosion of love is so overwhelming. I could never have done it twice.'

'Jonah complained endlessly about being an only child. Martin was quite offended. He didn't understand why Jonah would want to share him.' Nina would happily have had more children. Martin had been kind and pragmatic when it didn't happen. Look at the child we do have, he'd say. Look at our Jonah. How could anyone else possibly be as marvellous as him?

'Life is complicated enough with one kid,' Dima said. 'And Gus would say that having any more is bad for the planet.'

'Gus sounds like he's got his head screwed on. Nina tells me you're a lawyer, as well as an artist?'

'That's what brought me down here. One of my clients wanted me to see the site they want to develop. You can look at maps and photos until the cows come home but it's not the same.'

'You deal in property?'

'With, not in; I'm not buying and selling, but I do property law.'

'In that case, can I ask your advice on something? A legal matter?'

'You can try,' Dima said.

'I'm moving into one of those retirement villages. It's a minefield – what to do with my house, what I'm signing up to with service charges, all that.'

'Sadly I don't have any expertise in that area,' Dima said. 'It's quite niche. I'm more involved when people want to put stuff up or knock it down again.'

Nina had only recently found out about this latest idea of her mother's. She'd forgotten to move a brochure from one of the care homes she'd visited from the front seat of her car. 'We'll talk about what you might be doing with this later,' Annette had said. 'I have other ideas.' Her mind was already made up, and it wasn't Nina's business to try and change it. Nina still couldn't work out if she was serious.

'Will you stay in this area?' Dima asked.

'Of course. This is home.' Annette seemed to drift. 'No place like home. That's such a great movie. It was always Nina's favourite. Do you remember, darling? You liked the dog. What was its name again?'

'Toto,' Nina said. Surely people didn't forget those details. Dorothy. Toto. The yellow brick road.

'Toto. Of course. He runs away. Sets the whole thing off. I have no plans to run away from home. Simply to move somewhere more practical. Then Nina can stop fretting.'

'You weren't from here originally?' Dima asked.

'I went to art college here,' Annette said. 'Then we were in Surrey while Nina was growing up. I moved back when my husband died. Put down roots. I've got so many friends now, it would be madness to move anywhere else.'

Nina thought her mother was directing this comment at her but couldn't be sure.

When Dima left for the evening, Nina took Neville round the block. She came back to find that Annette had started on the washing-up, dunking plates into hot water with her good hand. They stood side by side at the sink, like they'd done when Nina was a girl, before dishwashers were commonplace. Her mother would wash, Nina would dry and her father would put everything away. The same pattern every day. It was one of her happiest memories, even more so for having been on repeat for so many years.

Chapter sixty-two

With her visitors all gone and her mother discharged from most of her clinics, Nina had more time on her hands. Harbour Walk was booked up for the whole of the season, which meant Chris and Petroc were busier. She'd tentatively offered to help them out with some of the admin. They had told her, very kindly, that they only ever worked with local people. The daytime social activities continued. Nina dropped in when she had nothing better to do. Invariably, she was the youngest person there. She could never stay for long, not wanting to leave Neville to his own devices.

Petroc still called in on Annette when he could. He'd been a great support in navigating her possible move into the retirement complex, getting her onto the waiting list for a rental with an option to buy. The waiting list was morbid, although turnover was slower than you might have thought when you saw some of the residents.

'Are you sure about this?' Nina had asked her mother when they'd gone for a recce. It was a new-build development, slightly inland, low rise with attractive brickwork, scattered around a man-made lake. Ample parking for residents and guests. Nina counted three BMWs and two Jaguars. There was a café and a small gym. The flats ('apartments') were pleasant. An escalating tariff of dizzying service charges meant you could buy in as little or as much support and communal living as you wanted. It was a one-stop shop for later life. A nursing home tucked at the end of a long driveway catered for residents who slipped into the dependent or extra care brackets. Nina thought it would only be a matter of time until a discreet undertakers' office opened on the site.

'I don't want to move twice, Nina. I'm too old. This place lets you progress through the stages. Like a school. Or an alcohol recovery programme.'

'You'll miss walking into town.'

'They have a bus. And there are taxis.'

'It seems so drastic,' Nina said. 'You're managing so well at home now. Almost back to normal!' She wasn't sure why she was putting up objections to something that made a lot of practical sense.

'It's a new chapter, Nina. Something different to look forward to. I don't really expect you to understand.'

*

Neville's schedule had also changed. Dogs were banished from the nearest beach for long parts of the day. They made up for it with blowy stomps over the cliffs (on a lead in case he got ideas about flying). Some days, he'd go off on his own jaunt courtesy of Nina's landlady, who took her own dogs to the beach on the other side of the headland and offered to take Neville (but never Nina) with her. At

7pm every day, the nearby beach reopened, and Neville and Nina rushed to join the laughing, splashy crowds. Even on the wettest evenings, you could rely on seeing one or two familiar faces peering out from under sodden hoods.

There was no good reason for Neville still to be in Cornwall. The 'couple of weeks' for Colin to finish his complicated commission had long passed. He'd sent her a link to the finished result, with a detailed explanatory email in case she was unclear how the narrative unfolded. (It was a storyline concocted by a class of seven-year-olds and had its own barely discernible logic.)

Then again, there was no good reason for Nina still to be there either. 'I don't know what to do,' she'd said to Niall. A consultation over Microsoft Teams. Not something she'd repeat. He'd set a disconcerting background of summer trees. He told her to think about what she wanted. She should make a list and rule out the things that were impossible. Martin alive. Her mother less determined to have everything her own way. Life to have been different. That sort of thing.

Epilogue

Two months later.

Neville couldn't decide if he was following or leading the pack. He skittered back and forth, colliding with a small girl. While Colin apologised to the parents, Nina admired the child's smart pink scooter.

'Doggy!' The girl pointed at Neville.

Everyone beamed at everyone else. Nina thought how comfortable and reassuring they must seem: a friendly woman, a plump man and their clumsy orange dog, sharing an early morning wander on an ordinary day. No one would guess their plans for later.

Nina waited for the family to move out of earshot. 'It's good of you to come, Colin. It means a lot to Jonah and me.'

'Happy to be here. Linda had already arranged to go and visit Gus or she'd have come too.'

'Muddy's with Dima?'

'He is indeed. Just until I get back. He's got a dog walker coming in twice a day.'

'Poor Dima. He hates being dependent on anyone.' She planned to keep offering help, of course. What else were friends for?

347

'Dima's thriving. He and Linda are happier apart. They should have done it ages ago. You'll see for yourself soon enough.'

They'd both said the same to Nina on her last trip home. She'd been twice since the beginning of May, helping Jonah with the move and talking crockery with Lina. London was looking at its best in the early days of summer.

'It's funny how quickly things can change,' she said.

'If you let them. Do you know the anniversary's coming up?'

'What anniversary?'

'Ours. The great supermarket emergency. I was taking Neville home from his walk and remembered I'd run out of Marmite.'

'Hardly an emergency.'

'You can't make soldiers without Marmite.'

'I suppose you can't.' She could picture Colin carefully cutting up hot toast to dunk into runny eggs, held firm in stripy egg cups. Nina didn't eat Marmite herself. She'd look on it more positively from now on. 'I almost didn't stop,' she said. 'Someone had challenged me to try some random acts of kindness. You just happened to be there.'

'Fortune favours the kind,' Colin said. 'Or the Marmite eaters. You did us all a favour that day.' The sun was climbing. 'Shouldn't we be turning back? Give ourselves plenty of time to get ready. I'll let his nibs know.' He called Neville, who ignored them both until Nina produced a Bonio from her pocket and stretched out her arms to invite him into a hug.

The way to have a seriously small wedding was to make it difficult for people to get there, Jonah had explained. Except the most important people. Also, he wanted both his grannies there. Since Annette couldn't travel, everyone else would have to work around her. He'd drive Maud himself and she could go back by plane from Newquay to Manchester. Nina could see that the grannies were getting on well.

Kate's family had been philosophical. Cornwall was better than their middle daughter's choice. She was planning one of those barefoot weddings in the Dominican Republic, happily not for another eighteen months. They were dropping unsubtle hints about carbon footprints and tourism pollution in the hope that she might change her mind.

Short notice helped too. Petroc and Chris were full. They'd recommended a venue, faux-rustic with alpacas and sweeping views of working farmland. A cancellation. You'd have to be very superstitious to let that put you off. 'Also,' Jonah said, while he was justifying the timing, 'it gives Granny something to look forward to. It's bad luck, hurting herself again so soon after the last time.'

A broken ankle was surprisingly less debilitating than a broken wrist. This time, the stairs in the house were probably to blame. The hospital had gone back into overdrive. Annette was to have scans in case she'd had mini strokes and they were speculating too about degenerative diseases. The only person not getting excited was Annette. 'Don't look so gloomy, darling,' she'd said as

Nina helped her into her room at the retirement complex. 'Trying before buying. That's the way to think of it. It's going to work out very well.' Her house was already on the market.

They borrowed a wheelchair for the wedding day. Colin pushed and Neville sat in Annette's lap, joining in with the music. Other than Dima and Linda (she'd need to start thinking of them separately), everyone alive who Nina cared about was in this purpose-built barn. It was artfully strewn with daisy chains. Real daisies. There must be a bald meadow nearby waiting for the days to go by until the next seeds grew up to have their turn at life.

In the end, Nina had decided against wearing a hat.

Jonah and Kate made earnest promises while someone played something stringed. She worried that they were too young. Then, she and Martin hadn't been much older, so happy and so confident about what lay ahead.

The photographer was even younger, one of the students from Sarah's college. Jonah and Kate hadn't wanted anything fancy, or expensive. She buzzed round taking informal shots. 'You're Nina, aren't you?' she said. 'The groom's mum.'

'Yes. Pleased to meet you.'

'Kate said to be sure to get a picture of you and Neville. She didn't say which one's Neville.'

'He's the dog. Over there with my mum. We can go and get him.' If the picture was halfway decent, she'd have it framed. Nina and the orange dog. It had a nice ring to it. Maybe her mother would like a copy to go in her new flat.

Tomorrow, when all this was over, Nina would leave the Holiday Box for the last time and drive back to

London, taking Colin and Neville with her. Neville would move in with her, of course, but could visit Colin and Linda and Muddy any time any of them wanted. He was her dog now. It had been surprisingly easy to update his registration.

Author's note

Much of the book is set in an approximate version of Twickenham. A few of the locations are real. Nina meets Neville for the second time in beautiful Marble Hill Park. The café she visits beside the bridge is based on Tide Tables. Turner (and others) painted the famous view of the Thames from the top of Richmond Hill.

Some of what Nina finds in Cornwall is also real. The train line south of Exeter hugs the coast. The sea and light are spectacular. There are a lot of memorial benches. But the Cornwall in the book is seen through Nina's eyes and she has only ever been there as a visitor.

Acknowledgements

Thank you to my family and friends. Many of you have been waiting a long time for me to stop banging on about writing my book and get on with doing it. My life is much richer than Nina's because there are so many people I love very much rallying around and cheering me on.

In 2023, I completed the MA in Creative Writing (First Novel) at St Mary's University, Twickenham, led by the wonderful Russell Schechter. I got some words down, learned to take criticism and avoid adverbs, and had the chance to read extracts from some exciting new novels-in-the-making. Thank you, Brittany, Emma, Marisa, Jodie, Christopher, Lucy, Kristina, Rachael and Amber.

About the author

Jane Clarkson lives in London. *Nina and the Orange Dog* is her first novel.